THE
IN-LAWS

BOOKS BY LAURA WOLFE

Two Widows

She Lies Alone

Her Best Friend's Lie

We Live Next Door

The Girl Before Me

THE
IN-LAWS

Laura Wolfe

Bookouture

Published by Bookouture in 2023

An imprint of Storyfire Ltd.
Carmelite House
50 Victoria Embankment
London EC4Y 0DZ

www.bookouture.com

Paperback ISBN: 978-1-80314-918-9
eBook ISBN: 978-1-80314-917-2

For the usual suspects: JP, Brian, Kate & Milo

Love is heavy and light, bright and dark, hot and cold, sick and healthy, asleep and awake—its everything except what it is!

William Shakespeare, *Romeo and Juliet*

PROLOGUE

They were afraid to look. Six figures stood near the edge of the bluff, toes inching as far forward as anyone dared. Reluctantly, their eyes pulled downward in the morning light. Someone gasped and turned away. Two people whimpered, hugging their arms around themselves. Another let out a guttural squeal. No one could produce a recognizable word. The sight was too gruesome, too unbelievable to be real.

Two hundred feet below, beyond the steep drop-off and among the rocky crags, a body lay motionless, torso twisted one way, the head facing the other direction. A leg splayed sideways at an unnatural angle. A streak of blood stained the skin's grayish hue like something from a horror movie. Even from so high up, it was obvious they were too late, that all signs of life had vanished. Several hours had already passed since one of them first realized something terrible had happened, that one of their group had not returned.

Now, someone doubled over, heaving for breath. Another person limped toward a spindly pine tree. Two more sets of eyes found each other, a furtive look passing between them. The air was thick with fear as a question seemed to circle through the group, buzzing like flies around rancid meat. No one wanted to say it out loud, but it hovered nearby just the same.

What if this wasn't an accident?

ONE

ABIGAIL

The forest waited for us, somewhere on the horizon. I wasn't used to sitting in the back seat, and I strained against my seat belt, feeling a little sick watching the bridge's steel slats flitting past the window, and water stretching below us. The breakfast I'd treated us to at The Grand Hotel sat like a rock in my stomach. But neither the rich food nor Dad's driving was the reason I felt queasy.

"Wow. Now that's a nice view." Dad glanced over his shoulder as touristy Mackinac Island shrunk in the distance. "This is quite an adventure you're taking us on, Abigail."

Mom rode shotgun, nodding her head along to the nineties music playing from the speakers.

I mumbled in agreement. The vibrant blue water outside looked endless. The scenery was so much more expansive than the manicured houses and fenced-in lawns of the Detroit suburb we'd left behind the day before. Mom and Dad still lived in the same spacious brick colonial on the rolling acre lot where I'd grown up. And now Pete and I lived in a modest townhome only ten minutes away from them, a little bit closer to the restaurants and shops on Main Street. Dad's foot found the brake, then the accelerator again, as we continued north across the bridge toward Michigan's upper peninsula. We would meet the others at the Hiawana National Forest in two hours.

I slid my hand forward on my knee. The diamond on my finger glinted in the wandering light, a steadfast reminder that Pete and I were getting married in September, just three months from now. We'd been engaged for seven exciting and hectic months, much of which I'd spent basking in the attention showered upon me, the bride-to-be. It amazed me how the words "I'm getting married in September" could make my friends swoon, the faces of complete strangers light up, and middle-aged men and women clasp their hands together and offer heartfelt advice on lasting love.

I braced myself as Dad punched the accelerator to pass a flatbed truck. Last night's stay at The Grand Hotel had been a bribe because I knew neither Mom nor Dad wanted to go camping, especially for three nights with Pete's parents. But they were desperate to please Pete and me, to appear accommodating. Any tension between the families would not be their fault.

Dad smiled at me in the rearview mirror, his cheeks pink with razor burn. "I can't remember the last time I went camping. Maybe with the Boy Scouts about forty years ago."

"It's good to try new things." I projected my voice from the back seat. "And it's only for three nights."

Mom's eyebrows lifted as she looked back at me. "You're absolutely right, honey. They say you stop living when you stop trying new things." Mom was a psychiatrist who had the uncanny ability to pluck inspirational quotes from her back pocket at a moment's notice, and I imagined her treasure chest of sage advice came in handy with her patients.

At last, the loud vibration quieted beneath the tires as our car reached the other side of the bridge. I released a breath, grateful to be back on a solid road. An empty seat sat next to me, and I envisioned Pete making a parallel drive with his parents from their home, which I'd never visited but Pete had described as a ramshackle house in a small town on the outskirts of Traverse City. He'd spent the last two nights with them to "talk about wedding stuff" as he'd put it. But I knew Pete was just as nervous about this weekend as I was. He was going along with it to make me happy.

Our wedding planning had gone relatively smoothly. We'd hired a wedding coordinator and Mom and Dad were eager to host an elegant celebration. The country club venue had been booked. My silk and lace Italian dress had been selected and fitted. The formal invitations had been printed and were stacked on my dresser, waiting to be mailed. The plane tickets for our honeymoon in Hawaii had been purchased, and I'd already moved into Pete's townhome. We'd even adopted a cat called Mango. But there was one looming obstacle we hadn't tackled yet: getting our parents to like each other. They'd met only once for dinner, and it had been nothing short of a disaster.

Mom's head tipped back. "Still, though. I don't understand why the Mitchells couldn't have just met us on Mackinac Island. That would have been simpler, wouldn't it? Plus, we'd have running water and beds to sleep in."

Dad chuckled. "Oh, come on, Kristen. Toilets are overrated."

I leaned forward, biting back my smile at Dad's joke. "It would have been simpler for us, maybe. But not for them." I clasped my hands together, finding my palms clammy. "The Grand Hotel would have been out of their budget, not to mention their comfort zone. Pete's parents don't eat out or vacation much."

Mom pursed her rosy lips, touching a polished fingernail to her temple. Her eyelids were smoky with eyeshadow, lashes heavy with mascara. She was wearing too much makeup for a camping trip, but I didn't want to tell her that. I knew she was trying her best in her own way, that she wanted to look nice for the second introduction. We rode on for a minute without speaking. A strange hum of anticipation buzzed through the car.

"Anyway, you're going to love our guide, Liam." I thought back to when I'd met Liam the previous fall. He was one of the guides with Team Wilderness, an outdoor hiking and team-building company that had led a two-night work outing for the public relations firm where I worked as a content writer. The experience had done wonders in improving communication and building camaraderie among my co-workers at Pegasus.

Dad tapped his thumb on the steering wheel. "We got Liam's emails with the packing list and all those other forms we had to sign."

"He seems like a nice guy, but we practically had to sign our lives away," Mom said, throwing her hands in the air.

I cleared my throat, trying to keep the conversation on track. "Like I said, when I found out that Team Wilderness does personal and family tours too, I thought this would be perfect for us. I mean, considering how your first meeting with the Mitchells went." I paused, staring out the window. "You and Pete's parents will probably be best friends by the end of this."

Mom craned her neck toward me, face brightening. "It's such a fabulous concept, getting people out into nature to open the lines of communication. I think we simply got off on the wrong foot with the Mitchells. It would be nice if we could all be friends."

I recognized the glint of nostalgia in Mom's eyes and remembered how my two sets of grandparents had attended nearly every one of my childhood birthday celebrations, even though each pair lived over an hour away. They'd always been eager to gather for Thanksgiving dinners, Christmas festivities, and Easter egg hunts. Maybe it was a rare phenomenon, but my grandparents had enjoyed each other's company. It had been an idyllic way to grow up and I'd hoped for the same dynamic in my adult years. Especially after hearing my best friend Betsy's frequent complaints about her parents and in-laws arguing over who went where for which holiday.

Outside the car window, a row of cottages lined another distant lake. Then the scenery turned to forest, occasional billboards dotting the landscape. The view repeated itself for miles as Mom and Dad chatted about the neighbors and a couple of languishing home improvement projects.

After a moment of silence, Mom looked back at me. "To be honest, Abigail, I'm not super excited about sleeping in the woods. But even so, I think this camping trip will be worthwhile. I barely learned anything about Darla last time, with Kenny rambling on the way he did."

"Well, we know Kenny's a cheapskate," Dad said, eyes fixed on the road.

"Dad!"

"I'm only saying, he could have offered to split the bill."

My parents and I had only met the Mitchells once before, seven months ago at an Applebee's restaurant halfway between their house and the suburb where we lived, a two-hour drive for everyone. The generic chain restaurant in the middle of nowhere wasn't the type of place my parents would usually have chosen, but options were limited. Everyone had been cordial enough, but my nerves had jittered through me, making it difficult to speak. The uncomfortable atmosphere had been exacerbated by the stilted conversation as it quickly became clear that my parents and Pete's parents had virtually nothing in common. Darla had spent the entire dinner leaning back in her chair, silently watching us as if observing rare birds through a window. Meanwhile, her gruff husband dominated the conversation, recounting the drama on the multiple reality TV shows he regularly watched. As Kenny spoke, Darla's stony eyes locked onto me with a stare so piercing it felt as if she'd sliced me open and was examining my insides, evaluating whether I was acceptable wife material for her son. I could only smile and look away. During a lull in Kenny's harangue, she patted my hand, leaning forward and saying, "I don't know why Pete has kept you hidden from us. We plan to see much more of you after the wedding."

"That's great," I said. And I would have meant it, but there'd been something strange in Darla's tone that I couldn't decipher.

When the bill finally arrived, Dad reached for it, eager to leave. "I got this one," he said, clearly expecting Kenny to offer to chip in or at least say thank you. But the other man only blew his nose, then left to use the restroom before the long drive home.

Pete usually had a magnetism about him. But during that dinner with his parents, he'd been somber and quiet, his face growing a deeper shade of red with every story his dad told. Pete told me later that he felt bad that I'd not had the chance to meet his family before he proposed, so that I could make an informed decision about marrying him. I punched him in the arm and told him to stop being ridiculous. But something about that dinner at Applebee's had poked a pinprick of doubt in my gut. I couldn't stop wondering how Pete could be so different from the people who had raised him.

Shaking the memory off, I straightened my shoulders. "So, Darla and Kenny are a little unique. But we shouldn't be judgmental."

Dad caught my eye in the rearview mirror. "Hey, give us some credit. We're easygoing."

Mom nodded. "I understand that some people are less…" She paused. "Less sophisticated than others. It was the lack of manners that bothered me."

Dad raised his chin, grunting in agreement.

Mom continued. "Tell me more about Darla. She barely said two words at that dinner."

"Hm." I squeezed my elbow, recalling what little I knew

about them. "Pete said she likes crafting. And I guess she's very spiritual."

"Oh! In what way?" Mom's voice went up a pitch.

"She reads palms and Tarot cards. She's into horoscopes. That sort of thing."

Silence greeted me from the front seat. Mom's background in the medical field meant she usually rolled her eyes at mystics, referring to their practices as pseudoscience. I didn't disagree with her, but this was the kind of judgment I'd been referring to a couple of minutes earlier.

Mom smoothed down a stray hair. "Well, I guess if it's just for fun, then it doesn't hurt anyone."

"Right. It doesn't hurt anyone," I said, my voice louder now.

Dad scratched his head. "A fortune-teller, huh? I've asked Pete about his parents and his brother a number of times, but he's tight-lipped about his family."

"It seems like he's a little embarrassed by them." I crossed my arms in front of me. "That's why I thought it would be good to have a guide with us and scheduled activities. Just to make sure everything goes smoothly."

Mom sighed, inspecting her fingernails, painted the color of ballet slippers and cut to a sensible length. "We can survive roughing it for three nights. Your dad and I really need this change of scenery. Or, at least, I do." Mom frowned as she glanced at Dad.

Dad's fingers ceased tapping the steering wheel. "Let's not start again, Kristen."

I noticed how Mom set her jaw as she turned away. I didn't know what the issue was this time, but my parents occasionally had these little spats. Although I'd learned to ignore them, they'd been happening more frequently in recent weeks. They'd even argued during our bike ride yesterday. Mom had wanted to stop and look for shells on one of the beaches, but

Dad insisted on keeping ahead of the crowds and continuing around the island. We'd ended up stopping.

"I'm only saying," Mom continued, "that it's refreshing to get out of the house. We don't have a lot of fun anymore."

Dad made a choking noise and shook his head. "Speak for yourself. I have plenty of fun."

"Ha." Mom faced the window.

"This will be good for everyone." I raised my voice, desperate to end the uncomfortable exchange.

Dad eyed me in the rearview mirror. "Anyway, you're marrying a good one, Abigail. Regardless of his parents. Your mother and I agree on that."

Mom nodded, giving a tight smile in my direction.

I closed my eyes, remembering how, as a little girl, I'd dreamed of marrying someone kind and handsome, someone with a successful career that would rival my own career aspirations, so I could raise a family in a similar setting in which I'd grown up. After only a few months of dating, I'd realized Pete was the man I'd been waiting for. My friends and family seemed to recognize it too, often commenting on how Pete's personable demeanor complemented my quiet nature, and how we brought out the best in each other.

Our car continued along the highway. As the miles passed, I had the strangest feeling that this drive represented the end of something. Although, I reminded myself, it would also be the beginning of something else.

A text from Pete buzzed through my phone, interrupting my thoughts.

Hey beautiful.

My eyes hovered over the words and then I wrote back.

Hi handsome. I miss you.

Bubbles appeared, then Pete's reply.

We're at a rest stop forty minutes out. Where are you?

I think we're just a little behind you. We'll meet you at the visitors' center. Look for Liam when you get there.

OK. Are you as nervous as I am?

You have no idea, I thought. But I simply wrote:

Yes. I hope everybody gets along.

TWO

ABIGAIL

Gravel cracked beneath the wheels as Dad parked our car outside the Hiawana National Forest Visitors' Center. I opened my door and sucked in a breath. The air was damp, infused with an earthy scent. Despite the sun burning through the clouds, the sky was darker here. Trees towered over us on all sides.

I stretched my arms over my head, spotting Pete's silver Rogue on the opposite side of the lot. My parents surveyed the area, taking in the array of cars, trucks, and SUVs equipped with elaborate storage racks. A few feet away, a guy with a crew cut who looked like he hadn't showered in days loaded equipment into the back of his pickup truck, coughing every few seconds and swearing when his bungee cord didn't connect the way he wanted. A fresh cut slashed the side of his face, the wound seeping red. His wife or girlfriend sat in the front seat, sobbing. I wondered what had happened to them.

"Well, we made it." Dad's voice was upbeat, but his face was flat as he took in the man and woman nearby.

The angry man stepped toward his girlfriend's open

window. "Will you just shut up, Samantha? I'm trying to get us out of here as fast as I can."

"I wish I never agreed to come out here with you!" she screamed between gasps of air. "I hate you!"

"None of this was my fault!"

I widened my eyes at Mom and Dad, noting their blank stares. We froze for a second, a similar realization seeming to occupy us simultaneously: there was no turning back now. We were heading out into the wilderness. With Pete's parents. A lot could go wrong. Dad's eyes flickered toward his car as if he was considering darting back into the driver's seat and making a run for it.

"We can leave our luggage for now." I waved them toward the visitors' center and away from the volatile couple. "Let's go find the others."

Mom rolled her shoulders back and smoothed down her hair, stepping behind Dad. We headed in the direction of a building resembling an oversized log cabin which sat at the edge of the lot. As my feet scraped over the gravel, my thoughts drifted back to the day I'd first met Pete. It had been a little over two years ago, and I'd arrived at Dad's commercial real estate company to meet him for lunch. But when I'd entered Dad's corner office expecting to find him sitting behind his mahogany desk, I'd found someone else staring back at me instead. A tall, dark-haired man about my age looked up, an easy smile stretched across his face. "Hi, I'm Pete," he'd said, stepping forward to shake my hand. He had the kind of deep voice that could fill a room. He wore a button-down shirt and expensive-looking shoes, giving him the air of a successful businessman or at least someone more grown-up than the guys I'd dated before him. Dad arrived a minute later, insisting that Pete join us for lunch.

That first meal was at the West Side Bistro with Dad sitting between us. Dad had thumbed toward Pete. "This guy put himself through college, Abigail. He's probably going to be running the whole company in a few years."

"Wow," I'd said with a bashful smile, secretly impressed. The lunch continued with me too nervous to take more than a few bites of my sandwich and Pete asking me plenty of questions and tossing a stream of compliments in my direction. His intelligence and modesty quickly won me over. The moment Dad stepped away from the table, Pete leaned toward me. "Can I take you out to dinner this Saturday?" He gave a lopsided smile as he raised an eyebrow. "Without your dad?" His extra clarification made me laugh.

On our first real date, we'd discovered a shared love of travel, and an interest in reading and learning about other cultures. We laughed at the same things, both of us enjoying a similar dry sense of humor. He was easy to talk to and I liked the way his lips curved to the side when he smiled, the way his biceps flexed beneath his polo shirt whenever he leaned forward to ask me a question.

The following weekend we'd embarked on a long meandering bike ride along a paved trail, ending at a riverside park. Pete had packed a picnic lunch and picked me a wildflower. I was sure there'd been sparks flying when he'd kissed me. We'd been together ever since. And, as Dad later admitted, he had positioned Pete next to his desk that day on purpose because he thought we'd make a good pair.

Now, a Jeep zoomed past, kicking dust around us. Dad hustled ahead and pulled open the door to the visitors' center. My heart thrummed against my ribcage, and I reminded myself to calm down, that the time for our parents to get to know each other was overdue, and this camping trip was a good plan.

I stepped inside the rustic lobby, my head angling around a family of four to find Pete and his parents in the corner. My fiancé stood tall, eyes brightening at the sight of me. He looked like a more rugged version of himself, dressed in his hiking boots and the water-resistant clothes he'd purchased from REI. "There they are!" Pete lunged forward and kissed my cheek. His jaw was rough with a day's worth of stubble and he smelled different than usual. The burned scent of sandalwood incense clung to his clothes, which I guessed was Darla's doing. Pete knew both of my parents well, and he greeted them in his usual way, Mom with a hug and Dad with a handshake, their heads dipping toward each other in curt nods. I wondered if he and Dad would ever part with the formality of their office relationship.

Kenny hovered a few feet away, shifting the weight of his tree-trunk legs from one foot to the other. A black zippered coat that had seen better days stretched across his heavyset frame. I glimpsed a hint of a grin behind the man's scruffy gray beard, and I smiled at him. Darla peered at us from beside her husband. She shared Pete's dark eyes, but hers were murkier, something mysterious lingering behind her stare. A shirt resembling an artist's smock hung from her shoulders, and she'd woven a strand of ribbon adorned with peacock feathers and colorful beads into a single, gray braid that tapered at the end and draped over her shoulder.

Pete slung his arm around me, pulling me forward. "And here's Abigail!"

"Hello," they both said at once. Darla stepped closer. I'd forgotten how stout she was, standing a few inches below me, and a good foot shorter than her son and husband. She offered a hand and I shook it. When I let go, she laced her fingers together and appeared to have stopped breathing. Despite her burrowing stare, I could see she was just as nervous as I was. The fingers of Darla's left hand loosened their grip on something, revealing a purple, cone-shaped crystal. Kenny joined in the greeting, extending a hand. My cheeks ached as I maintained my wide smile and shook the hand of my future father-in-law, realizing he was a complete stranger to me.

"And, Mom and Dad." Pete waved behind me. "You remember Abigail's parents, Kristen and John Cates."

"Nice to see you again," Mom said.

"We're looking forward to this." Dad extended his hand along with what I assumed was a white lie.

Pete's parents nodded, not speaking as they exchanged handshakes.

Mom raised her gaze to the wooden beams crisscrossing the ceiling. "We're a little out of our element here."

"We have a friend with a camper." Darla's fingers stroked the crystal's shiny surface. "She lets us borrow it sometimes to stay at the county park. But we've never stayed in tents before."

"This will be a true adventure then." Mom smiled, but I recognized the manufactured enthusiasm stretching through her voice.

"The stars will be so clear up here." Darla's eyes were suddenly wide, childlike. "Perfect for my astrology charts. Do you read your horoscope?"

Mom rotated to the side, touching the nape of her neck and looking slightly distressed. "No. I haven't in years, but I'm sure the stars will be beautiful."

Dad cleared his throat. "Kenny and Darla, I'm sure you're aware that I've known your son for—goodness—it must be five years now. Pete worked for me even before he started dating our daughter." Dad gave Pete two pats on the shoulder. "He's a solid guy. So impressive. A real self-starter. You've sure done something right."

A sheepish grin spread across Pete's face as he stood between Dad and me.

Kenny shook his head. "Well, John. We can't claim any credit for our son. Pete has always done his own thing, had his own plan." Kenny kicked at the floor, something brewing in his slate-blue eyes. Was it jealousy? I touched Pete's arm, remembering that he and his parents weren't always on the same wavelength. He'd often told me how Darla and Kenny had been so focused on his brother Trent's constant behavioral issues that Pete was all but forgotten much of the time. They'd offered him little encouragement over the years. There'd been no vacations to Disney World or road trips for college tours like my parents had provided for me. It hadn't helped that the Mitchells barely scraped by financially. Sometimes, there hadn't even been enough money for food or to pay the heating bill.

Darla chuckled, deep and throaty. "We have no idea where Pete came from. Kenny and I used to joke that they gave us the wrong baby at the hospital."

"Either that or aliens swapped him out." Kenny smirked, eliciting an awkward laugh from the rest of us. "Now Pete's brother, Trent. He makes more sense. He's definitely my son."

Pete released a breath, and I could almost feel the solid frame of his body withering next to me. His parents' words seemed borderline cruel. I touched his hand.

"I guess I'll never measure up to Trent." Pete moved his hands to his hips, his words heavy with sarcasm.

Darla seemed to notice the uncomfortable looks on everyone's faces and snapped back to herself. "Oh, come on, Pete. We love you, of course. You were always the easy one."

"We think Pete is such a wonderful young man," Mom said. "And he has really brought out the best in our daughter."

Kenny motioned toward me. "We've only met Abigail the one time at Applebee's. Then Pete whisked her away as soon as we paid the bill."

Pete made a pained noise, a sigh crossed with a yelp. "John paid the bill, Dad. Not you."

"It doesn't matter." Mom waved everyone off. "It was Applebee's, for God's sake, not the Four Seasons."

"She's right," Dad said. "It was nothing. After this weekend, I suspect we'll all know more about each other than we ever wanted to. Leave it to our kids to dream up something like this."

"You got that right." Kenny grinned, and I wondered if he and Dad were already finding some middle ground.

I nudged Pete. "Is Liam here?"

"Yeah. He's setting up our gear out in the back. He said to come and find him once everyone was here."

As we headed toward the door, Mom hung back, leaning close to my ear and whispering, "Liam is going to have his work cut out for him with our group."

I glanced around at the others, knowing Mom was right. I hadn't been prepared for so much awkward conversation right off the bat. We filed outside where I noticed the unhappy couple's truck was no longer parked in its spot. I wondered what had gone so terribly wrong that it caused them to scream hateful words at each other, to shatter what had perhaps been a previously content relationship.

The balls of my feet pressed into the ground as I shook away the lingering image of the couple. I guided my thoughts back to our two sets of parents, to my upcoming wedding, and the three nights ahead. I closed my eyes and hoped Liam could work his magic.

THREE

ABIGAIL

We trekked along the side of the enormous log building and rounded the corner. I recognized Liam's lanky frame in the distance. His sandy blonde hair was pulled back into a thin ponytail as he hunched in a clearing, inspecting a backpack. Six more backpacks lay on the ground in two neat rows, along with piles of other supplies provided by Team Wilderness.

"Hey, Liam." Pete's voice boomed across the landscape. "We're back with the whole crew."

Liam spun around to face us, a sweaty sheen reflecting off his forehead. "Hi, everyone." He nodded toward me. "Nice to see you again, Abigail."

We shook hands. "Thanks for doing this, Liam."

"Are you kidding? I love working with smaller groups. This is going to be a blast." His eyes traveled to Dad, then landed on Mom where his gaze rested a moment too long, almost as if he was checking her out. My stomach turned at the thought. "And what a good-looking crew we've got here." Liam winked at me. "These must be your parents."

"Yes," I said, introducing them. I could see Mom's shoulders relaxing, and the relief on Dad's face that there was, in fact, a professional camper in charge.

Mom clasped her hands together. "Thank goodness at least one of us knows what we're doing out here."

"I haven't lost anyone yet. Knock on wood," Liam said, tugging at a strap on his backpack. The rest of us chuckled nervously as Liam surveyed the remaining pile of gear. "Okay, I've already secured our camping permits and registered our route with the Park Service. And I've received everyone's waivers. I'm hoping to get us on the trail in about thirty minutes." He waved toward the spread behind him. "I've got all the packs back here and I've divided the extra gear, so no one has too much weight."

"Sounds good," Pete said.

Liam paced in front of us. "Just to refresh, we'll want to keep clothes to a minimum to reduce the weight. But it gets cold at night up here, even in June, so definitely pack some layers, including a waterproof outer layer. Make sure to bring any medications you may need, but leave non-essentials behind. Extra pairs of socks are vital."

"Got it," Pete said.

I nodded toward Mom and Dad. We'd already separated our camping clothes, toiletries, and other supplies when we'd changed into our hiking gear at the hotel.

Liam continued, "There are lockers in the visitors' center where you can secure your valuables, like purses, wallets, and phones."

"Phones?" Pete asked.

"You can bring a phone with you for photos if you want, but there's probably not going to be any signal out there. I'll carry most of our food in my pack. You can bring your own trail mix or granola bars or whatever too. And I have a first-aid kit in case of any unexpected injuries."

"What about tents?" Now it was Dad who piped up.

"I have a single tent for myself. Then we have two tents for the six of you, so we'll figure out how to split up once we get to our campsite."

"Two tents?" Mom mumbled under her breath as something close to horror flashed across her face.

"Don't worry, Kristen. They're big tents," Liam said. "And we'll all be so tired by the end of each day that it won't matter anyway."

I glanced toward Mom. "We had the same setup for the work trip. It wasn't a big deal."

Mom managed a weak smile, then stared at the ground.

"How many miles?" Kenny asked.

"Only five today. But tomorrow will be more like seven or eight, some of it uphill."

Kenny whistled. "Oh, boy."

"I chose the route based on the results of everyone's Physical Capabilities surveys. The hikes will be challenging, but achievable. This is where team building comes in. We're really going to have to encourage each other, lift each other up." Liam's eyes were bright. "And there's one motto we all live by when hanging out in the woods: Leave no trace." He motioned toward us. "Everyone, say it."

"Leave no trace," we all repeated in unison.

Liam bobbed his head in approval. "Take only pictures. Leave only footprints. We don't leave any garbage or belongings behind. You can dig a hole in the ground to go to the bathroom, but then you cover it up and bury the compostable toilet paper too. Got it?"

I looked around at the others, who shifted their weight and picked at their nails as if waiting for someone to suggest trashing the whole idea and grabbing pizza and a few beers at the closest restaurant. Instead, Pete clapped his hands twice, angling his chin toward the parking lot. "Daylight's burning. Let's get our stuff."

It took a few minutes to gather our things and load them into our packs. We returned multiple times to the visitors' center to use the bathroom, secure our extra belongings in lockers, and fill the filtration water bottles Liam had given us. At last, Liam helped me heave my giant backpack onto my shoulders. My knees almost buckled under the weight.

"Ugh. I forgot how heavy these things were."

To my left, Pete helped his parents get their packs secured. Darla tugged at the straps, face pained. "I don't know if I can make it."

Pete rubbed his forehead. "Mom, we haven't even started hiking yet."

Kenny put his arm around his wife, massaging her shoulder and kissing her on the cheek. "C'mon, Darla. You can do it. I believe in you."

I stared at them for a second. This was a side of Kenny I hadn't seen yet, the encouraging and loving partner. Pete must have gotten that quality from his father. I watched Kenny, noting the familiar square jawline beneath his beard and catching a glimpse of what Pete might look like thirty years from now.

Liam hoisted Mom's pack onto her shoulders and secured the buckles for her. "How's that?"

"Oh." Mom craned her neck to the side, grimacing. "I agree with Darla. This is heavy. I don't think I'm going to manage it either."

Mom and Darla looked at each other, eyes connecting in shared misery. A moment later, they burst into laughter.

Pete leaned close and whispered in my ear. "Looks like our moms are bonding already."

I lowered my gaze, slightly alarmed by Mom's unusual reaction.

As the two women pulled themselves together, Liam secured his pack with ease, despite it being double the size of everyone else's. "Okay, if everyone feels like their packs are relatively comfortable, we should really get going. We have a route that's a little off the beaten path, and it's important we get to our campsite well before sundown."

We arranged ourselves behind our guide and told him we were ready. Dad gave Mom a little squeeze of encouragement. I was happy to see whatever tension had bubbled between them during the car ride had dissipated.

Pete grabbed me from behind and kissed me on the cheek. "I love your adventurous side, you know that?"

I smiled, looking away. While I appreciated Pete's constant compliments, sometimes they felt a little forced. That's how this one felt only because I wasn't convinced Pete actually wanted to be here. He'd gone along with my crazy camping trip idea because he'd seen how much it meant to me. But, as far as dream vacations went, Pete was more of a luxury, tropical resort type of guy.

Pete pulled at the straps near his armpits, adjusting his pack. "I still can't believe we're really doing this, that we got our parents on board."

"Me neither." I stepped closer to him, remembering the extreme amount of planning and convincing that had been required to reach this point. The parents had eventually agreed that three nights in the woods with a professional guide could be beneficial—or an unforgettable adventure, at the least. But as I watched my parents and Darla and Kenny hovering in front of me, the doubts about this forced outing gnawed at my insides. The wind rustled the tree branches overhead, whipping the leaves into a fury. My nose caught a whiff of decay in the air, and a ripple of unease traveled through me. Something cold and lifeless seeped through my veins as we followed Liam into the woods.

FOUR

ABIGAIL

I marched, one foot in front of the other, Pete by my side, and two sets of parents in front of us. The weight of my pack had settled, feeling bearable now. Still, my breathing was more labored than usual. The trail was wide, allowing us to walk two by two, and our pace was surprisingly quick, thanks to the flat ground and our fresh legs. Liam kept turning back, telling us facts about the forest, the types of trees we passed—the white pines, maples, hemlocks, and birches—and the various other flora that bloomed this time of year. He seemed at ease, completely in his element. Just as he'd been on the outing with my co-workers.

"Any bears around here, Liam?" It was Kenny who spoke.

"Yes. There are black bears in the upper peninsula. Wolves too. And even cougars, although sightings of big cats are super rare."

Mom gasped, head swiveling toward the dense trees in every direction. I scanned the branches above, searching for a big cat coiled above us, camouflaged and ready to pounce. Liam must have noticed the charged silence because he stopped walking and turned toward us, a look of mild amusement stretching across his face. "The predators in these woods are a good thing. It's a sign of a healthy ecosystem. Trust me when I say the animals, even the big ones, are way more scared of us than we are of them. As long as we hang our food from a tree at night—which I always do—the bears and other animals won't bother us. I can almost guarantee it."

The others nodded, reassured by Liam's plan, by the odds being in our favor. But Mom angled her pale face toward me. It seemed she had also noticed that extra word Liam had added. *Almost.* He could *almost* guarantee the predators wouldn't bother us. I raised my eyebrows and gave her a thumbs-up, refusing to reveal that I was just as scared as she was.

"You got a gun?" Kenny's question made everyone stand up straighter, tilting heads toward Liam for an answer.

Liam swiveled around again, the previous look of amusement having drained from his face. "Nope. Not necessary. I've got a knife and bear spray." Liam patted a compact red-and-black bottle clipped to the side of his pack, then pulled his stare from Kenny and addressed the rest of us. "There's seriously no reason to freak out. I've led dozens of these expeditions in this park, downstate, up in Canada, and a few other national parks. I haven't had a single run-in with a bear or any other predator. Okay?"

This time we all nodded.

"Great." Liam clapped his hands. "Let's keep going at this pace for another forty minutes or so. Then we can stop for a snack break." He continued ahead, waving us along. Pete and I brought up the rear.

Pete looped his arm around me, pulling me close. "Don't worry. I'll protect you from all the beasts in the forest."

I looked my well-dressed suburban fiancé up and down, a faint chuckle escaping my mouth. "With what?"

He gazed at the sky, pretending to think about it. "I don't know. But by the time the bear eats me, it'll probably be too full to eat you too."

"That's so romantic," I said with an added eye roll.

"Don't you forget it." He gave my arm an extra squeeze and we caught up to the others.

Dad angled his head toward Kenny. "Do you play any golf, Kenny?"

"Nope. Can't say that I do." Kenny wiped his nose with the back of his hand without elaborating.

"Do you watch any sports?"

"Not too much."

Dad glanced back at me as Kenny began recounting a TV show he'd been watching where a survivalist is dropped in a remote location with only a backpack and water bottle.

"This guy has to find his way back to civilization before dying of dehydration, starvation, or getting eaten by a wild animal." Kenny shook his head. "He eats caterpillars and tree bark and drinks his own piss. It's unbelievable!"

I watched Dad hike quietly next to Kenny, feeling a little bad for him and his failed effort to find common ground.

The group of us trudged along, with Mom mentioning more than once that her heel hurt and Darla complaining about the pack straining her shoulders.

"So, what's your other son like?" Mom asked Pete's parents. "I haven't heard much about Trent."

"Trent takes after me, I think," Kenny said over his shoulder. "Likes bowling and fishing."

"He's younger, right?" Mom asked.

Kenny shook his head. "Nope. He's two years older than Pete. He works for the electric company. It's a pretty good gig."

"Oh, he's an electrician." Mom's voice went a pitch higher. "That's such an important skilled trade."

"Trent's not an electrician," Pete called out from behind

her. "He answers calls and cleans the company trucks. That's it. No skill involved."

"Pete!" I said, punching his arm.

Darla narrowed her eyes at Pete as if to tell him to shut up. Then she refocused on Mom. "Trent finally moved out last year. We're proud of him. His best friend died in an accident when they were seventeen. It's been hard on him." She frowned, shaking her head.

"That was over ten years ago." I heard the exasperation in Pete's voice, remembering all the stories he'd told me about his parents coddling his brother, who constantly acted out, while they left Pete to fend for himself. "It was Trent's fault Freddie died. He tipped the boat over on purpose."

Kenny stopped walking and glared at Pete. "It was no one's fault."

Pete jutted out his chin, glaring right back at his dad. They were gridlocked like that for a couple of uncomfortable seconds.

Finally, Mom clucked. "A tragedy like that at such a young age can have a lasting impact on a person."

Darla nodded, huffing her way up a slight incline as the group moved forward again. "He's had a hard time of it."

"Trent barely made it through high school. That's why we're so happy about his new job," Kenny said, then motioned toward Pete. "Not like this one, who's always been going places."

I glanced at Pete, whose mouth had flattened into a straight line.

Darla flipped her braid over her shoulder as she turned to look at Mom. "But now Trent's got his own place on the other side of town. He's making an honest living. He's a good son. He comes over every Sunday for dinner."

"Unlike Pete." Kenny added this last part under his breath, but we all heard it.

"Dad." Pete stopped walking, the vein on his neck bulging.

"I live over four hours away from you. I can't pop by every Sunday for dinner. I have an actual career. And a life. Besides, Trent is a screw-up with no social skills. He makes everyone around him feel uncomfortable."

Darla shook her head and clucked. "He's still your brother, Pete. And while we're on that subject, you didn't have to cut him out of the wedding party. You should have asked him to be your best man. I'm sure you hurt his feelings."

The way Darla's stare tightened on Pete, then bore into me, gave me flashbacks to the uncomfortable dinner at Applebee's. I laced my fingers together and looked at the ground as we trudged along the trail.

"Can't you at least make Trent a groomsman?" Darla asked, refusing to drop the topic.

"Not really, Mom. We've already decided on one best man and one maid of honor—Oliver, and Abigail's best friend, Betsy. There aren't going to be any other groomsmen or bridesmaids. Abigail and I want to keep it simple."

"But to just cut him out..." Darla said, her voice cracking.

"We didn't cut him out." Pete sighed. "He's an usher, along with Abigail's cousin. That's an important job. Anyway, Trent assured me he was totally fine with the arrangement."

Darla puckered her lips. It was clear she was taking the usher assignment personally, even if Trent wasn't.

I thought back to the one time I'd met Pete's brother, Trent. It was several months ago, when I'd been spending most of my time at Pete's townhome but hadn't officially moved in yet. Trent had unexpectedly shown up on the doorstep one night, blinking against the glare of the porch light. When I'd joined Pete in the foyer, he'd reluctantly introduced me to his older brother, whose greasy hair looked as if it needed a good wash. I'd said hi and smiled, but Trent had only grunted in return, training his eyes on Pete. "Can I spend the night? I need a break from Mom and Dad."

"You should have called me first." Pete had tipped his head toward the ceiling, clearly annoyed.

My hackles had gone up at the way Trent paced in the entryway with his hands shoved into his pockets, his face refusing to look in my direction. After a couple of additional brief exchanges, Pete had allowed Trent to stay over for the night, but he'd insisted I go home, which, given how uncomfortable Trent had made me feel, I'd been happy to do. The next day, Pete arrived at my place with flowers, apologizing for his brother's rudeness.

"Besides, Mom," Pete continued, interrupting my thoughts, "you and Dad could just as easily drive over and visit me and Abigail. But you don't."

Darla craned her neck to look at her son, her face falling. "I guess you're right. We're going to make more of an effort to do that sort of thing a lot more often. Especially now that Trent is standing on his own two feet, and our family is growing." Her eyes flicked toward me, followed by a smile.

I smiled back, although the thought of Darla and Kenny stopping by for regular overnight visits sat in my stomach like a bad piece of fish. Family gatherings for the holidays were one thing, but I didn't want them interfering with our weekly routine. Still, I reminded myself that these were the sort of compromises married people made all the time. No one had perfect in-laws. My grandparents had been the exception, not the rule. I'd heard enough of my friends complain about the weekends spent with their new relatives, how they sometimes felt uncomfortable, out of place, the one who was asked to take a photo of the rest of the family. Maybe that was simply part of the deal.

Some chatter filtered through the trees up ahead. Pete stopped and moved to the side as a group of four campers in colorful windbreakers filed past us. They nodded and smiled, voices chirping as they marched down the trail with walking sticks in hand. "Don't miss the view at Crystal Lake. It's spectacular," one of them said before they disappeared beyond the bend.

"Are we going to Crystal Lake?" Darla's voice sounded breathless as she followed behind our guide.

Liam looked over his shoulder. "Not this time. Our route is a little more remote, so we don't have other people around."

Kenny nodded. "Yeah. Sounds good."

"No tourists," Pete added from beside me.

Mom widened her eyes and looked at Dad. "I think Crystal Lake sounds nice."

Dad shrugged and we all continued following Liam down the trail.

A few minutes later, we reached a clearing where five large boulders dotted a meadow. Liam stood to the side to let us slide past him. "We can take a break here. Grab snacks, water, whatever."

"Oh, thank goodness." Darla collapsed onto the nearest boulder and slipped her pack off her shoulders. Mom did the same, then unlaced one of her hiking boots. The rest of us lowered ourselves onto the other rocks.

"How's everyone doing so far?" Liam paced in front of us, dropping his massive pack into the tall grass.

"So far, so good." Dad took a swig of water, his forehead shiny with sweat.

Pete stretched his arms in the air. "It feels great to get some exercise after sitting in the car for so long."

Darla placed a palm on the small of her back. "My back sure aches."

"I have a blister on my heel," Mom said.

"No worries. These are minor problems that we can fix right now." Liam knelt by his pack and unzipped a side pocket, removing a first-aid kit. He located a Band-Aid and handed it to

Mom, who ripped it open. "Darla, let's see if your straps need adjusting." Liam lifted her pack but made a face before heaving it up and down a couple more times. "Did you pack bricks in here? This feels way heavier than it should."

Darla sighed as she stood up and hunched over her pack, unzipping the main pocket. "I'm sorry. I had to bring my crystals." She removed a mesh bag filled with shimmering, translucent rocks of various colors, including the purple one she'd been gripping when we arrived at the visitors' center.

Pete threw his head back. "Mom! Are you kidding me? Why would you put a bag of rocks in your backpack?"

"They are crystals, Pete. They bring out important energies. The energy that we all need to survive this camping this trip."

I looked toward Dad, who stared at the horizon, rubbing his jaw. Mom chuckled, shaking her head in disbelief.

Kenny faced us, scratching his beard. "Alright, everyone. Just back off. Darla has her reasons for doing what she does." He walked over to his wife and touched her on the shoulder. "I'll carry those for you, hon."

Darla nodded at him as Kenny gripped the weighted bag, his loyalty toward his wife earning my admiration again.

Liam's face was blank as he turned toward Mom, apparently eager to change the subject. "Abigail told me you're a psychiatrist, Kristen."

"Yes."

He let out a low whistle. "That's really something."

"So cool," Pete added.

Kenny lowered the bulging mesh bag. "You know, Darla's a healer too."

"Oh." Mom tilted her head, eyeing the crystals. She tucked in her chin as if searching for the right words. "That's not quite the same thing, though."

"What do you mean?" Kenny asked.

"I mean, I went through years and years of schooling and hands-on training." Mom pursed her lips as she motioned toward the bag. "Darla has a handful of supposedly magical crystals that have never been scientifically proven to do anything."

Dad stepped toward Mom as if preparing to intervene before the conversation spiraled downward.

"I read palms too," Darla said. "And Tarot. And I'm just getting my feet wet in professional astrology."

"Huh." Mom was stone-faced, but I could tell she was struggling to keep it together, that she considered Darla a con artist and didn't appreciate the comparison of the other woman's mystic hobbies to her professional medical career.

Darla raised her chin. "I can read your palms later if you want. No charge."

"That's okay. I don't really believe in that kind of thing."

"Just because you don't understand it, doesn't mean it's not real." Darla's voice had hardened.

Kenny nodded. "Darla's helped a lot of people. She does a good business."

"Okay." Mom turned, raising her eyebrows so only I could see.

"Moving on." Pete gave a little headshake, exasperated by his parents. Dad kicked at a long tuft of grass, clearly biting his tongue.

Liam approached Mom. "Hey, Kristen, have you ever treated anyone crazy, like someone with multiple personalities, or something like that?"

Mom flinched as if he'd thrown a bucket of spiders on her. "We don't like to use the term 'crazy.' It implies a negative connotation for people with mental health issues, which are illnesses, just like cancer or heart disease."

The sparkle vanished from Liam's eyes. "Oh, sorry. I didn't mean anything by it."

"That's okay. And, no, I haven't encountered anyone with multiple personalities. Most of my patients suffer from varying degrees of depression and anxiety."

Liam lowered himself onto a corner of Mom's rock, something dark passing over his face. "Man, I wish I'd had someone like you to talk to after my mom died."

"Oh." Mom straightened up. "I'm so sorry, Liam. I didn't realize you'd lost your mom."

"Ovarian cancer."

"How long has it been, if you don't mind me asking?" I noted the calm tone of Mom's voice, seeing how easily she slipped into psychiatrist mode.

"About three years now." Liam looked around, realizing that everyone was watching him. He cleared his throat. "That's actually the reason I became a wilderness guide. I felt so empty after she was gone. Lost. I probably should have talked to a therapist, but instead, I developed a drug addiction and spent six months in rehab. I'm not proud of that, of course."

There were a few offers of "I'm sorry" and "That's too bad." I nodded along with the others because I already knew about his mom's tragic death and Liam's battle with addiction. He had shared the same story with me and my co-workers during the work outing eight months ago.

Mom leaned in, touching her chin. "People use drugs and alcohol to dull their pain all the time. You should be very proud for getting clean." Everyone else mumbled their agreement.

Liam rubbed his eye with the back of his hand. "Once I got clean, I really thought about what kind of life I wanted to live. What made me happy? It wasn't the material stuff. I realized the times I felt the most alive, the most at peace, were when I was out in nature." He motioned toward the trees surrounding us. "Something happens out here in the wild. I can't explain it. It's good for the soul."

"I totally understand," Darla said. "Good for you for listening to your intuition. So many people don't."

Liam lowered his gaze. "Anyway, I wanted to share this magic I found with others, to let them see it too. That's when I joined Team Wilderness about a year and a half ago. It's been such a blast. And I get to help people."

Darla clasped her hands together. "You're good at your job because your heart's in it."

Mom nodded. "I agree with Darla on that."

"Thanks. And, hopefully, throughout the course of the next few days, you'll be able to open up more to each other too. Maybe share some parts of yourselves that the others don't know about. We'll have lots of good talks around the campfires." He motioned toward Darla. "And if that includes palm and Tarot card readings, then so be it."

I dipped my head in approval. "Sounds good."

Liam stood up. "Now let's get back on the trail. We still have about three miles to go, much of it uphill, but the next stop will be our campsite."

The rest of us helped each other hoist our packs. As I slid my front buckle together, a shadow slipped through the trees on the other side of the trail. It was dark and fleeting, darting into the foliage before I could make out any details. By the time I turned to get a better look, it was gone. "What was that?"

Pete looked at me, then followed my stare toward the forest. "What?"

"I don't know. I thought I saw someone—or something—run through the trees over there."

Kenny narrowed his eyes. "I didn't see anything."

"Yeah. I heard a branch snap," Darla said.

"Oh my God. What if it was a cougar?" Mom's mouth opened as she peered around.

Liam put a hand in the air, amusement tugging at his lips. "It was probably a deer. Or a bird. Nothing to worry about." He surveyed the group, then locked eyes with me as if begging me to keep things moving. "Everyone ready?"

"Yes." I forced a smile. "Let's go." But my molars ground into each other because the shadow I'd seen had been tall. Not a deer or a bird. It was more like a person. One who hadn't wanted to be seen.

FIVE

ABIGAIL

We continued along the trail with our guide leading the way. I kept my eyes straight ahead, shaking off my anxiety from whatever I'd glimpsed in the woods. Apparently, it had rained the night before and the earth was still damp, the air saturated with the scent of moss and wood. But the smell was refreshing, the kind that filled your lungs with a burst of oxygen. I kept pace with Mom while Dad and Pete followed behind us, chatting about a new client who owned some desirable office buildings downtown.

Mom leaned close, lowering her voice to a whisper. "I was right."

"About what?"

"Liam's got his hands full with this group."

"He can handle it. I'm sure he's seen worse." I remembered how Liam had smoothed things over with my co-workers. He'd done it in a way that they didn't even realize what had happened. Through physical activity requiring teamwork, he'd gotten them to connect on a deeper level, to create a unified atmosphere where there'd previously been nothing but conflict and resentment. We'd been in a different forest then, a state park just an hour's drive from work because it had been October, too cold to head so far north. There'd been a ropes course to start, followed by a hike, then setting up camp with real bathrooms a short walk away. I was eager to see how he'd alter his plan for our group in this more remote location.

Liam halted, causing the rest of us to stop too. The trail split in front of him. A wooden arrow pointed to the right, indicating that Crystal Lake was a mile ahead. The Crystal Lake trail was as wide and well-traveled as the one we were on. "We're going this way." Liam pointed the other way, to the unmarked trail on the left. Branches overhung the narrow path, which was nothing more than a line of dirt. I could barely tell it existed at all.

"Are you sure?" Dad's eyes ricocheted between me and Mom. "Is that even a trail?"

Mom yanked at the hem of her shirt. "Crystal Lake sounds so lovely. Those other hikers were just raving about it. Maybe we should go that way instead."

"Nope. We're not taking the easy route. This is the way to our campsite. It's the route I registered with the park." Liam angled his head toward the overgrown path, a mischievous smile twitching on his lips. "The road less traveled, as they say."

An uneasy giggle slipped from my mouth.

"We trust you, Liam," Kenny said as Darla nodded beside him.

"Let's do it!" Pete yelled from behind me.

We forged onward, this time in a single-file line. Darla was walking in front of me and every so often, leaves and branches whipped back as she pushed past them, and then hit me in the face, causing my eyes to close and my lips to tighten. Mom winced and grunted behind me, and I realized the same thing was happening to her.

"This sucks," I said.

Darla laughed. "It was your idea, sweetheart."

I tightened my lips, knowing she was right and letting the comment slide. A few steps later, I caught a movement behind the trees in my peripheral vision. Ignoring the flutter in my stomach, I hoped it was merely a trick of the light. But when I peered toward it again, I realized the dark shape was the same one I'd seen several minutes earlier. Now the tall and lumbering figure was heading toward us, leaves crunching and branches snapping. I couldn't get a clear view, and for a split second, I feared we'd inadvertently stumbled upon a Bigfoot. I gasped, stopping suddenly so that Mom ran into my back.

"Abigail—" she started to say, then stopped, spotting the figure too. As it approached, a man wearing a backpack materialized. The others turned toward us, following our nervous stares and becoming aware of the man's presence.

Liam cleared his throat. "Hello." He stepped off the trail and into the brush, closer to the scruffy stranger.

The man dipped his head but didn't speak. He was built like a scarecrow, tall with sinewy muscles straining through his arms. A layer of grime coated every inch of his skin. His dirty, blonde hair clumped into long ropes resembling dreadlocks. A full beard covered his face. But it was his eyes that caused my breath to catch in my throat. They were pale blue, vacant, sunken into hollow sockets.

"Are you lost?" Liam asked.

The man jerked his head. "No, sir."

"Which way are you headed?"

"That way." He pointed behind us and I released a breath, thankful we were heading in opposite directions. The man sniffled, and I studied him again, realizing something about his face, his crooked nose, looked vaguely familiar. Still, I was sure I'd never met this person. I must have seen someone who looked like him at the coffee shop or on a TV show.

"Can I trouble you for some extra food?" The man's scattered stare darted around the group.

Mom's fingers fumbled for a zipper on the side of her pack. "I've got a couple of granola bars you can have."

I wanted to say, *What if we need those?* I hoped we wouldn't find ourselves in a desperate situation and have to resort to swallowing caterpillars and chewing on tree bark like the people on those survival shows Kenny had been telling us about. But I assumed Liam had packed plenty of food and Mom couldn't really take back the offer now anyway. I helped her by unzipping the outer pocket of her pack. Two oat and honey bars with shiny green wrappers lay inside. I pulled them out and handed them to the guy, noticing the slight quiver in my fingers as he greedily swiped the bars from my palm.

He lowered his forehead, no longer making eye contact. "Appreciate it," he said before turning and hiking away from us through the trees.

Liam raised his hand. "Safe travels."

We all hovered, silent, as we watched the man hobble away, devouring one of the bars as he went.

"Wooee!" Kenny tipped his head back once the man was out of sight. "That guy could sure use a hot shower."

Mom tightened her lips. "He was so thin. I hope he's okay."

"I wonder how long he's been living out here," Dad said.

Liam shrugged. "Lots of people live out in national parks, sometimes for weeks or even months. Usually, people who want to get away from society. It's a lifestyle."

"Like fugitives," Kenny said matter-of-factly.

"Okay." Pete stepped forward, interrupting. "I'm sure that wasn't what Liam meant. Let's keep going so it's still light when we get to the campsite."

Liam gave a tight nod. "Agreed! Let's stay focused. Our campsite has a creek running through it. After we complete our chores, you'll want to have time to relax and enjoy the view." He turned and continued up the rugged trail, which had taken on a steep incline.

My feet felt damp inside my clunky hiking boots, despite the moisture-wicking socks I'd purchased. The temperature hovered in the high seventies, but the air felt warmer as sweat gathered in my armpits and beaded across my forehead. I worried about how the older members of the party were holding up. I found myself looking over my shoulder as we marched along, not only to check on Mom and Dad but also to make sure that strange man wasn't lurking in the weeds or behind a tree. I couldn't shake his face from my mind.

"You guys been watching the new season of *The Bachelor*?" Kenny shook his head. "There are some real characters on there."

"I haven't seen that one," Dad said, his voice flat. I couldn't remember Dad ever watching a reality TV show in his life. He preferred college sports, a Tigers' game, or business reports on the news channels.

"How about *Keeping Up With the Kardashians*?" Kenny asked.

Mom released an audible gasp. In her mind, the Kardashians represented everything that was wrong with society. I stayed quiet to avoid admitting that I occasionally caught an episode while I folded laundry. The show was an escape into a different kind of life, one with glamour and drama and lots of makeup.

Pete huffed. "Dad, no one here watches *The Bachelor* or *The Kardashians*." I glanced back at Pete, finding his features tight, fists clenched. "Remember what we talked about."

"Right." Kenny swatted a fly away from his head. "I forgot that my hobbies embarrass you. That our family embarrasses you."

"No. That's not—" Pete grunted. "It's just, why don't you ask people something about themselves? You barely even know my future wife. Or her parents, for that matter."

Liam twisted toward us, leaning forward. "Hey, Kenny. If

you don't mind me chiming in, I think that's a great idea. Remember the main purpose of this outing is for everyone to get to know each other better."

Kenny mumbled something, then looked over Darla's shoulder at me, a flicker of shame in his eyes. "Abigail, I'm sorry. I don't always have the best manners. You seem like a nice young lady. What is it that you do for a living again?"

"I work for a public relations firm as a content writer. The firm I work for does a lot of projects for auto companies and a couple of banks. We have some high-profile business leaders too. Anyone who needs a little push to help change their public image."

"So, they pay you to make them look good?"

"Yes." I smiled. "Basically, that's it in a nutshell."

"Well, that's really something. Good for you."

"Thanks."

"I drive a forklift. Auto parts," Kenny said. "That's what's in the boxes I stack in the warehouse. Or sometimes I remove the boxes and stack them in the trucks." He offered a smile. "So I guess we have something in common. We both work for the auto industry, in a way."

"Yeah. That's true." I stared at Kenny's wide back as we continued walking, remembering the way he'd defended his wife, and had carried her heavy bag of crystals without complaint. Now, after only minor prodding, he was making a genuine effort to connect with me. Maybe my first impression of him at Applebee's as being rude and self-absorbed had been rushed and not entirely correct. Underneath his rough exterior, Kenny seemed like a decent guy.

Kenny's gaze slid past me, landing on Mom. "Kristen, I already know you're a psychiatrist. I take it there are plenty of patients to go around."

"That's very true. No lack of troubled souls in this world."

Kenny yelled back to Dad. "And, John, how's the real estate business going?"

"It's going well. Partly thanks to Pete. He's such a hard worker. Did he tell you he is the first employee in the company to get promoted twice in under three years?"

"Well, no. I don't think you ever told me that, Pete. That's real good."

Now Darla turned back to look at her son. "Good for you, Pete. You're a Virgo, of course, so your determination is no surprise." No one responded. "Abigail, what's your sun sign?"

"Mom!" Pete protested from behind me.

"C'mon, now, Pete. Whether you like it or not, this is how I get to know people."

I raised my voice. "I'm a Gemini."

"Oh. That's interesting." Darla breathed through her mouth, her feet landing heavily on the uphill path.

"What do you mean?" I asked when Darla failed to elaborate on what exactly was "interesting."

"You and Pete are both ruled by Mercury, but you have some conflicting traits. Geminis are typically positive people who enjoy expressing themselves creatively, while Virgos are hardworking but critical."

"Well, hopefully they can work it out," Dad said from the back, a hint of sarcasm in his voice.

"I'm sure we can," Pete added in the same tone, but louder.

Darla glanced over her shoulder, a stiff smile on her lips. "Opposites attract, I suppose."

Mom coughed. "But, Darla, if you don't mind me playing devil's advocate, doesn't everyone have all those traits to some extent? I'm critical sometimes, and positive other times. There's a famous study that shows most people who are fed general information in a 'fortune-telling' scenario believe that the general information specifically applies to them. This was true no matter what general information was told to them. It's called the Forer effect."

Darla laughed, deep and throaty. "Skeptics will always try to disprove my craft, Kristen. I don't tell anyone's fortune. There is no predetermined fate that cannot be altered. I simply identify strengths and weaknesses, possible pitfalls that may be overcome."

Mom's feet moved slower. "Yes. I'm only saying that what you're doing isn't based on anything real. There's no science to back it up."

I tossed Mom a stern look. A sour expression pulled down her features. I could tell she was struggling to be polite, although her true feelings were clearly surfacing.

Darla's moon-shaped face flipped back again, staring Mom down. "There's no science to back up the five major religions of the world either."

Mom continued walking, looking at her feet. I braced myself for the dam to break, but it seemed she didn't have a ready response. Mom was a Methodist who made it to church when it was convenient. I'd long suspected her occasional Sunday visits were more of a social appearance than for her to attain spiritual guidance. But the mention of religion had thrown the conversation into dangerous waters, and Mom didn't wade out any further.

"Tell you what, Kristen," Darla said as the bright blue and green feathers in her braid fluttered in the breeze, strings of beads clinking. "I brought my Tarot cards with me. I'll do a reading for you later once we get settled into camp."

There was a beat of uncomfortable silence.

"I think you should go for it, Kristen," Liam said from the front. His encouragement caused my toe to catch on the ground, but maybe the activity fit into his plan to get people talking.

Darla placed her hands on her lower back. "You can take or leave the insights, of course."

Again, I braced myself for Mom's response. To my surprise, maybe reminding herself of the goal of the outing, she only said, "Sure, Darla. That will be a new experience for me."

A familiar grunt sounded from behind me. I swiveled around to face Pete, who shook his head, eyes fixed on the dirt path. "What a bunch of bullshit," he muttered under his breath. He looked like he'd rather be anywhere else, like he'd prefer to be swallowed by a sinkhole than to continue this hike with his parents who were revealing a side of his upbringing he'd mostly kept hidden.

My heart sunk as I closed my eyes, digging my fingernails into my palm, wondering if this trip had been a terrible mistake.

SIX

ABIGAIL

I walked beside Pete for the next hour. He was unusually quiet and sullen as the four parents and Liam chatted about species of birds and pine trees. I wasn't sure if Pete's silence stemmed from his embarrassment of his parents, but I thought his reaction was a little extreme. I wished he'd loosen up a little and give everyone a chance to get to know each other. Or maybe something else was eating at him. In either case, I felt bad that his feelings were hurt.

My back ached under the weight of the pack when Liam finally shouted the words I'd longed to hear. "We're coming up to our campsite. Once we hit the creek, we're there."

"That's a relief." Mom wiped her brow with the back of her hand. "I could really use a break."

The rest of us voiced our agreement. We turned a bend, where the sound of water met my ears, the soothing cascade immediately calming me. Trees scattered across a rolling expanse. A stream rushed over rocks in the distance, with dense woods beyond. The scene was breathtaking, almost otherworldly. I could see why Liam found solace in this setting.

"Wow." Dad's chest expanded as he took in the view.

Liam waved everyone forward. "See. This is even better than Crystal Lake. And we have it all to ourselves."

"It's just beautiful." Darla reached for Kenny's hand.

"Pretty nice. Good job, Liam." The adventurous glimmer had returned to Pete's eyes. He lifted the pack off my back and set it down.

"So, the first thing we'll do is set up the tents," Liam said. "There are simple instructions inside each tent bag. How about the men set up one tent in this clearing here," he motioned toward a flat area, "and the women set up the other tent about eight or ten feet away? I'll set up my single tent right here." He pointed downward. "These will be our sleeping arrangements too."

I saw the way Mom's face fell for a moment before she recovered. I knew she'd been hoping to share a tent with me and Dad.

"Boys versus girls." Kenny pumped his fist in the air, oblivious to Mom's disappointment.

Darla kicked away a few rocks, inspecting the ground. "This should do." She transferred her weight from foot to foot. "But you'll have to excuse me. Nature calls."

"Go for it." Liam waved her away as he handed each group a canvas bag and stood nearby, observing as the rest of us read directions and doled out the responsibilities. He dipped his tanned face in approval, then stepped away to help the men organize their gear. After Darla returned, I noticed how Dad, Kenny, and Pete took turns hustling into the woods and returning. I had to pee too, having already held it as long as I possibly could.

"I have to go, too. Be back in a second," I said, interrupting Darla's reading of the assembly instructions to Mom.

"I'll go with you." Mom dropped the rod she'd been holding, leaving Darla to make sense of the directions.

Mom and I found our way behind the trees to a thick clump

of shrubbery, squatting behind it on opposite sides and both returning to the campsite a couple of minutes later to help Darla insert rods into tiny sleeves and assemble the other pieces. With only a few missteps, which we quickly corrected, our tent was up. Liam returned from digging through his pack to stake the four corners of our structure into the ground, a task he did with ease. Kenny's laughter bellowed from a few feet away, and I noticed the men had also finished putting together their tent. I was amazed everyone was getting along so well, and I couldn't stop my eyes from traveling to Liam, so confident in his role as our leader.

"Do we want to make a campfire tonight?" Liam asked after we'd gotten our sleeping bags laid out inside the tents. "We'll cook our food over the camping stove, so we don't really need one. It's up to you."

"I love campfires." Mom gave a wistful smile. "They remind me of going to summer camp when I was a girl."

"Yeah. Let's do it." Kenny shoved a handful of trail mix into his mouth, smacking his lips.

Liam peered around. "Okay, look for a good spot. Sometimes you can find a place where other campers have had one."

We spread apart, wandering between the trees, searching for ashes or a clearing where we could build a small fire.

"There's something here," Mom yelled from further down an incline and behind a small pine tree. A crease formed along the center of her forehead. "This is so strange."

We headed toward her as she stared at the ground, eyebrows furrowed. I followed her line of vision to a circle of ashes. A decaying log rested nearby, forming a bench of sorts. Beside the ashes, someone had taken twenty or thirty smallish stones and spelled out three words:

WATCH YOUR BACK!

"Watch your back." It was Darla who said the phrase out loud, her voice cracking.

"What's that supposed to mean?" Kenny asked.

"Oh, no." Darla's forehead wrinkled as she looked up at the sky, then at me and Pete. "I feel a very negative energy surrounding us."

Pete and I glanced at each other. "It sounds like a threat," he said.

Mom pulled her frightened stare from the ground and looked toward our guide. "I hope not. Why would anyone want to threaten us?"

"I don't know. I've never seen a message like this before." Liam shifted his narrow hips, staring off into the trees beyond the creek. A second later, he registered the unease on our faces. "I'm sure it's just some weird thing from whoever camped here before us." He stepped forward and kicked the rocks, erasing the words.

"So much for 'Leave no trace.'" Kenny shook his head, chuckling to himself.

"Did someone here do this?" Tension stretched through Pete's voice. "It's not funny."

"None of us could have done it," Dad said. "We've all been together the whole time."

My hands reached for opposite elbows, hugging my arms close to my chest. I didn't reply because Dad's statement wasn't entirely true. After arriving at the campsite, each of us had wandered into the woods at one point or another to relieve ourselves, while the ones who stayed back were preoccupied with setting up tents. Mom and I had slipped into the forest together, but as far as I remembered, everyone else had ventured out alone. The slope in the landscape and the little pine tree could have obstructed our view of someone laying out the message.

"Of course none of us did it, honey." Mom forced a smile toward Pete, but uncertainty clouded her eyes.

Darla's face had lost its color, her fingers laced in front of her. She seemed to have traveled somewhere else in her mind.

Kenny pointed to the ground, face solemn. "Maybe it's not a threat. Maybe someone is trying to tell us to be careful about building a campfire here. They're saying, 'Watch your back. Embers might fly up and light your clothes on fire.'" He looked around, considering. "This could be a high-wind area."

I eyed Kenny and noticed the way Mom and Dad did the same. At first, I thought he was joking, but quickly realized he was serious. I supposed his theory was almost as plausible as it was laughable.

Liam exhaled. "That's probably all it is. A friendly—and very vague—warning to keep our eyes on the campfire. Maybe the person ran out of rocks to really spell it out for us." Liam smiled, clearly not as bothered by the message as the rest of us. "Anyway, I saw a better spot over there, closer to the creek. Everyone, gather some sticks and I'll build a circle of rocks to contain the fire."

As the others scattered to find sticks, I put my head down, feeling Pete's palm on the small of my back. "You okay?"

"Yeah. That message was a little creepy though."

He took both of my hands in his and squeezed. "I think Liam's right. It must have been from the previous group. I really don't think it had anything to do with us."

I leaned into him, feeling the heat of his body. "Probably not."

Pete draped his arm around me as we joined the others at the newly designated fire pit, the strange message still etched in my mind.

We set up the wood for the fire, not yet lighting it. Liam unpacked our food, waving away our offers to help prepare dinner. "You guys go explore. Just make sure you stay within range of being able to see our camp. We don't want anyone getting lost out here."

"What's for dinner?" Dad asked.

"Burgers."

"Abigail doesn't eat meat," Mom said, throwing a concerned look in my direction.

"Oh, yeah. I know. Neither do I." Liam glanced at me because we'd discussed the meal plans last week. "I'm using the plant-based stuff."

Kenny frowned.

Liam looked around at the others. "Don't worry, you won't know the difference. And it's so much better for the environment. And for the animals, obviously."

"Thanks, Liam." I'd stopped eating meat three years earlier but had only gotten Pete partially on board with my veggie lifestyle. It was a relief to have an ally in Liam.

Dad rubbed his hand together. "Well, thank you for doing the cooking. I'm starving."

While Liam set up the little camp stove and prepared the food, the rest of us wandered toward the creek, following it upstream for a while and peering into the clear water. Gray and black pebbles covered the creek bed and it was obvious that this was the place where the rocks from the strange message had originated. I crouched down and plunged my fingers into the current, shocked by the water's icy temperature.

"These stones look almost like onyx." Darla's voice directly behind me made me jump. I turned toward her as she bent down, dipped her hand into the cold water, and scooped up a few stones. She tossed a couple back, holding a black one up to the fading sunlight, inspecting it. Her lips puckered. "Nope. Not onyx, but it's still pretty." She tucked the stone into her pocket.

As we marveled at the water, clear as glass, I was surprised to see Pete and Mom on the other side of the creek, pointing at an object beneath the surface. Dad and Kenny each held twigs, poking them at something.

"We found a crayfish." A boyish wonder lit Dad's eyes as I wandered toward him. He lowered the twig. He and Kenny laughed as Darla and I watched the crustacean pinch the stick in its claw. We spent the next twenty minutes discovering tiny wonders along the creek—a school of minnows, a slug, a rogue piece of sea glass. We shared each discovery with the others. Again, I couldn't believe how well everyone was getting along. Even Pete seemed to have gotten over his earlier annoyance with his mom and dad. I glanced toward our guide, who hunched over the tiny stove, flipping burgers and placing them onto tin plates.

He lifted his head and gave me a slight nod. "Hey, guys. It's time to eat!"

A few minutes later, we sat around the camp stove, everyone holding a thin plate on their lap. We passed around a bag of potato chips, taking bites of the juicy burgers inside soft buns.

"Wow. Good job, Liam." A bit of juice ran down Mom's chin and she wiped it away.

Kenny nodded. "I'm impressed. You a professional chef too?"

The rest of us laughed as a sheepish grin overtook Liam's face. "Nah. This will be our best meal, so enjoy it. It's impossible to keep anything cold for longer than a few hours. Tomorrow night is ramen noodles. But at least my pack will be about two pounds lighter in the morning."

"I wonder what that other fellow is eating tonight." Kenny's eyes darted toward the woods, and we all knew he was referring to the guy we'd crossed paths with earlier.

Darla's eyes seemed to darken as she scanned the woods, something I'd seen her do several times when we'd been exploring the creek.

Mom lowered what was left of her hamburger bun, glancing over her shoulder. "What if that hungry man was the one who left that weird message with the rocks?" She shook her head. "But that doesn't make any sense. Why would he threaten us?"

Pete shrugged. "Just someone messing around, probably. Like Liam said."

"Wait a minute. I think you're onto something, Kristen." Kenny picked at his teeth. "It looked like he's been living outdoors for a while. Fugitives are known to hide out in National Parks, as I said before."

Pete made a loud sound like something was stuck in his throat, causing all of us to turn toward him.

Kenny ignored Pete's throat clearing and continued talking. "A guy I knew in prison did that. The police couldn't find him for months."

A thick silence filled the air as Kenny peered around the circle. Dad lowered the potato chip he'd been about to eat. Mom gasped. I looked at Pete, confused. *Prison?* But Pete only kicked the ground and dropped his head into his hands.

"Did you say prison?" Mom sat up straight, touching her throat. She locked eyes with me as if to ask if I knew anything about this.

I managed a slight shake of my head, feeling like my blood had turned as cold as the creek water, rushing just as fast. Pete had told me some troubling stories about Trent, including how he'd gotten suspended from high school after threatening a classmate in the school parking lot, but he'd never shared this bombshell about his dad with me. I studied Pete, gathering from his body language that he'd been aware of his dad's criminal past, that he'd hidden it from me. The betrayal rose up in me, heating my face.

Liam leaned forward, mouth opening but no words coming out. It seemed even the expert peacemaker was at a loss for words.

Darla patted Kenny's knee. "Kenny got into some trouble about six years ago. He had some gambling debts. Unfortunately, he and his friend tried to steal a car."

"My buddy had a gun. It was so dumb." Kenny frowned. "I did my time though. Learned my lesson. I stay away from the casinos now too."

"How long were you in?" Now it was Dad who spoke, his face unnaturally still.

"Twelve months. It was something else in there. Let me tell you. Not much to do except watch TV."

I exhaled, temples throbbing. Twelve months in prison. I wondered what that did to a person. No wonder Kenny watched so much TV.

"Dad. Goddammit!" Pete threw his plate down.

Liam stood up and put his hands in the air, attempting to deflect the loaded stare between the father and son. "Whoa. Whoa. Let's all take a breath."

"I wasn't ready to do this." Spittle flew from Pete's mouth. "This wasn't the time or the way to tell them about that." I could see the fury tightening Pete's face, the rage burning in his eyes, the strain in his neck. It seemed he wanted to strangle his dad. Instead, he stood up and stomped off into the woods as the rest of us remained in place, silent and stunned.

SEVEN

ABIGAIL

I jogged after Pete, finding him crouched against a tree trunk on the other side of the campsite. His red-rimmed eyes couldn't look at me.

"Pete—"

"I'm sorry." He covered his face with his hands. "I swear I wasn't trying to hide anything from you."

"It's okay." I touched his shoulder. "But I don't understand why you never told me about your dad."

"I was going to tell you. But not in front of everyone like that." Pete gritted his teeth, the tiny muscle in his jaw pulsing. "He has no shame, no ability to read other people."

I crouched next to Pete, wanting to comfort him, but also feeling a tinge of anger. We'd been together for over two years. There had been plenty of opportunities to bring up difficult subjects. I'd always provided a soft place for him to land. But lately, I'd also gotten the feeling he'd been holding something back from me, that he felt most comfortable presenting himself in the light he thought I wanted to see him in: as a confident businessman and a loyal and caring partner who'd risen above his upbringing. Now I realized that Pete had never been quite as confident as he'd led me to believe.

As Pete swore under his breath and punched the tree, it was obvious that Pete's family was the source of his insecurity. There'd been a thick tension between him and his parents as we hiked. They were opposites, and not in a way that complemented each other. Pete was a people person who had the uncanny ability to adapt to any conversation with ease, entertain the room, and make the people around him feel important. His polished personality was one of the reasons he'd been so successful at Dad's company. It must have been frustrating for him to deal with his somewhat unrefined parents out in the open—Kenny's unfiltered commentary and Darla's unquestioning belief in the mystic arts.

Conversation from the campsite filtered through the trees, low and muffled. I wondered what the others were saying, how Mom and Dad were processing Kenny's unsavory revelation.

"I'm not my dad." Pete searched my face, visibly desperate for a sign of forgiveness or, at least, acknowledgment.

"I know that. Of course, you're not." I pulled in a few deep breaths, letting my weight fall into him. "It's just that I would have liked to have known the whole truth. Like how you shared your fears about Trent and your neighbor's dog with me."

"But this is my dad. Trent is different. Something's always been off with him."

My thoughts spun toward Pete's brother, back to the night Trent had shown up on Pete's front steps and ignored me. The next day, Pete had stopped by my place with flowers, and we'd talked about Trent's behavior for a few minutes. Then, in a quiet voice, Pete had shared a disturbing memory. When he was twelve, their neighbor, Mr. Flynn, who lived across the street, had a dog named Molly who loved to play fetch. Both boys had doted on the happy dog, slipping her treats after school or taking her to the nearby field to throw a tennis ball. One afternoon, Pete had gotten a weird feeling and happened to glance out his bedroom window. On the street below, he'd spotted Trent leading Molly away from her house and toward a patch of woods. The next day, a long-faced Mr. Flynn had knocked on their door asking if they'd seen his dog. Molly had been missing since the previous afternoon and he couldn't find her anywhere. The boys had helped him search for days, but the poor dog was never seen again. When Pete confronted his brother, Trent claimed he loved the dog and hadn't done anything to her. But Pete had a hard time imagining what else could have happened. When he mentioned the incident to his mom, she'd shooed him away and told him never to speak about it again.

Now, I examined Pete's face, seeing the strain at my mention of Molly the dog. I placed my hand on his arm. "Whatever your dad did wouldn't have changed anything between us. I just want to know the real you."

He sniffed. "Yeah. I messed up. I'm so sorry."

"Is there anything else about them you need to tell me?"

Pete blinked, chest rising and falling.

"Pete?"

"No. That's about the worst of it."

I squeezed his hand. "Your mom's not an axe murderer?"

A smile curved across Pete's lips. "No. She's a lot of things, but not an axe murderer."

"Okay, then let's head back there and do some damage control."

"I love you." He kissed me, and I could feel the heat pulsing off his body. I could smell the sour scent of his sweat. This was about as real as it got. Still, something turned in my gut. Maybe because of the way Pete had hesitated when I'd asked him if there was anything else I should know, like he'd thought of another dark secret but then decided to bury it. Then again, I supposed Pete didn't know everything about me either. Maybe all relationships were a careful balance of truth and half-truths.

Maybe the worst parts of ourselves were more comfortable hiding in the shadows.

We returned to the circle, to the silent bodies and uncomfortable smiles.

Kenny kicked his foot out. "Sorry about that, Pete. I didn't realize my past was a big secret."

Pete raised his eyes. "It's my fault. I shouldn't have kept the information from everyone." He looked toward Mom and Dad. "I'm sorry."

Dad looked tired as he lowered his eyelids. "It doesn't change anything, Pete."

I noticed the way Pete's shoulders relaxed at Dad's reassurance. Still, a hint of embarrassment lingered on my fiancé's face as he stared at the unlit pile of sticks.

Our guide finally spoke. "We're more than our mistakes." Liam's voice was calm and introspective. It seemed he was talking just as much about his own troubles and addiction as he was about Kenny.

Mom set her plate down and gestured toward me. "When you were gone, I was reminding the others that everyone makes mistakes. Some are worse than others, but the important thing is that we learn from them."

"Yeah," I said, biting the inside of my cheek and aware that Mom had, once again, morphed into psychiatrist mode. But I knew her well enough to notice the way she'd glossed over Kenny's felony record and cemented the understated smile on her face. She was masking her true feelings.

Kenny crossed his thick arms and leaned back. "Well, I learned my lesson in there, that's for sure."

I leaned into Pete, hoping it was true.

Mom turned the conversation toward my childhood and how she'd caught me swiping a candy bar from the Kroger checkout lane once when I was six, how she'd walked me back into the store and made me hand back the unopened chocolate bar to the checkout lady and apologize. I'd locked myself in my room when we'd gotten home, proclaiming I was never coming out. According to Mom, that had lasted about fifteen minutes before I'd slunk down the stairs and asked if dinner was ready. The others laughed, faces turning pink in the waning daylight.

I looked at Darla. "Do you have any funny stories like that about Pete?"

"Oh, well. I don't know if I can remember any right now. I always had my hands full with Trent, even though he was the older one. He was a real terror when he was a kid." Her eyes held a dazed look. "Pete was usually off on his bike somewhere or reading a book in his bedroom."

Kenny grunted. "He loved that bike. The blue one. Remember?"

Darla nodded. "Sure did."

The rest of us waited for them to add something more, another memory or anecdote about Pete as a boy. But Darla and Kenny didn't say anything else, only stared at their hands. Pete shifted his weight, and I gleaned another insight into why he didn't particularly enjoy spending time with his parents. He'd been the well-behaved child, but also the forgotten one.

Liam stood and stretched his arms above his head, clearly sensing the previous conversation lay dead in the water. "What do you all say we wash off our plates in the creek and then get this bonfire going?"

Dad popped up. "Sounds good."

"And don't forget to refill your water bottles. The water looks clear, but we can't see the deadly microbes that might be lurking in it. Make sure you only drink through the filtration straws. Otherwise, you risk getting sick." Liam pulled out a pack of Graham crackers and some marshmallows and set them aside. He placed the remaining food in a large plastic bag, asking the rest of us to add any food we'd brought with us, so as not to attract the bears. We did as we were told. Liam strung up the bag so that it dangled from a tree branch at the edge of the clearing.

After the food was hung, the water collected, and the plates cleaned and dried, we found our seats around the pile of sticks and branches. A stark forest surrounded us, the sky darkening above the wavering shadows.

Liam dug into his pack for more supplies. "If anyone needs to go to the bathroom again, now's a good time. You know, before it gets really dark."

I raised my eyebrows at the others. "And by 'bathroom,' I think he means pee in the woods."

Darla chuckled at my comment as she ran her fingers along the string of beads dangling over her shoulder.

We all scattered in opposite directions, disappearing behind wide tree trunks and dense bushes to relieve ourselves. Once everyone had returned to the circle, Mom passed a bottle of hand sanitizer around.

Liam used his handheld gas lighter to get the fire going. "Oh, good," Dad said. "I was worried we were going to have to rub two sticks together."

"Nah. I wouldn't do that to you."

The fire spread and crackled as night descended on our corner of the wilderness. The flames cast long shadows across us, everyone's faces looking strange in the flickering light. An owl hooted. The wind blew the smoke toward the creek, rustling the nearby leaves. It was peaceful.

Liam passed around sticks and marshmallows, and we began roasting our dessert. "So, not to get too serious, but does anyone have anything they want to say to Pete and Abigail before they get married? Maybe some advice. Or something you hope for them."

Darla scooted forward, waving her hand. "I do. I hope Abigail gets pregnant right away. I would love to be a grandma as soon as possible."

"Oh." I almost dropped my stick into the fire. I looked at Pete, who closed his eyes in dramatic fashion. Then I turned to Mom and Dad, whose faces were frozen. My mouth had gone dry, but I managed to find my voice. "I'm not ready to be a mom just yet, Darla. I'm sorry."

Darla's lips pulled down in the corners. "You should reconsider. I have a strong feeling about it. A very strong feeling."

Pete set his jaw. "Mom, it's not your decision."

I removed my marshmallow from the flames, doing my best to soften my voice. "It's just that I want to focus on my career for a while first."

Mom sat up straighter. "If you don't mind me chiming in, Darla. I told Abigail that the best thing John and I did after getting married was waiting for two years to have a baby. It gave us time to enjoy being with each other."

"No." Darla tugged at her long braid. Even in the dim light, I could see a pink splotch blooming across her neck. "Don't wait. That's a mistake."

"Mom. That's enough. You're totally out of line. You need to respect our decision." Pete's voice had hardened.

Liam's stunned eyes darted between Pete and Darla. "Okay, yeah. This might not be my place, but I agree with Pete and Abigail on this one. A big decision like that can't be forced or rushed."

Darla bit her lip as she looked up at the stars, chin quivering. "I'm sorry, but this is very upsetting for me."

Kenny stood up and gave his wife a quick hug, whispering something in her ear. She nodded, but not before I saw tears filling her eyes. Her reaction was confusing, and I couldn't help wondering about her reason for the artificial timeline. Had she been diagnosed with a brain tumor or a deadly form of cancer and was worried she'd never get to meet her grandchild? Wouldn't Pete have mentioned that to me?

Liam continued poking at the fire, not speaking. I recalled

Mom's earlier comment about Liam being in over his head, and I realized she might be right.

Darla coughed into her hand. I would feel terrible if she was battling a terminal illness. Maybe it was something she'd hoped to keep quiet. I sat up, peering over the flames. "Darla, how about we do the palm reading now? Or Tarot. Whatever you want."

Pete gave me a sideways glance as if to say, *Are you serious?*

"Yes. Let's do that. I'll go first." Mom's unnaturally high voice drew my attention, and I could tell she was faking her enthusiasm for Darla's sake. I wondered if she was just being amenable or if she'd had the same thought as me about Darla's days being numbered.

Liam clapped his hands a few times. "Okay. Darla, you're up. I can't wait to hear what you know about us."

Darla offered a sly grin as she swallowed down a marshmallow and wiped her palms down her thighs. "I'll start with palm reading." Her stare latched on to me. Maybe it was the petulant look on her face or the way the flames danced in her dark eyes, but a knot tightened in my stomach. Clearly, she was still miffed by my response to her plea for me to have a baby right away, even though she'd been the one who'd crossed a line. But Darla was in control of our fortunes now, and I had an uneasy feeling that things between Pete's family and mine were about to get even worse.

EIGHT

ABIGAIL

"Place your hands in mine, palm up." Mom and Darla sat facing each other as the fire crackled beside them. Darla's voice suddenly sounded different, almost eerie. "What do you hope to get from this reading, Kristen?"

Mom shook her head. "I really don't know. I'm only curious, I guess."

"Relax your hands and fingers." Darla closed her eyes and manipulated each of Mom's fingers, bending them backward and forward. Then she leaned closer studying something none of the rest of us could see. "You have an air hand. That's not surprising, given your analytical nature. Your love of knowledge."

Mom fluttered her eyelashes. "How do you know it's an air hand?"

"Square palm, long fingers." Darla continued staring at Mom's right hand, giving no further explanation. "Your fingers are somewhat inflexible. This can indicate a rigid worldview or merely someone who is set in their routines."

"She loves her routines," Dad said from the other side of the fire as a smile twitched on his lips.

"Everyone loves routines." Mom frowned. "It's human nature."

Darla ignored the comments as she tapped one of Mom's shiny fingernails. "These aren't your real nails."

"No. I had some acrylics put on at the salon last week. I thought the lighter color was nice." Mom smiled, clearly waiting for a compliment from Darla but none came.

"These fake nails may obscure some important observations about your demeanor."

The smile vanished from Mom's face. "I didn't know this was a fingernail reading. I guess I shouldn't have bothered going to the nail spa." She gave an incredulous laugh.

Darla showed no reaction. She only turned over Mom's hand, inspecting it. "You have a strong Line of Heart. I can see that you love your family deeply, both in the past and the present."

Mom's face softened.

Pete muttered something and shook his head.

Darla ran a finger over Mom's palm. "Your Mount of Venus is quite elevated. This indicates a warm and loving personality, someone who others can trust."

I nodded toward Mom. "That's pretty accurate, Mom."

Mom's eyes skittered toward me, and I noticed how she didn't contradict the positive parts of Darla's reading.

Darla traced another line, peering closer as a deep crease formed across her forehead. "There's a clean break in your Line of Life." Darla closed her mouth and opened it again. "Contrary to popular belief, a short Line of Life doesn't necessarily signal a short life. But a break like this can possibly indicate a major illness or health problem or..." Darla raised her gaze to meet Mom's eyes. "Have you battled cancer recently?"

"No."

"Another illness?"

"No."

"Are you taking care of yourself? Eating healthy? Exercising?"

"Well, yes. I eat lots of fresh fruits and vegetables. And I'm out here hiking for three days, aren't I?"

"You need to get screened. As soon as possible."

"I just went to the doctor last month." Mom tried to pull her hand away, but Darla gripped it tighter. "Everything was fine."

Darla pressed her thumbs into the center of Mom's right palm. "It might not be cancer. It could be something else. Regardless, please get checked out, just to be safe."

"Okay." Mom's voice was stiff. "But I'm sure I don't have any health problems."

Darla grasped the tops of Mom's fingers. "I'd like to reiterate that there is no predetermined fate. Everything can be changed by taking the correct actions. You can use this knowledge to overcome future obstacles, so please don't worry about what I just told you."

"I'm not worried." Mom's face was pinched, and it was obvious she was struggling to keep her true feelings contained, to stop herself from stating facts that would surely poke holes in Darla's insights. I appreciated her biting her tongue if only to avoid unnecessary conflict.

"Your Line of Fate, which I see here," Darla traced her finger up the middle of Mom's hand, "tells me about your destiny as related to financial success. It can give insights into your career aspirations. But ultimately, you are in charge."

"Of course I am," Mom said under her breath.

"Your Line of Fate indicates a strong passion for your chosen career. However, I see that you weren't always sure this was what you wanted to do. You started down a different road, then changed your mind."

Mom tilted her head. "Hm. I think you're off on that one. I've known my career path for quite a while."

"Didn't you used to want to be a veterinarian?" I asked, remembering a story she told me years earlier.

"Maybe for about two weeks when I was twelve. I hardly think that would have left a line on my hand."

Darla dipped her head, again ignoring Mom's comment. "Your Line of Marriage is clear and straight." Darla glanced at Dad. "As far as I can tell, she's not cheating on you, John."

"Phew!" Dad pretended to wipe the sweat from his brow as the rest of us chuckled. "That's reassuring."

"It makes sense that you have a prominent Ring of Solomon." Darla pointed between Mom's index and middle fingers. "That usually indicates an interest in psychology. Not everyone has this, but you do."

"Cool," I said.

"Woah." Liam nodded, excited.

Dad raised an eyebrow. Pete showed zero reaction.

Darla's stare hovered on Mom's palms. "I can go into some additional details if you'd like. Or we can end the reading here."

"I think I'm good." Mom pulled her hands back into her lap. "That was interesting, Darla. Thank you."

"My pleasure."

Mom sighed. "It's just that I can't help wondering if you're seeking out certain lines and marks on my hands because you already know I have a strong marriage and that I'm a psychiatrist who loves her family."

Darla narrowed her eyes. "That's not the way I do business, Kristen. Most of my clients are complete strangers. I don't know a single thing about them."

"Huh." Mom raised her chin and turned toward the fire.

Kenny leaned to the side, avoiding a swirl of campfire smoke heading toward his face. "Darla has a real gift. A few months back, she knew someone was going to die before it happened."

I tilted my head. "Really?"

Darla's eyes were glazed as she stared at the fire. "I didn't know for sure, of course. But I'd turned over some troubling Tarot cards and had a strong feeling. After the reading, I warned Lydia to leave that job. She was gunned down at her desk by a disgruntled co-worker three weeks later. She didn't listen to me. She had a choice." Darla tipped her head toward Mom. "Just like you."

I sat up a little straighter, noticing a skeptical look pass between Mom and Dad.

Darla snapped back to herself, looking around at us. "But no need to worry. Situations like that are rare. These readings are meant to be encouraging."

Liam pulled his knees to his chest. "Darla, other than that death premonition, I think this is really fun. Maybe I should figure out a way to work palm reading into all my wilderness outings."

"It can be a useful tool." Darla's gaze landed on me. "Abigail, I'd love to do a reading on you next. I want to get to know the woman who is marrying my son."

"Okay." I glanced toward Pete, who crossed his arms but didn't object. It seemed he'd given up on trying to rein in his parents.

Darla must have seen my look because she motioned toward her son. "Oh, don't worry about Pete. I tried to do a reading on him last night, but he wasn't open to it. I wasn't more than two sentences in when he backed out. He doesn't believe in my Tarot cards either. It's a real shame."

Pete shrugged. "I guess it's not my thing." He looked from Mom to Dad, who gave him slight nods of approval.

I loosened my arms and wiggled my fingers as I traded seats with Mom. There was a part of me that agreed with Pete and my parents. It was more than possible that Darla's observations were nothing more than an elaborate party trick. Still, there was a sliver of my psyche that was intrigued, that wanted to believe at least some of it was real.

Darla went through the same steps with me, studying the shape of my hands, the length and flexibility of my fingers, and —this time—the curvature of my fingernails. She inspected my left hand first, then switched her focus to my dominant hand.

"You have an air hand, just like your mom." Darla frowned. "Pete has a fire hand. I know at least that much about him." Her eyes shot toward Pete, then back to me. "Now, I'm not going to lie, it would be better if you both had the same hand types. People with the same hand types are generally the most compatible."

Mom huffed, which drew a death stare from Kenny. Darla mirrored her husband, pinning her eyes on Mom for a beat longer than necessary. Mom seemed to shrink into herself.

At last, Darla turned toward me, forcing a smile. "Of course, that doesn't mean that you and Pete can't be happy together."

Pete threw his stick into the fire. "Mom, this is so ridiculous. The shape of our hands has nothing to do with how happy we'll be."

Darla straightened her shoulders. "I'm talking now, Pete. Please, save your comments for later."

I bit back a smile at Darla's commitment to the reading. I couldn't help feeling like I was back in seventh grade at a sleepover with my girlfriends, shaking the magic eight ball to find out if whatever boy we were crushing on liked us back.

Darla proceeded to manipulate my fingers just as she'd done with Mom. "You are guided by your core morals, but also open to new ideas, new ways of thinking about the world around you. You often find creative solutions to problems."

I nodded because the things she was saying about me sounded true. A little too true.

"Your Mount of Venus is less elevated than your mom's but still prominent."

"What does that mean?" I asked.

"It means you're sympathetic and warm. You value

universal love over romantic love."

I made a face at Pete, who only shook his head.

"Your Line of Life starts very low on your hand. This is consistent with your quiet nature." Darla followed the curved line upward, then stopped. "Huh."

"What is it?"

"You have the same clean break as your mom." Darla blinked.

My body tensed. "That doesn't sound good."

"As I told your mom, a short Line of Life doesn't necessarily mean a short life. This break can be interpreted in different ways, but it's possible you're facing a disruption to your health. Is there a disease or ailment that runs in the family?"

I looked toward Mom, who shook her head.

"No. Not that we know of," I said.

"Do me a favor and check your carbon monoxide detectors when you get home. Make sure the battery is working."

Mom mumbled something under her breath. "Darla," she said louder. "I'm sorry to interrupt, but my daughter and I share the same DNA. Isn't it more likely that the lines on our hands match because they're hereditary traits and less likely that it's an indication that two perfectly healthy people share some deathly illness or will be in the same fluke accident?"

A gust of wind ruffled the feathers in Darla's hair. "I can see you're a true skeptic, Kristen. And that's fine. I'm only sharing what I see. It's up to you to do what you want with the information." Darla pulled my hands closer. "Would you like me to continue, Abigail?"

A log crackled and popped from the fire as sparks flew into the air. I nodded.

"Let's take a look at your Line of Marriage. That's what we're all here for, after all." Darla pulled my pinkie away from the rest of the fingers. A troubled expression passed over her face, but she masked it quickly. "I see one longer line here. That must represent you and Pete. But I also see some shorter lines here." She ran the edge of her fingernail along the other line. "Have you had a few other serious relationships?"

My stomach folded as I glanced toward Pete, then Mom and Dad, and finally Liam. No one made eye contact with me. This was hardly the time or place to discuss my previous relationships and I couldn't help wondering if this was an elaborate ploy by Darla to unearth my romantic history. I shrugged, ignoring the heat that prickled across my face. "I dated a couple of other people when I was in college, one of them for almost two years."

"He was a jerk," Mom said, and Dad grunted in agreement.

"And that's it?"

"Yes. I mean, I guess I had a boyfriend for a few months in high school too."

Darla lowered her eyes, but not before I'd glimpsed the flash of something in them—*worry? Anger?* I wasn't sure. I wondered again how much of me she could really see. Or was she merely selling a bag of magic beans? She peered down her nose. "Those other relationships have left a mark on you. But that's not always a bad thing." She refocused on my palm, pointing out a few other lines, elevations, and circles.

The reading ended a couple of minutes later. I thanked Darla but secretly acknowledged Mom was right, that I hadn't really learned anything new about myself. There'd been Darla's insistence that I get screened for diseases, but I'd never had any major health issues, nor did I have any symptoms. I doubted I'd go to the trouble of following her advice, outside of checking the batteries on our carbon monoxide detector which I already did once a year. I knew Mom wouldn't heed the advice either. Yet something about the palm reading had left me unsettled. I couldn't shake the look on Darla's face when she'd studied my Line of Marriage. She'd hidden it well, but I could tell she hadn't liked whatever it was she'd seen.

NINE

ABIGAIL

Dad stood, stretching his arms toward the night sky. "I just realized I didn't take my medication."

"Oh, sorry." Mom touched her forehead. "I forgot to remind you."

"I have one pill I take in the mornings and another I take both morning and night." Dad faced Darla and Kenny, for some reason feeling the need to explain his medication regimen.

"He had a mild heart attack about two years ago," Mom added.

Kenny shook his head. "That's a shame, John. Everything good now?"

"Yes. It's completely under control. I eat much healthier these days and exercise more than I used to. Honestly, I feel like I'm in the best shape of my life. I'll be right back." Dad walked toward his backpack, which rested near the tents. Liam placed another armful of sticks on the fire. Kenny said he needed to pee, and ducked out of sight, into the woods.

I pulled Pete aside and lowered my voice to a whisper. "Is your mom in good health?"

Pete's lip curled up on one side. "Yeah. As far as I know.

Why?"

"Nothing. It's just that talk of us having a baby was a little strange. I was wondering if there was a reason for the rush."

"There's not. She can be impulsive like that. I'm so sorry. When she starts getting her weird feelings or visions or whatever, it's best to ignore her."

"Okay."

Pete wrapped his arms around me and I leaned into him.

A couple of minutes later, everyone was back around the fire. Pete shared a seat with me on a folded blanket, looping his arm around my back and pulling me toward him.

"Look at the stars." We peered upward and took in the show of twinkling lights. "They're beautiful."

"Almost as beautiful as you."

"Stop." I giggled and pretended to push him away.

"I see Pete hasn't lost his knack for flattery." Kenny smiled at us. "He didn't get his smooth-talking from me, that's for sure."

Mom yawned and several of us followed in a chain reaction. Liam slid his feet forward, popping the last Graham cracker into his mouth. He'd traded his hiking boots for his vegan leather Birkenstocks, which he'd made a point to tell us all about. I admired Liam for caring so much about the environment and animals. He was completely relaxed, totally in his element out here. I wiggled my toes in my flip-flops, thankful for his advice to pack an extra pair of shoes for after the hikes.

Liam looked at us. "All the fresh air and exercise are tiring. I bet everyone will sleep well tonight."

"I guess that depends on how loudly Kenny snores." Dad motioned in Kenny's direction as the rest of us chuckled.

"Before we turn in for the night, how about a scary ghost story around the campfire?" Liam's eyes gleamed in the oscillating light. "I've got a good one. It's perfect for this location."

"Okay," I said before anyone else could disagree. "I love scary stories."

Pete cleared his throat. *"The call is coming from inside the house..."* He spoke in a deep voice, repeating the well-known line. Everyone laughed.

"No. It's not that one." Liam pointed at Pete. "You're pretty good at that, though."

Kenny looped his arm around his wife. "We're ready for your spooky story, Liam. Go ahead."

Liam rubbed his hands together, a boyish smile tugging at his lips. "Okay, like all the best scary stories, this one is true. Or so I've been told." He paused, looking around. "And it happened right in this very forest."

Mom squealed and grabbed Dad's hand. "Sorry. I'm a wimp about this stuff."

"Is it really true?" Kenny asked.

Dad raised his eyebrows.

Liam put a hand in the air, signaling for everyone to be quiet. "About forty years ago, a group of campers, not so different from us, planned a four-day getaway through these very woods. They were two married couples who were lifelong friends, Dan and Leah Norton and Steve and Suzy Macabee. But almost as soon as they began their first day of hiking, terrible things began to happen. First, they encountered poison ivy and broke out in horrible itchy rashes all over their bodies. The next night, a bear found their food and ate most of it. On the third day, someone in the group got bitten by a snake."

"Oh my gosh. Snakes!" Mom covered her face with her hands. "I didn't even think about snakes."

I motioned for her to be quiet.

Liam continued. "A couple of the campers wanted to turn back. But the other two insisted on continuing their loop and powering through, and that's what they eventually agreed to do. But they were hungry and tired and scared. They were at each other's throats." Liam peered around at each of us. "What two of the campers didn't realize was that their spouses had planned something evil. You see, a few weeks before the camping trip, Dan Norton had spotted his wife, Leah, on a date with his best friend, Steve Macabee. There was no mistaking what was going on between them. Dan saw them holding hands and kissing. He watched his wife leave the romantic Italian restaurant with Steve and go to a hotel."

Darla gasped.

"I see where this is going," Dad said.

Liam shifted his weight. "When Dan told Suzie what he'd seen, she was filled with rage. The two betrayed spouses concocted a plan to murder their other halves and make it look like an accident. They knew about the deep, rocky ravine that sits just a few miles from here, the one that's now known as Norton's Gulch. They knew that the trail was narrow and the drop-off was steep and deadly. There was nothing to catch a person's fall except for the sharp blades of pointed rocks. And so they lured their cheating spouses to that very ledge and encouraged them to check out the view. And just as Leah and Steve began to admire the dramatic landscape, two sets of hands pushed them from behind, plunging them to their deaths."

"Oh my God!" Mom peeked through her fingers. "I can't listen."

Liam grinned as if he'd succeeded. "Dan Norton and Suzie Macabee returned to the suburbs and played the roles of grieving widow and widower. They told the details of the first miserable few days of the trip, saying they wished they'd listened to the others and turned back sooner, that they should have known the trail was too narrow, too slippery after all that rain, and that someone was likely to lose their footing.

"Whispers followed them for years as people wondered if their spouses really died in an accident. But investigators only had their word to go on. There was never enough evidence to arrest them, much less convict them. It wasn't until Suzie was on her deathbed that she confessed to what they'd done. Dan had already died by then. They'd never had to pay for the murders." Liam paused again, seemingly enjoying the tension in the air.

"And so it is said that the spirits of Steve Macabee and Leah Norton, the two murdered adulterers, haunt these woods, looking for someone to suffer the consequences for their untimely deaths. Some have claimed to hear their screams echoing through the trees. Others have seen their ghostly shadows floating along the path next to the gulch. Still, others, have felt hands touch their back as they skitter along the Norton Gulch Trail."

Darla closed her eyes. "I believe it."

Liam raised an eyebrow, continuing the story. "And so tomorrow as we hike along the narrow trail next to Norton's Gulch, don't linger too long to take a photo, don't creep too close to the edge, or you just might be the one who pays the ultimate price." He leaned back, smiling.

I covered my face, squealing. "Why did you tell us that? I'm not going to be able to sleep tonight."

Liam shrugged. "It's part of the local lore. There really was a woman named Leah Norton who fell and died down there in the eighties, hence the name, Norton's Gulch. Some people are skeptical about the rest of the story."

"Man. What a way to go." Pete gave a nervous laugh as he patted my leg.

"You have a real knack for storytelling, Liam," Kenny said. "That's really something."

Darla folded her hands. "That warning we found earlier—watch your back. After hearing Liam's story, I realize it may have come from the spirits."

I sucked in a sharp breath, my head whipping toward the spot where Mom had stumbled across the message. I didn't understand how Darla's statement could be true, yet goose-bumps erupted across my skin. "This is getting creepy."

Pete tipped his head down, shaking it back and forth.

Dad grunted. "With all due respect, Darla, I don't think that message had anything to do with Liam's fictional ghost story. Or with any of us, for that matter."

Darla stared toward the woods, ignoring Dad's comment. "I'll try to connect with their spirits tomorrow. I've always had a strong sixth sense." She tilted her head toward the stars, humming softly as Mom widened her eyes.

"Well, on that note, maybe we should call it a night," Dad said, stifling a yawn.

My head weighed heavy with fatigue. "Darla, maybe we can do a Tarot card reading tomorrow."

Pete's arm dropped from my body. Mom shot me a look that indicated she wanted to strangle me.

Darla's eyes snapped toward me. "Sure. We'll do it first thing."

As she stood, an agonizing noise pierced through the air, coming from somewhere far beyond the shadowy tree line. It was shrill and drawn out as if the creature producing it was being eaten alive.

"What was that?" My spine straightened, the tiny hairs on the back of my neck standing on end. I searched between the trees, but nothing was visible in the narrow gaps and blackened hollows. The light from our little campfire only extended a few feet.

Dad tugged at his collar. "It sounded like a scream, didn't it?"

Mom was standing now, hugging herself. "There must be an animal over there." Her lips pulled back and I could tell she was imagining a predator, a bear or maybe a cougar.

Pete stared beyond the creek. "It was probably a bird. Maybe an owl. Or the wind." He pointed toward the hanging bag of food, which swung back and forth on the creaking tree.

"Or the spirits of Leah Norton and Steve Macabee," I said,

trying to quell my own terror by making light of the unsettling noise. Once again, I studied the lines of shadowy trees for any movement but saw nothing.

Liam put his hands up. "It was most likely just a coyote. They cry out like that sometimes at night. But don't worry. They're not interested in us."

"Good to know," Pete said.

Darla's eyes appeared to have doubled in size. "That didn't sound like a coyote. It sounded like a person, like someone screaming for their life."

Mom's face froze with terror as Dad placed a comforting arm around her.

I remained silent to avoid causing problems, but I secretly agreed with Darla. The scream *had* sounded human. I remembered the frantic couple in the parking lot earlier, the bloody slash on the man's face, and how desperate they'd been to leave this place. I wondered again what had happened to them. Maybe my imagination was spiraling, or I was picking up on Mom's radiating fear. Or perhaps Liam's ghost story still lingered in my consciousness, but something in the air had shifted. Our campsite felt dangerous as if we were sitting ducks for hundreds of creatures lurking in the never-ending forest. The wavering tree branches made it appear as if the forest was alive, a monster that could consume us with no warning or provocation. What else was out there? Who else? The face of the hollow-eyed man we'd crossed paths with earlier surfaced in my mind. What if he was a fugitive as Kenny had suggested? Had we just heard him attack someone? It would have been easy enough for him to follow us here, to hide undetected in the woods.

"I assure you, we're perfectly safe here." Liam looked around at everyone's blank faces. "We're all tired. Let's get a good sleep so we can tackle tomorrow's challenges head-on."

After a few minutes of convincing ourselves the scream had

originated from a distant coyote, we said good night to each other.

"I wish we had our own tent," Pete whispered, then kissed my ear. I smiled and playfully batted him away.

After we said goodnight, Pete retreated to the other tent, and Mom and I stayed together, removing our sleeping clothes and toothbrushes from our backpacks. We brushed our teeth as best we could, slurping up water and spitting it into a patch of weeds lit by my flashlight. At last, we were inside the tent. I slipped my legs into the water-resistant sleeping bag, which felt cold and slippery against my skin. A rock poked my back, a stark contrast to the firm mattress and crisp white sheets I'd enjoyed at the hotel the night before. Mom positioned herself next to me, releasing a sigh. Darla's sleeping bag was laid out on my other side. Outside the tent, the light from Darla's flashlight illuminated her shadow, which traveled along the length of the structure, stopping and crouching every few seconds.

"What's she doing now?" Mom whispered.

"Something with her crystals."

Mom closed her eyes, but I imagined her eyeballs rolling back into her head. "I love Pete. But this is quite a family you're marrying into, Abigail." Mom spoke in the quietest of whispers, but I could hear the note of disapproval in her voice as if she was telling me to think again.

A moment later, Darla opened the tent and tumbled on top of us, zipping the door closed from the inside. "I hope I didn't let any bugs inside," she said as she climbed over me and into her sleeping bag, resting her arms on top. "I placed some amethysts around our tent. It's a natural sleep inducer."

Mom chuckled. "I guess I'll take all the help I can get."

"And what's that one for?" I pointed to the polished oblong rock gripped within Darla's fingers.

Her eyes flicked toward me, the whites visible around her dark pupils. "Black tourmaline. It's for protection."

TEN

ABIGAIL

Sleep did not come easily. The tent lay in blackness. Only a hint of light was cast from the stars and moon. Darla breathed through her mouth next to me, the black crystal gripped inside her thick fingers. On my other side, Mom tossed and turned. An hour later, they'd both fallen asleep, but other noises outside kept me awake. An owl hooted every thirty seconds or so, piercing through the faint babble of the creek. The wind blew through the trees, creaking the branches. I squeezed my eyelids closed and tightened my fingers around the slippery fabric of my sleeping bag. I pictured the men huddled into their nearby tent and Liam in his single one. I wondered if they were asleep.

The more I tried to relax, the more my mind spun with thoughts. It was only the first night, and I already wondered if I'd made a mistake. Maybe I shouldn't have forced the families together, especially out in the wilderness. Maybe I should have believed in myself, in my decisions, no matter who became uncomfortable as a result. But I wasn't a strong person. I didn't possess Pete's confidence or Mom's strong will. Instead, I over-thought things. My chest caved at the thought of people being mad at me. I so wanted their approval. Anyway, it was too late now. We were here in the deep, dark forest with Liam guiding us along a remote trail for another two days. I had to stick to the plan and hope for the best.

I flinched when the owl hooted again. I tried meditating, closing my eyes, loosening my limbs, and following my breath through my nose and into my lungs. On the second inhale, something moved outside the tent. My eyes popped open and then I froze, my muscles suddenly rigid. I couldn't see anything, but footsteps padded nearby. A throat cleared. I wasn't sure whose, but when it happened again, I realized it was Kenny. The footsteps faded as a twig snapped further away. I guessed he'd probably gotten up to pee in the woods again. Two minutes later, feet tiptoed past the tent, then bumbled around before something else rustled. The faint sound of a zipper. At least he was trying to be quiet, to not wake everyone else.

I burrowed deeper into my sleeping bag, touching the bottom seam with my toes and trying not to think about the tortuous scream and what could have caused it. There was something mildly comforting in knowing someone else was awake and able to look out for the rest of us. I rolled onto my stomach and finally drifted off to sleep.

* * *

The sunlight woke me. I didn't know what time it was, but Darla had already left the tent. Mom lay next to me, eyes still closed.

I sat up, pulled on my sweatshirt, smoothed my hair into a ponytail, and took a long drink from my water bottle, then ventured outside into the crisp air. Darla's crystals lined the perimeter of our tent, a rainbow of shiny rocks sparkling in the sun. The campsite looked different in the bright morning light. Less scary.

Liam lifted a pot off the stove and dug in his pack for something. "Morning, Abigail. Instant coffee?"

"Yes, please," I said.

He poured the steaming liquid into a tiny tin cup, and I noticed he'd already collapsed his tent and rolled it into a tight cylinder, which sat near the bag of food he'd lowered from the tree.

Pete and Dad hunched on a nearby log, holding their cups and talking about the benefits of waiting another year before selling an office building downtown. Pete was bright-eyed, but Dad was not. Purplish bags puffed out under his eyes. Still, his face lifted when he saw me.

"There she is."

"Hi, guys."

Pete stood and gave me a hug, kissing the top of my head. "How'd it go?"

"Pretty good," I said, although that hadn't been entirely true. I glanced toward the woods, noticing Darla and Kenny strolling in the distance, stopping every few feet to collect pine cones. "How about you?"

Pete nodded. "It was fine."

Dad shrugged. "Not the most comfortable, but we made the best of it."

I sipped the bitter coffee, flinching as it scalded my tongue.

"The coffee takes some getting used to." Liam glanced toward my drink. "I'm whipping up some pancakes in a minute. After we eat, we can pack up and get on our way."

"Sounds good."

Mom crawled from our tent a few minutes later, resembling an animal emerging from hibernation. Her eyelids blinked into the sunshine and her tangled hair pouffed up on one side. The makeup accentuating her features the day before had all but vanished. She joined us, accepting a cup of coffee. I made my way to the creek, setting down my drink and splashing the freezing water over my face. Mom followed, doing the same.

Darla approached with pine cones in hand. "Morning!" Her cheeks were rosy and her hair was neater than yesterday, slicked back into a fresh, tight braid. She'd left out the ribbons, beads, and feathers today. "Did you both sleep as well as me?"

Mom smoothed down her shirt. "You know, it's crazy, but I really did."

Darla bobbed her head up and down. "It's the crystals. They have that effect."

Mom smiled in a way that didn't quite reach her eyes.

In the distance, metal clinked on metal. Liam whisked batter in a tin bowl, working hard on our breakfast. I couldn't help but be impressed by his early morning energy.

Darla stepped toward me. "Abigail, maybe we can do the Tarot card reading now, while Liam is making pancakes."

"Okay. Yeah."

"I'll get them." She rushed toward the tents. Mom and I followed, walking at a slower pace.

"Honey," Mom said, lowering her voice. "Maybe you shouldn't encourage her. Her antics are clearly upsetting Pete."

I waved her off. "He'll be okay. It's just for fun. I want her to like me."

"Yes, but she *should* like you, regardless, because you're marrying her son. And what was all that about pressuring you to have a baby right away?" Mom shook her head. "So inappropriate. Especially when she barely seems to know her own son."

"That baby conversation was weird." I cupped my coffee in both hands. "But she's dropped it, so I will too."

Mom eyed me. "That's very mature of you."

We were back at the extinguished campfire now. Kenny helped Liam with the pancakes, pouring out the batter, one circle cooking at a time because that was all that fit on the tiny pan.

"Okay. I've got my cards." Darla raised a thick deck in her hands as she approached. "Let's sit here." She pointed to a flat area of compacted dirt a few feet behind Pete and Dad.

I lowered myself, sitting cross-legged and she positioned herself next to me.

"Let's do a simple five-card layout."

"Sounds good," I said, having no idea what that meant.

"A relationship reading is most logical. So, basically, I'll ask questions about you and Pete and see what the universe has to say."

Darla divided the cards, and I realized she had three separate decks, each with a different color scheme and design. She shuffled each deck and placed them in front of me, then set a unique crystal on top of each one. "Which deck are you most drawn to?"

I studied all three, looking back and forth between the blue, pink, and yellow crystals, but pointing to the one with the light blue crystal on top. Darla pushed the other two decks aside and told me to draw five cards from the deck I'd selected. She laid them face-down in front of us and closed her eyes. "Today we are seeking answers concerning the relationship between Abigail and Pete. Please reveal Abigail's current energy." She flipped over the card on her left, staring at it with a slight tilt of her head.

The image on the card depicted a blindfolded woman with her arms bound to her sides. She stood with her head down, surrounded by swords.

I looked from the card to Darla, searching her face for clues. "That doesn't look promising. Is that a bad one?"

Darla puckered her colorless lips. "There is no good or bad in Tarot—only information you can use to inform yourself." Darla drummed her fingers across the face of the card, and I noticed again how her voice had dropped an octave just like it had during the palm readings. "This is the Eight of Swords. It generally signifies apprehension or feeling trapped." She stopped, looking up at me. "Can you relate to that?"

"No." I glanced toward Pete, who had his back turned and was still talking to Dad. I adjusted my voice to a loud whisper. "I mean, I guess I am a little nervous about the wedding. It's such a big turning point. So, yeah, apprehension makes sense, I guess. But it's not because I don't love Pete."

Darla gave a solemn nod. "Of course. Marriage is a huge commitment for anyone. Oftentimes, the apprehensions revealed by the Eight of Swords are imagined ones that can be overcome merely by opening yourself up to your partner."

I dropped my head, relieved that was all the card had revealed. "Okay. That's good."

"Now we'll check in on Pete's energy." Darla flipped over the card on the right. "The Ten of Cups, reversed." She was silent.

"What does that mean?"

"When this card is reversed, it usually points to a potential disconnect or delay, typically related to achieving a goal or maintaining family harmony."

I felt my mouth open as I repeated Darla's words in my mind. A disconnect. A delay in achieving a goal or maintaining family harmony. Did the card refer to our wedding? Was Pete having doubts?

"Don't read too much into this." Darla waved her hand in the air. "The disconnect could refer to anyone, not just you. In this case, I'd guess that Pete's feelings probably relate more to me and Kenny. Or Trent. I'm sure he feels we're messing up his image when it comes to your family."

"Oh, I don't think he feels that way," I said. But my polite response was a little too automatic, and I could see Darla didn't buy my line.

"Anyway, that's the thing about Tarot. It's more of an art than a science. We often have to rely on our intuition to discern a card's true meaning." Darla tapped the cards as I nodded along. "Now we ask the cards to reveal the bridge that connects Abigail and Pete." She flipped over the middle card, the one lying horizontally. "The Four of Wands." Darla smiled. "Now this makes perfect sense. The Four of Wands indicates a celebration, such as a party or a big event. Right now, the idea of your wedding, the excitement of walking down the aisle, is something that bonds you together and keeps you connected."

I recognized the truth in her statement. "Pete and I talk about the wedding all the time. It's all-consuming."

"Let's reveal an outcome to avoid." She flipped over one of the two remaining cards. "Two of Swords." Darla blinked, mouth pressing into a straight line.

"What's that one mean?"

She shook her head. "The cards are telling you and Pete not to ignore red flags. Basically, listen to your gut."

"Okay."

"Now let's see the highest potential for your relationship." Darla flipped over the last card, finding another card stuck to the bottom of it. "Oh, I didn't notice that extra card." She froze for a second as a shadow passed over her face, her pupils expanding and contracting in an instant.

I leaned forward. "What is it?"

She shielded the cards with her hands. "Maybe I flipped the wrong one. I haven't read this layout in a while. This must have been the outcome to avoid. Or maybe there are two potential outcomes here."

"Breakfast is ready." Liam's voice cut through the air. He stood next to the little stove in the distance. Kenny held a plate stacked with pancakes. Dad and Pete motioned for Mom to go ahead of them.

"Let's go eat." Darla slapped her hand down. Her face had taken on a grayish hue.

"Wait. What did those last two say?" I tried to angle my head around her hand.

Darla swiped her fingers over the cards, forcing them into a pile, but not before I'd glimpsed the image—a body lying face-down with a line of swords impaling the figure's back. "What was that last one? Was that person dead?"

Darla gripped the cards. "Not necessarily. There are multiple meanings for every card, but I couldn't see how this last one was relevant to your situation." She tapped her finger on the edge of the deck. "You know what probably happened? I bet you chose the wrong deck. I saw you staring at the amethyst and then you went for the sapphire at the last second."

"Oh." My mouth had gone dry. I guess I had been considering that other deck with the pink crystal too. My stomach churned with something other than hunger as I stood and followed Darla over to the food.

Pete made a beeline toward me. "How'd it go?" He smirked as he neared.

"I don't know." I stood still, waiting for Darla to pass, and lowering my voice. "I guess I chose the wrong deck."

Pete held his plate in one hand, cutting his pancake with the edge of his fork with the other. "Let me tell you a secret. There is no wrong deck because the whole thing is completely made up. She can give you another reading in ten minutes and all the answers will be different."

"Yeah. You're probably right." I glanced toward Darla, who was thanking Liam and Kenny for her breakfast. Her pants pockets bulged, and I could see that's where she'd stashed the cards and crystals.

Pete shoveled a forkful into his mouth. "These aren't the worst. Go get one." He nodded toward Liam and Kenny.

I headed toward the food, my insides hollow and shaky from drinking coffee on an empty stomach. I knew it was important to fuel up before the long hike ahead. Pete was most likely correct that Darla's readings were nothing more than a choreographed hoax, but something about the Tarot reading, particularly Darla's face when she'd flipped over the last two cards, had left me on edge.

I took a plate from Liam, noticing the slight tremor in my hand. "Thank you. These look delicious."

Liam winked. "Don't thank me until you taste them."

I spied over my shoulder at the others. "Everything going okay from your end?" I asked.

"Yes, ma'am. We're right on schedule. And we've got a full day ahead."

I nodded, chewing.

Liam chuckled, eyeing my parents and Pete, who sat in the distance. Kenny had moved over toward Darla, both standing near the edge of the woods. "This is quite a group you put together."

"Thanks." I swallowed and raised my eyebrows. "I warned you, didn't I?"

"Yeah. But I have to admit, I wasn't expecting a convicted felon," Liam whispered.

"Me neither." My eyes darted toward Kenny.

"Liam," Kenny called from across the clearing. "I gotta question for you."

Liam raised a hand in Kenny's direction, heading toward him as I continued eating. The pancakes were dense, but I choked them down. My nerves needled through me, so I steadied my feet against the ground. I told myself to stop it, to stop freaking out over Darla's stupid Tarot cards. Last night's mysterious scream. That weird guy in the woods. I closed my eyes, listening to the birds. It worked for a few minutes. But the calm was temporary, like a patch of sunlight peeking through a wall of clouds.

I wandered over to the others, where Mom and Darla were bickering about the best flowers for the wedding. Liam asked

Kenny a question about prison food, maybe meant as a joke, but it led to a rambling speech about the high value of cinnamon rolls in prison. Common sense told me that all these personalities weren't going to be able to hold it together much longer. Still, I never could have predicted the thing that happened next.

ELEVEN

ABIGAIL

Dad set down his plate and headed toward his pack, groaning as he crouched down and fumbled with the pockets. I intervened between Mom—who was insisting lilies would look the best with my dress—and Darla—who felt wildflowers were essential for good luck. I promised them I would take both into consideration and send them a photo of my bridal bouquet before submitting the final approval.

Mom nudged me with her elbow. "It's your day, so you get to choose your flowers." She paused, whispering in my ear. "Lilies would look gorgeous though. And we're the ones who are paying for everything."

I silently counted to ten, reminding myself to be patient. Having spent most of my life with Mom, I knew she had a strong sense of right and wrong, a passion for fairness. I could see she was annoyed that she and Dad were paying for the entire event, while Pete's parents contributed nothing, even though that was the societal norm and she and Dad were much better off than the Mitchells.

Several feet away, Dad muttered under his breath. He

ducked into his tent. By the time I finished my pancakes, he'd emerged from the makeshift shelter with a stooped posture.

"What's wrong, John?" Mom asked.

Dad patted his pockets. "I can't find my pills."

She gasped. "Any of them?"

"Yeah. They were in my backpack. Now they're gone." Dad's eyes scanned around the campsite.

"Are you sure you packed them?" I asked.

"Yes. I took a pill last night, the one I take twice a day. They were in a pillbox in the side pocket of my backpack. It's orange with a white lid."

A wave of panic rippled through me as I motioned to Liam. "My dad misplaced his pills. They're for his heart. Have you seen them?" I looked around at the others.

Liam's mouth opened. "Seriously?"

"They manage his blood pressure and his stress levels." Worry pulled down Mom's face as she surveyed the surroundings.

"Has anyone seen a pillbox?" I said again. "Orange with a white lid."

Kenny, Darla, Pete, and Liam shook their heads.

"This isn't good." Pete rubbed his elbow and frowned. "I'll check my stuff."

Liam picked at his thumbnail as he stepped toward Dad. "Don't worry. We'll find them before we head out." He gestured toward Dad's tent. "Let's break down your tent. Maybe they slipped under someone's sleeping bag or got caught in some clothes."

"They can't be far." Kenny eyed the immediate area. He and Liam removed the sleeping bags from inside. Liam shook each bag, open side down so that anything loose would fall out. The exercise revealed nothing but a dirty sock.

Mom faced me and Darla. "You two check our tent and I'll

search outside. Maybe the box fell out of his pack in the dark last night."

We separated and rummaged through our things for several minutes, every pocket coming up empty.

Behind me, Liam hunched over his pack, metal carabiners clanking against each other. He cursed under his breath, fingers fumbling with the connectors.

I abandoned my pack and stepped toward him. "What's wrong?"

His movements were frantic as he dumped out his pack, scattering the contents. He stood and patted his pant pockets and tipped his face toward the sky. "What the hell?" He looked around at the surrounding woods.

"What is it?" My voice was louder now and drew everyone's attention toward us.

Liam paused before sharing the source of his distress. "Something of mine is missing too."

"What is it?" I asked.

He blinked rapidly. "The bear spray."

My stomach felt as if it had dropped out of my body. Dad shook his head. Everyone else looked as if they were teetering on the edge of a cliff.

Mom clung to Dad's arm. "Did someone take these things while we were sleeping?"

Liam kicked his pack. "No. I don't think so. My carabiner was broken. It didn't close all the way. It must have fallen off the clip while we hiked yesterday. I can't believe I didn't replace it."

"We should go back to the visitors' center," Mom said. "It's not safe out here anymore."

Everyone stood silent, arms crossed and eyes twitching this way and that. Liam's discovery had knocked me sideways too, but I could see Mom was eager for any excuse to leave this backwoods excursion.

Liam raked his fingers through his thin ponytail. "Wait.

Let's think about this. The missing bear spray is probably no big deal. In all my years doing this, I've never once used it. I just don't like that it's out there somewhere."

Mom pointed to the forest. "That guy from the woods. What if he came here while we were sleeping and took our things? We all heard that horrifying noise last night."

Liam held up a palm. "Let's not jump to conclusions. That noise we heard was more likely an animal."

Mom continued as if Liam hadn't spoken. "And, John, we need to get you home." The panic in Mom's eyes had been replaced with a sheen of something else, something shinier and more energetic. *Hope?* "We can be at the visitors' center in a few hours. Then we'll drive to the nearest pharmacy."

Dad held up his hand, looking from Mom to me. "No. No. I'll be fine. You're overreacting a little bit, don't you think? You know that medication isn't essential. It's only a precautionary measure."

"Like vitamins?" Kenny asked.

Dad frowned. "Kind of like vitamins, I guess."

Pete stared at Dad. "But they're for your heart. That's not something to mess around with."

Dad waved him off. "My heart attack was nearly three years ago, and I'm much fitter now. I've forgotten to take the pills plenty of times before and nothing has ever happened."

"But what about your stress levels?" Mom said with a tight jaw. "This can't be good for you."

Dad waved toward the sky. "We're outside hiking through nature. Nothing reduces stress quite like that."

Liam nodded. "That's true."

"But there are other stressors here." Mom spoke through her teeth, making a visible effort not to look directly at Darla and Kenny.

Dad ignored her. "Anyway, Abigail and Pete have put so much planning into this." He smiled at me. "I can go two more days without the pills with no issues. And who knows? I'll probably find them later today."

Darla checked her pockets again. "I bet they'll turn up when we least expect it."

"That's usually how it happens," I said, although I didn't want to subject Dad to any unnecessary risks. I remembered how scared I'd been the afternoon Mom had called me at work, telling me in a shaky voice that Dad had collapsed on the sidewalk and was in the hospital. It had been about six months before he'd introduced me to Pete. Now I studied my dad's face. He clearly didn't want to be responsible for cutting the trip short, but I couldn't tell how much he was watering down the truth about the importance of his pills to make things work.

Pete swatted at a bug. "No one would be upset if you want to turn around and go back, John. I promise." He and Mom locked eyes in a moment of solidarity.

"Yeah. We can go back, Dad. It's okay." A strange mixture of emotions swirled inside me.

Dad's lips pulled back. "No. There's no reason to change the plan. Everything is fine. I feel great. The pills are probably mixed up in someone's things. And even if they're not, it doesn't matter because, as my wife well knows..." He paused, raising his eyebrows at Mom. "I take the pills daily and they're still in my system. There's no issue resuming my medication in two days."

Mom and Dad went back and forth over Dad's rationale a few times, but Dad wasn't budging. He was adamant that taking the pills every single day wasn't essential and that we continue the trip as planned. Eventually, we all agreed to let him decide for himself, and that having lost the bear spray wasn't ideal, but the chances of us needing it were extremely slim. Everyone scattered to pack their things and prepare for the long hike ahead.

Liam sat by the creek, stacking the rinsed dishes in a separate bag that fit into his pack. I thought back to the previous wilderness outing with my public relations company, and to a similar incident that occurred. A pair of socks belonging to my colleague, Edward, had disappeared while he was sleeping, leaving Edward with only his wet pair from the day before. We'd hunted for the missing pair of dry socks, turning our belongings inside out with no luck. Finally, another co-worker lent Edward his spare pair. But a minute later, Liam returned with the missing socks, a glimmer in his eyes. He had orchestrated the whole thing, explaining that by hiding Edward's socks, he had forced us to work together without us realizing it. Now I looked over my shoulder, making sure no one was within earshot as I approached our guide.

"Do you have anything to do with this?"

"Huh?" Liam's hands stopped moving.

"The pillbox? Or the bear spray?" I whispered, but louder. "Is this like last time? Another case of missing socks? Because, if so, you've taken it way too far."

"What?" His eyes popped, the whites showing all around like a trapped animal. "No! Are you kidding me? I'd never mess with bear spray. And what kind of monster would steal someone's medication? I wouldn't do that." He glanced over my shoulder toward the others. "Especially not to someone in my group."

"Do you have any idea what happened to his pills?" I struggled to soften my tone. "I mean, they didn't just disappear." I thought of the noises I'd heard the night before, the footsteps, the light hum of a zipper. "I heard Kenny get out of the other tent last night. Everyone else was asleep. I thought he was going to relieve himself, but maybe he did something with Dad's pills. Or the bear spray."

"Kenny? Why would he do that?" Liam appeared leery of my suggestion. "We can't just accuse the guy. He probably got up to take a piss in the woods. I bet your dad misplaced his pills and my bear spray fell off my broken carabiner as I hiked."

I dropped my head, realizing how unlikely my claim sounded now that it was spoken out loud. Liam was probably right. Just because Kenny had left his tent last night, it didn't mean he had swiped Dad's pills or the bear spray. It had been relatively early when I'd been lying there, listening to the night-time sounds. Then I'd fallen asleep and had been out cold for another six hours, during which anyone could have gotten up without me knowing, including Dad. It was more likely that Dad had tucked the pillbox into a hidden pocket somewhere and forgotten it.

Liam stood up, giving my arm a playful punch. "Listen, Agatha Christie, I've got some good stuff planned for today. Your dad doesn't seem concerned about the pills at all, so maybe we should buckle our seat belts, so to speak, and continue this wild ride in the name of your future."

I hugged my arms around myself. "Yeah. Alright. But nothing too crazy, okay? I don't want anyone getting injured."

A piece of hair had fallen from Liam's ponytail and hung near his eyes. "Obviously. I always strive to avoid injuring my campers." He pushed the hair back. "Anything else we should clear up?"

"No," I said, but then remembered there actually was something else. "Wait. Yeah. Why were you staring at my mom?" My question was a little direct, but I'd spent enough time talking to Liam by now that I felt comfortable asking him.

"What? I wasn't staring."

"You were yesterday. It was a little creepy, to be honest."

Liam bit his lip, gazing off in the distance for a second. "Okay, I might have stared for a second. I just couldn't believe how much the two of you look alike. It was crazy, almost like you could be sisters or even twins. I mean, if you were closer in age."

I glanced toward Mom. It was true that we shared a strong resemblance. We both stood five feet nine inches tall with wavy chestnut hair and round faces. Fine wrinkles etched Mom's skin, especially around her eyes, but she had dyed the gray out of her hair, was physically fit, and appeared much younger than her fifty-six years. She normally dressed more formally than me, but out here in the woods, we were wearing similar clothes. It was understandable that Liam had done a double-take when he'd seen us together.

"Got it," I said.

He adjusted the stack of plates, face reddening. "It won't happen again."

I got the feeling he'd been temporarily smitten with Mom, and I hoped I hadn't embarrassed him too much. "Cool." I nodded toward the others. "I should go apply my bug spray." I started back toward the others. Over by the clearing, Mom and Darla debated over the correct way to fold up the tent as Pete intervened. Something shifted in my peripheral vision, sending a prickly warning up my spine and over my scalp just as it had the day before. My feet halted, and my head swiveled toward the distant movement. A vague shadow darted behind the trees. Maybe it was a deer like Liam said. I couldn't breathe as my eyes searched among the dense trees, a practice that was becoming routine. I waited for several seconds, hoping for another glimpse if only to put my mind at ease. But there was no more movement. Whatever I'd seen was gone.

TWELVE

ABIGAIL

Twenty minutes later, we were back on the trail. Liam forged ahead as Kenny wheezed with each step, then broke into a cough, the kind that comes from the chest. He made a show of clearing his throat and spitting into the woods. It was gross by anyone's standards. I winced as Mom looked back with a similar look of disgust on her face.

"Sorry about that, ladies. I got hooked on cigarettes when I was in prison. There wasn't much else to do. I quit last year but this stupid cough never goes away."

"That's good that you quit," Mom said.

Liam looked over his shoulder. "Hey, good for you, Kenny. They say nicotine is more addictive than heroin."

Kenny lifted his chin and chuckled. "Well, I guess you would know, Liam."

"Dad!" Pete glared at Kenny. "What's wrong with you? Why would you say something like that?"

"It's okay," Liam said without looking back. "No offense taken. Heroin wasn't my drug of choice anyway."

Liam's dismissal diffused some of the tension in the air, but the obvious question lingered. *What was your drug of choice?* No one asked and Liam didn't offer, so we all kept walking.

Liam cleared his throat. "So, are you guys all set with the wedding planning?"

Pete nodded. "Yeah."

At the same time, Mom said, "Not really. There are still so many details to work out."

"Like what?" Darla asked.

Mom rolled back her shoulders. "Well, Darla, I've been meaning to tell you that we've had to reduce some of the guest list. The venue holds a hundred and fifty people, but John has some important new clients he has to invite, so we were hoping you could narrow your list down to thirty, tops, including you and Kenny."

"Thirty? But Kenny has three brothers, plus their families. That will just about fill up all the spots. And everyone already got the 'Save the Date' postcards you sent out."

Mom cocked her head. "Their families?"

Pete turned toward Darla. "Mom, we're having a formal wedding. No kids. I told you that a couple of months ago, remember?"

"I don't remember that! What is everyone supposed to do with their children while they drive across the state?"

"They can hire a babysitter like everyone else," Mom said. "We're not paying $200 a plate for a six-year-old who would be happier eating macaroni and cheese."

"Or they don't need to come," Pete added.

"This is just—" Darla's voice splintered and she didn't finish her sentence.

I kept my eyes trained ahead and stepped over a rock, wishing I could run behind the trees and hide.

"Wait a second," Kenny yelled. "You said a hundred and fifty guests, but we can only bring thirty? That hardly seems fair."

Mom raised her chin. "I'll tell you what, Kenny, when you pay for half of the cost of the event, you can invite half the guests."

I held my breath. Dad widened his eyes at Mom, who seemed to have lost her ability to remain polite.

"I see." Kenny walked in front of me, his hands balling into fists. His breath heaved in and out with each step as we traversed the rocky trail in relative silence. Darla muttered something I couldn't understand, and Kenny whispered a few words back to her. Their movements were rigid, and it was clear they were offended.

"What's the plan for the rehearsal dinner?" Dad asked. "Darla and Kenny, I take it you've got that covered."

Kenny coughed again. Darla shook her head. I wondered if Mom and Dad had secretly met behind a tree back at the campsite and planned to ambush Pete's parents over the finances.

"I'm paying for the rehearsal dinner." Pete projected his voice. "It's going to be at the City House Tavern in the private room. We won't have many people at all. Maybe fifteen or twenty."

Mom clucked in disapproval.

"Not everyone has the kind of money you have, Kristen," Darla said with a scowl.

Mom shrugged. "Maybe Kenny can steal another car."

Everyone stopped. Darla gasped as Pete's eyes stretched wide.

Mom's hand flew to her mouth as if she couldn't believe she'd been the one to speak those words.

Kenny tilted his head, pounding a fist in his opposite palm as his nostrils flared. "What did you say?"

"Nothing." Mom now covered her entire face with her hands. "I'm sorry. That was uncalled for. I'm just tired."

I stepped forward, stunned by Mom's outburst. "She didn't mean that. Sorry, Kenny."

"The dinner isn't a big deal, Kristen," Pete said, keeping his voice calm. "Couples pay for their own weddings and rehearsal dinners all the time."

Mom managed a slight nod. "I suppose you're right."

"It sounds like it's under control." Dad's face was pinched and, despite his words, I sensed he wasn't completely satisfied with the solution.

The atmosphere felt heavy as we pushed forward for several more minutes, no one speaking. The trail led us down a slope, through dense brush, then into a swarm of flitting gnats. Pete swore at the tiny flying insects as Mom and Dad flailed their arms. One of the bugs flew into my eye and I blinked rapidly but failed to flush it out. Kenny coughed and spit behind me. We all moved faster to get through the swarm, and soon we found ourselves overlooking an expanse of water rushing in front of us. This one was wider than the little creek at last night's campsite, more like a river. The current moved faster, creating white rapids and whirlpools in places. A few logs lay haphazardly across the water, not quite touching each other and a couple of feet short of the shore on each side. Liam stopped, spun toward us, and rubbed his hands together, evil villain-style. "Alright, folks. We've arrived at our next challenge. The river crossing."

"We're crossing that?" Darla appeared stunned, her arms dropping to her sides.

"Yes. It's not too difficult, but it's going to take some team-work." Liam's smile broadened as he touched his chin. "Who wants to go first?"

Mom's face was colorless as she studied the rapids.

Pete trotted toward the edge, raising a hand in the air. "I'll do it."

"Good man, Pete," Dad shouted over the rushing water.

The rest of us watched Pete as he pushed his toe against the nearest log, testing its stability. He stepped gingerly onto it, then inched across the makeshift bridge until he reached the next log. Then he repeated the steps. But when his foot stretched for the third log, he tipped sideways, flailing his arms.

"Careful," I said as the others gasped.

Pete's athleticism saved him. He recovered and took three quick steps across the final log and jumped to the opposite shore. We clapped and cheered, while Pete bowed and removed his backpack.

"I'll go," I said, following the steps Pete had taken over the logs, only pausing once to catch my balance.

Dad went next, taking twice as long as Pete, but keeping his balance. Kenny's journey didn't go as smoothly. Between the second and third logs, he slipped, plunging his right foot into the water.

"Dang it!" Kenny regained his footing, as he pulled his dripping foot back up on the log.

Liam clapped his hands. "That's okay, Kenny. Good save."

As Kenny removed his soaked boot, Pete returned to the other side, moving quicker as he carried both Mom and Darla's packs over the river for them.

"Okay," Liam turned toward Darla and Mom, "you're up. I want the two moms to work as a team. No one else can help."

Mom and Darla silently eyed each other. Worry pulled down Dad's face. He looked around at the rest of us as if waiting for someone to object. Kenny only shrugged.

Darla pressed her hands against her thighs. "I don't want to fall in."

Mom stepped backward. "Me neither."

Liam motioned them forward. "It's only about two feet deep if you do."

"I bet it's cold."

"Just do it," Kenny yelled.

Darla went first as Mom yelled "good job, Darla" every couple of seconds. I couldn't help noticing the lack of enthusiasm in her voice. Darla traveled at a pace so excruciatingly slow that I worried we might not make it to our next campsite before sundown. After a long pause, she crawled across the final log, hurling the weight of her body toward the earth as soon as she was within two feet of shore, and blessedly landing on solid ground with a grunt.

I looked across the river, where Mom stood. Her face had gone white, her arms outstretched as she inched toward the first log.

"You got this, Mom," I yelled.

Liam gave me a stern look. "Darla's coaching her."

Mom closed her eyes. "The swirling water is making me dizzy."

I dug my fingernails into my palms as Darla told Mom where to place her feet. "Look straight ahead," she said. "Don't look down."

Mom held her gaze in front of her as her foot almost slipped off the log. I thought back to my crossing a few minutes earlier and realized I'd looked at my feet as I'd stepped on the logs. So had Darla.

"Actually, Mom. You should—"

"Shhh!" Liam held his finger to his lips. "Only Darla can help her."

I tightened my lips as Darla offered a series of encouraging words and detailed tips about exactly where Mom should place her feet. I breathed a sigh of relief as Mom reached the second log. But as she neared the gap between the second and third logs, Darla said, "Take a big step with your right foot to find the next log."

The third log sat to her left, not the right. Before I could shout out, Mom's toe reached forward, then plunged into the water as her body toppled over itself with a splash. She screamed as she stood up, shaking out her soaked arms, looking at the logs, and then glowering at Darla. "You did that on purpose!"

"No, I didn't. I meant to say 'left foot' not 'right foot.' I got turned around."

Mom huffed as she trudged through the knee-deep water, tripping once and swearing as her nail caught on the submerged log. Finally, she made it to shore.

Darla rubbed her hands as she approached Mom. "Sorry. I misspoke. I was thinking my right, but it was your left."

Mom smiled in a way that wasn't really a smile. "It was an accident, I guess."

My jaw tightened as I studied Darla's face, noticing the way her lip twitched ever so slightly in the corner. An uncomfortable sensation crept through me, one that told me Darla had lied, that she'd caused Mom to fall on purpose.

"You okay, Kristen?" Liam yelled from the opposite bank.

Mom winced. Water dripped from her arm as she held up her left hand, which was now missing a polished pinkie nail. "I lost a nail too."

"I'll be there in a second." Liam tightened a shoulder strap on his pack. He was the only person left to cross the river. As expected, he skittered easily across the first log as if running on flat ground. But when he hopped to the second piece of wood, his foot landed at an angle. Just as Mom had done, he fell sideways into the water as the current rushed over his body. But unlike Mom, he was wearing his backpack, which was almost completely submerged.

"Oh my goodness!" Mom stepped forward as if to help.

Liam popped up, but he was soaked. "Oh, man! I can't believe I just did that." He shook the water from his arms.

"Are you okay?" Pete asked.

"Yeah. Yeah. Just a little cold and wet." Liam bypassed the rest of the logs and waded through the water until he reached us. "It's no big deal." Rivulets of water trickled from his hair and down his face. He looked away, flattening his lips and clearly embarrassed. "I just didn't want Kristen to feel lonely."

Mom chuckled, and I was relieved she could still find some humor in the situation.

"It happens to the best of us," Dad said as Liam peeled off his drenched shirt.

"I'm going to put on some dry clothes." Mom ducked behind a clump of bushes, emerging a couple of minutes later in dry hiking pants and a T-shirt, but her hair was still dripping.

"Let me check the damage." Liam unzipped his pack. "Oh, man. Crap!"

I looked at Pete, who made a face. "Is something wrong?"

Liam's eyes were glazed as he shook his head. "Our food got wet when I fell in. I guess I didn't seal the ziplock bag all the way." He held his dripping pack out in front of him and pulled out the bag of food. The few items in separate wrappers were protected, but everything we'd already opened—the crackers, cookies, pancake mix, and dehydrated fruit—was waterlogged.

I couldn't pull my eyes from the ruined food. "Oh, no." Another surge of panic prickled through me. We'd already lost the bear spray and Dad's medication and now most of our food was inedible. It had been nearly three hours since we'd eaten breakfast, and my stomach was twisting with hunger.

"We still have two nights to go." Mom squeezed a section of her wet hair as she stared off into the trees.

Darla crossed her arms. "You shouldn't have given your bars to that stranger, Kristen."

Mom grunted.

Liam tipped the bag over, draining out some of the water, and holding up a separate sealed bag. "At least my clothes are dry." He stared at the compromised bag of food. "Okay, let's not panic. The ramen looks fine. That's our dinner tonight. And I have a few cereal packs. We'll have to cut back but we won't starve."

"We'll just be really hungry," Dad said.

I patted the top of my pack. "I have a couple of granola bars."

Mom closed her eyes. "Maybe we should turn back. Nothing good is happening out here." She glanced at me. "Sorry, honey."

We all stared at each other, then back at the river we'd just crossed.

Liam edged forward. "The problem with that solution is that we're already almost halfway around the loop I've mapped out, so reversing course wouldn't save us from much of anything. Also, another group has probably already reserved our previous campsite for tonight."

I looked around at the other faces. Worn expressions of hopelessness, fatigue, and annoyance surfaced through the sideways glances and nervous smiles. It seemed every person in our group would have been happy to call it quits, to hitch a helicopter ride back to civilization. But there was no helicopter. Liam's statement about being halfway around the loop back to the visitors' center had deflated the air out of everyone. We'd all heard what he'd said. The easiest and fastest way to end this journey was to continue the predetermined route. So, we straightened our shoulders and nodded at each other, reluctantly agreeing to inhale a few breaths of courage and follow the path toward our next campsite.

THIRTEEN
ABIGAIL

We took a break at the edge of the river to regroup, resting along the rocky shore and eating a meager lunch of broken granola bars, dry cereal, and damp crackers. With our blood sugar raised, the sun shining, and the water rushing past, the situation suddenly seemed less ominous than it had only minutes earlier.

Kenny chewed with his mouth open, then slurped some water from his bottle. "Man, what I wouldn't give to be on my living room couch, watching *Real Housewives*. Now that's an entertaining show."

"I haven't seen it," Dad said.

Darla chuckled, crinkling her nose at her husband. "Oh, you with your shows."

Kenny caught Pete glaring at him and changed the subject. "Hey, Abigail. I was telling Darla how nice it is to get to know you. We've never gotten to meet any of Pete's previous girlfriends."

"Really?"

"Yeah." Darla nodded. "Pete dated someone for almost two years when he was away at school. We never met her."

Kenny touched his graying beard. "He's ashamed of his roots."

"No, Dad. That's not what it was." Pete breathed in loudly, looking like he was working hard not to flip out. "We just never got serious enough to warrant an introduction." Pete's demeanor lightened as he scooted closer to me and looped his arm around my shoulders. "It wasn't anything like what Abigail and I have."

I gave him an affectionate nudge and smiled.

Kenny shrugged. But next to him, Darla pinned her arms to her sides, peering toward the woods. The sun slipped behind a cloud, casting a shadow across her face.

"Everything okay, Darla?" Liam plucked a blade of crabgrass from the ground. "You look like you've seen a ghost."

Darla blinked, snapping out of whatever trance she'd slipped into. "I'm fine. I guess I got lost in my thoughts for a second."

Kenny laughed. "She does that a lot."

"I was just thinking how nice it will be to have a fresh start." Darla gestured toward me and Pete. "Pete has kept his distance from us for so long, but I can see that you're not like that, Abigail. And once you get to know Trent, I think you'll like him too. You're the kind of person that will be happy to join us for family birthdays and Thanksgiving dinners."

I smiled, aware of Mom's gasping breath. Her face looked gaunt beneath the moving clouds, and I knew it was because she'd assumed Pete and I would spend all major holidays with them as we'd done for the last two years. Or maybe she was envisioning spending all of her future holidays with the Mitchells.

I looked back and forth between the staring moms. "We can figure it out later."

Pete pushed himself to his feet in a clear attempt to end the conversation. "We should hit the trail."

"Yeah, it's clouding up a little." Liam pulled his damp boots over his dry socks. "Everyone have an outer layer handy, just in case?"

I nodded, eyeing the sky, which had morphed from a bright blue to a dull gray. Clouds had piled themselves on top of each other and the air tasted thick in my mouth. A storm was headed our way.

We followed Liam back into the woods, one foot in front of the other as swarms of gnats surrounded us. About forty minutes into our post-lunch trek, the skies opened, unleashing a torrent of rain that battered through the canopy of trees and bombarded our heads. We huddled together, hoods pulled over our foreheads and trading pained looks. I hunched beneath my water-resistant windbreaker, quickly realizing that "water-resistant" did not carry the same guarantee as "waterproof." My damp shirt stuck to my skin, and my pants were plastered to my legs.

"This is miserable." Mom closed her eyes. Dad rubbed her back, not speaking.

It was all I could do not to collapse to the ground and sob and apologize to everyone for my stupid camping trip idea.

Liam flinched as a lightning bolt splintered across the sky, the rain lashing us. "We should stay put until the storm passes. From the forecast the other day, it looked like this was a fast-moving one."

Mom's head popped up. "Wait. You knew about this storm?"

"No." Liam pulled his hood further forward. "I mean, not really. There was only a thirty percent chance of rain the last time I checked. I thought it would blow over."

I blinked my eyes, realizing the rain was mixing with my tears. "I'm sorry, everyone."

Pete's freezing fingers squeezed my hand. "It's not your fault."

"The storm will pass," Dad said.

Kenny lifted his head. "You know what? This might seem terrible, but it's a heck of a lot better than prison."

I looked at Kenny, noting the sincerity in his eyes, and couldn't help giggling at his comment. Even Mom laughed.

We waited like that for another twenty minutes, holding each other up and offering encouraging words and funny stories about other times we'd gotten caught in storms. Finally, the sky brightened and the rain tapered off.

"Okay." Liam pulled his hood away from his head. "Good job, team. We survived that, so I think we can survive pretty much anything."

"We got this," Pete said, clapping his hands a few times with what seemed like forced enthusiasm. Nonetheless, the rest of us hitched up our backpacks and followed Liam. My feet were soggy and my hair stuck to my head. Each one of us looked worse than the next. We marched onward, over wooded hills and along a muddy path that cut through a wispy meadow.

We hiked on for another hour and a half, stopping only one more time for water and bathroom breaks. My shoulders ached under the weight of my backpack and a cramp pulsed in my right calf. Just when I thought I couldn't take another step, Liam halted and turned to us. "Remember Norton's Gulch from my ghost story?"

"How could we forget?" Dad said and the rest of us laughed nervously.

"We're coming up to it now, and then we'll be at our campsite. You can look at the scenery but stay close to the wall of rocks on the right side of the trail and away from the drop-off. The trail is probably slippery from all that rain."

We followed Liam around a bend in a single-file line. As we turned the corner, the earth dropped off on the left side of the trail. The cliff plummeted nearly straight down with jagged rocks protruding at the bottom of the gulch.

Pete whistled. "Holy, moly! You weren't kidding." He

edged toward the ledge and peered down. "Look at this." The rest of us joined him.

Liam held up his hands. "Don't get any closer, guys."

The sight was dramatic and breathtaking. Spindly trees dotted the vast and rugged terrain, struggling to grow. Sprigs of wildflowers grew among the rocks. A beam of sunlight stretched across the landscape, reflecting off the rain droplets that still clung to the vegetation. I felt like I was viewing the scene from too high up, and my head became dizzy for a second. I hadn't realized the long, slow hike at a slight upward inline had led us to such a high altitude.

"They should put a guard rail along here," Mom said, backing away.

Darla held her arms up, taking in a deep breath. "I bet if we're all quiet, we can feel the spirits of the lives that were lost here."

Mom turned toward me, flattening her lips, but we stayed silent so Darla could do her thing. Ten seconds later, her eyes popped open as she nodded. "Yes. The spirits are definitely here with us. I feel their energy."

"Cool," Liam said.

Pete gave a slight shake of his head. I stepped back, hugging the side of the trail that didn't plunge hundreds of feet downward.

"It's quite a view, isn't it?" Liam surveyed our reactions.

"Sure is. But no one's surviving that fall." Kenny laughed as a fresh layer of sweat formed across his forehead.

Suddenly, Mom stood up straighter, her face beaming. "Are those pink lady slippers?" She pointed to a cluster of tiny flowers growing at the edge of the trail, inching closer to them.

Liam leaned forward. "Yeah. I think you're right, Kristen. They're rare, but they do grow up here this time of year."

Mom hunched down. "I love those flowers. They remind me of my grandmother. She lived in the woods and these little flowers grew all around her house." Mom raised her eyes, pointing into the gulch. "Look, There's more of them."

I studied the flowers, which were pretty, but didn't look like anything spectacular to me. I could see they held a special meaning for her, though.

Mom inched closer to a sprig of flowers, closer to the drop-off.

"Hey! You're getting way too close to the ledge." I glanced at Dad, not believing Mom was being so careless and that he wasn't paying attention.

Mom's head popped up. "Oh my gosh! You're right." She looked around and backed away. "I didn't realize how close I was. Hopefully, there'll be more of them. I'd love to pick some and take them home."

Liam shifted his weight. "Technically, Kristen, we aren't allowed to uproot any plants from this park. And it might be against state law to pick this flower. I'm not really sure about this specific variety. But if you want to take just one, none of us will tell," he said with a wink.

We all assured Mom that we'd keep our eyes out for more of the pink lady slippers and would keep her secret if she took one home. We lined up on the trail, taking in the view for another minute or two.

Liam shifted his pack higher on his back. "We're almost to the campsite, folks. Only a tenth of a mile to go. No more hills either."

"Good," I said, imagining the relief of removing the stifling backpack and changing into dry clothes.

As Liam guided us onward, I glanced over my shoulder for one last glimpse of the impressive and treacherous gulch. My muscles relaxed once we rounded a bend and the earth evened out on both sides. We continued along a winding trail through the woods, and soon, we arrived at an oblong clearing, where a few large boulders and clumps of greenery dotted the damp earth.

"We're here." Liam smiled as he waved his arms toward the clearing. "Good job, team! When everyone's ready, let's set up our tents first just like we did yesterday."

Everyone dropped their packs. I tipped my head toward the sky and exhaled. "I'm going to change into dry clothes first." I dug through my things, retrieving the pants I planned to wear tomorrow, plus a long-sleeved T-shirt and my flip-flops. The others hunched around me, locating their clothes too.

I hugged my shirt and sweatpants to my chest, looking first at Darla and then at Mom, who had already changed once after falling in the river but was now soaked again from the storm. "Let's go over there and change behind the trees."

They followed me along the perimeter of the campsite until we ducked behind several rows of trees.

"Thank goodness. I have one more dry shirt." Mom talked to herself a few feet away as I changed. She stepped toward me, wearing a fresh outfit, but a line of mud smeared down the side of her cheek.

My fingernails were rimmed with dirt too, and I guessed I didn't look much better.

Darla's black sneakers crunched toward us as she pinned her other clothes under her arm. "That's better. Should we set up our tent now?"

"Let's do it." I cut across the clearing, searching for an ideal spot. That's when I saw something that made my feet stop, my breath catch in my throat. Darla and Mom plowed into my back.

"What's wrong?" Mom asked.

I pointed downward. Words in all capital letters were scrawled into the mud with what looked to have been a stick.

SOMEONE IS LYING!

"Someone is lying," Darla read out loud.

Mom narrowed her eyes. "What in the world?"

I inspected the letters carved into the dirt, wondering who could have written this.

"It's just like that last message with the stones." Mom spoke in a whisper and her voice was barely audible.

Darla lifted her head, waving her free arm toward the men, who had already changed and were assembling their tents. "Kenny! You guys! Get over here."

Kenny stood. "Everything okay?"

Liam marched toward us with Kenny, John, and Pete a step behind. They slowed as they neared, gazes following our line of vision toward the ground.

Pete placed a hand on the back of his neck. "Seriously? What is this?"

"Did one of you do this?" Mom peered at the others. "It's not funny."

"No." Liam huffed out a breath scanning the surrounding forest.

Kenny thumbed toward the half-constructed tents. "We've been together since we got here."

"We only left each other for a minute to change our clothes," Dad said, placing his hands on his hips.

If any person in the group had been responsible for the words, I would have guessed it was Liam. He did all sorts of things in the name of his role as wilderness leader because he knew what brought people together and drove them apart. But now fear pulsed through me because it was unlikely Liam could have done this. We'd been with him the whole day, nowhere near this location. Even when Mom and Darla and I went into the woods for a couple of minutes, Dad and Kenny had been next to him, at least as far as I knew. It was pretty much the same thing that happened at last night's campsite.

Kenny jabbed his finger toward the ground. "Is this supposed to be talking about one of us?"

Pete set his jaw. "How could it be? No one out here knows us."

"I don't like the feeling of this." Darla's stare darted across the surrounding trees.

"It must be that guy." I pulled my eyes from the woods to face the others. "The one we saw in the forest who was hungry. What if he's following us? Leaving these messages and stealing our belongings?"

Mom nodded. "Yes. That must be what's happening." Fear wavered in her voice. "First he told us to watch our backs, and now he says that someone is lying."

Liam massaged his forehead, leaving dirty prints on his skin. "No. That doesn't make sense. The message is recent, otherwise, the rain would have washed it away. Whoever did this was just a few steps ahead of us, not following us."

Kenny's eyes widened. "Somehow that guy knows our route!"

"Maybe he works for the Park Service," Dad said. "You had to register our route, right?"

Liam glanced toward Mom, then stared at the words, not responding. I couldn't fully gauge his reaction. "Yeah, but... I really don't think that guy worked for the Park Service."

I lowered my face, realizing Liam was right. That other hiker appeared to be a far cry from someone in an official role.

Pete gestured toward the ground. "This message doesn't even make sense. How could that random guy in the woods possibly know if anyone here is lying? Not to mention watching our backs."

Mom clutched the back of her head. "Maybe he was angry we didn't give him more food and now he's trying to scare us. It looked like he was on drugs."

"No offense, Liam," Kenny added.

Liam raised his eyebrows at Kenny's comment but didn't respond. Our guide paced back and forth, cracking his knuckles. "Here's the good news. If that lone hiker was still nearby, one of us would have seen him. He's probably moved on by now. On top of that, I'm not convinced it was him that did this."

"Who was it?" Kenny asked.

"Probably whatever group stayed here before us. Just like last night. Who knows what kind of weird game they were playing? Or maybe someone thought it was funny to try to scare the next group of campers. People are immature sometimes."

"You could be right," Dad said. "That explanation makes the most sense to me. The tree branches must have shielded the words from getting hit by the rain. Also, I recall that other hiker was headed in the opposite direction when we passed him."

"That's true," Mom said.

Liam rolled back his shoulders. "Okay, so we'll keep our wits about us and not let our imaginations run wild." Liam peered around the group as we nodded. "Everyone take a few deep breaths, and let's finish getting those tents set up. Then I'll make some ramen, maybe half portions so we have something to eat tomorrow night? I have a fun activity planned for after dinner too."

Mom's features lifted. "Ooh. What is it?"

"A scavenger hunt." Liam smiled. "It's always a favorite."

"Sounds fun." I held his gaze as the others began to migrate toward the tents. I hoped he'd whisper in my ear that the message was all a big joke designed to get people talking or some bullshit like that. But he offered no such reassurance. He only bit his lip and turned to join the others.

The messages at the campsites seemed personal, left by someone who knew about us, about the wedding. An image of Trent emerged from the dark corners of my mind, the story about the missing dog leaving a bitter tang in my mouth. Even the memory of him pacing Pete's front porch made me uneasy. I found Pete and pulled him aside, lowering my voice to a whisper. "Do you think your brother could have followed us out here?"

"Trent?"

"Yeah." I motioned toward the ground. "Those messages..." My voice trailed off.

Pete placed his hands on my shoulders. "I don't think he's capable of planning something like this. Besides, he was signed up for a bowling tournament this weekend. Dad told me all about it like it was the freaking Olympics or something."

I scratched an itch on my elbow, thinking about it. "But Trent could have lied."

"What reason would he have to follow us here?" Pete gave a slight shake of his head. "I swear, when I talked to him last, he was totally fine with being an usher at our wedding. It was my mom and dad that were upset about that, not him."

"Okay." I shoved my hands in my pockets, scanning the woods for any movement, and fighting the urge to mention that Trent hadn't had any reason to hurt their neighbor's dog either. Still, Pete knew his brother better than me, and I hoped he was correct. There was nothing out there that I could see. Maybe Liam's theory about previous campers leaving the messages had been accurate. But I noticed the way Darla perched in the distance, aiming her stony stare out into the forest. I couldn't shake the feeling that something else beyond our planned wilderness outing was going on here.

And I had no idea what it was.

FOURTEEN

ABIGAIL

Twenty minutes later, all three tents were set up with sleeping bags inside. Pete stood beside me, complimenting my assembly skills. I stared at the bare-bones structure, envisioning my bed at home—the soft cotton sheets and firm mattress. It was likely our cat was curled up in a ball and purring on my pillow right now. "I wonder what Mango is doing. I bet she misses us."

"She's fine. I'm sure she's either sleeping or tracking litter all over the laundry room."

Pete liked to make snide comments about our cat, but I knew he loved her just as much as I did. He often wagged his shoelaces around for her to play with before he left for work or laid out empty boxes for her to explore.

"You know you look even more beautiful without any makeup on. How is that possible?" Pete nuzzled his prickly face into my neck.

I pushed him away, aware of the layer of dirt-encrusted sweat on my skin. I eyed our parents standing only a short distance away. "I'm not feeling particularly sexy right now. Sorry."

He pulled back, studying my face. "Is that weird message bothering you? It's nothing. You know that, right?"

"Yeah."

"And if that guy comes near us again, I'll beat the hell out of him."

"Thanks, but hopefully that won't be necessary." I picked at a speck of dirt on the back of my hand.

"Abigail, what's wrong?"

I lowered my voice, avoiding eye contact. "It's just that, I don't think our parents are getting along too well."

"Yeah. I noticed that too." Pete rubbed his forehead. "Not to say 'I told you so,' but I was afraid this was the way the camping trip would go. I tried to warn you, remember? But you were so excited about the idea of one big happy family. I didn't want to ruin your plan."

I swallowed, knowing everything he said was true. "Do you think this can work?" I motioned between us, my heart racing. "With them? And us? And my parents? You know, for the long-term?"

"What?" Pete's eyes grew wide, almost scared. "Are you saying you're not sure about getting married?"

"No. Of course not. I just worry about all of our holidays from here on out being stressful, instead of fun. I always hoped for everyone to get along, like my grandparents did..." My voice trailed off. "And I'm not ready to have a baby."

Pete grabbed my hands and squeezed them tight. "Please don't let my parents scare you off. I'm not like them. Hopefully, you know that by now."

"I know. But I like your parents. They're nice and honest. I never have to guess what they're thinking." Then I remembered Darla's evasiveness with the Tarot cards, her silence during our dinner at Applebee's, and the way she often seemed to get lost inside her head. "At least, I don't have to guess with your dad."

Pete shook his head. "I love them deep down too, but they can't be trusted. They've always had their own agenda."

"What does that mean?"

"Nothing." Pete pressed his lips together, eyes flicking toward the tents. "Just that they look out for themselves first."

I waved away his comment. "I'm sorry I said anything. I'm just tired. And hungry." I blinked, finding my eyes had filled with tears.

"We'll figure it out." Pete and I hugged, and I could feel his heart pounding against my ear.

Laughter drew my eyes toward the others. Mom and Dad watched Liam boil a pot of water that they must have gathered from the pond. Kenny sat on the trunk of a fallen tree over by the water, swatting at bugs. My eyes swept over the landscape, and I noticed someone was missing. "Where's your mom?"

Pete looked around. "I don't know. She must have wandered off somewhere."

"You want some bug spray, Kenny?" Liam yelled.

"Sure. I could use it."

Liam rummaged through the bag of food, which was meager at this point because he'd removed the ruined items and placed them in a separate trash bag attached to the outside of his pack. "Any of you have bug spray handy?"

"I can get some." I turned back toward the spot where we'd lined our backpacks in a row between the tents. I scanned across them, looking for my pack and the bug spray I'd slipped into the outer side pocket. That's when a pop of color caught my eye on the third pack from the front, causing me to forget what I'd been doing. Something orange and white peeked out from a partially open pocket. I dropped to my knees, fumbling with the zipper and hoping it was what I thought it was. My fingers tightened on the plastic object, pulling out Dad's pillbox.

"Dad! I found your pills." I held up the box, relief filtering through me as the pills rattled inside.

Dad's head swung toward me, features lifting.

Mom touched her brow. "Oh, thank goodness!"

Kenny abandoned his post by the water to see what we were doing. Liam and Pete also walked toward me.

Dad was next to me now, taking the box from my hand. Confusion stretched across his face. "That's crazy. We searched the heck out of everyone's stuff yesterday."

"Where were they?" Pete craned his neck to study the packs behind me.

"In a pocket of someone's pack." I pointed to it. "Dad, is that one yours?"

"No. Mine's the one on the end with the black zippers."

Kenny stepped closer. "That's my pack. But I don't know how those pills got in there."

I sucked in a breath, waiting for someone to say something. Mom and Dad exchanged a leery look.

The veins in Kenny's neck strained as he said, "I swear those pills weren't in there before. I checked."

We hovered in silence for a moment. Finally, Liam gave a solid pat on Kenny's shoulder. "There are so many pockets. You probably missed that one."

"Are you kidding me?" A flame of anger flickered in Pete's eyes as he glared at his dad. "How did those pills get in your backpack in the first place, Dad?"

Kenny tugged at the ends of his beard. "You're outta line, Pete. I said I didn't take them."

A twig cracked from behind the tree line. I turned to find Darla stomping over to us, carrying a handful of pine cones and angling her face at her husband. "What's going on?"

Pete spoke first. "Abigail found John's pills. They were in Dad's pack."

Kenny raised his palms in the air. "I have no idea how they ended up in there. Maybe I accidentally picked them up without realizing it." He nodded slowly. "That must have been what happened." Kenny's eyes were glassy. His voice sounded genuine, but I didn't know him well enough to know if he was lying. I couldn't imagine what his endgame would have been if he *had* purposely swiped the pills. Preventative heart medication wasn't exactly the type of thing people bought on the streets. Besides, Kenny didn't have any history of dealing drugs, at least as far as I knew.

Liam stepped between the father and son. "Let's not make accusations. That's not productive. Besides, everyone's things were mixed together."

"I'm sorry about all of this, John." Pete slumped forward, looking defeated.

Dad held up the pills. "Hey. It's no big deal. I'm sure it was nothing more than an innocent mishap. We found the pills and that's the important thing." He shifted his feet, and I wasn't quite sure if he really believed what he was saying.

Everyone nodded and mumbled things like, "yes," and "that's right." But a strange energy coiled around us, making it difficult to breathe.

Mom nodded at the pills. "I guess it wasn't that hungry guy from the trail after all."

"Hey, Kenny, you got the bear spray in there too?" Liam asked in a half-joking voice as he eyed Kenny's pack.

"No, sir. I sure don't."

Liam waved his hands in the air. "I'm just messing with you."

"You should take the pills now." Mom strode toward the water bottles, pulling Dad with her. A few paces away, she glanced over her shoulder, most of her eyeballs showing as if she was checking for a predator.

Pete sighed, following a few steps behind my parents.

"It's okay," Darla said again, nudging Kenny. "I know you didn't do that on purpose."

Kenny tightened his lips and hobbled toward his pack, digging through the other pockets.

"Where were you, Mom?" Pete placed a hand on his hip.

Darla raised the armful of pine cones. "Just wandering. Looking for treasures."

I stood in place and stared at the ground, trying to make sense of it all, to accept the most benign explanation for the unexpected reappearance of the pills. But the strange message from across the clearing had etched its way into my mind, refusing to leave me alone. *Someone is lying.*

I recalled the noises I'd heard last night as I lay awake in the tent. It had been Kenny who'd left his tent and cleared his throat in the middle of the night. I assumed he'd gotten up to relieve himself, but he could have swiped Dad's pillbox then. *Someone is lying.* The accusation was terrifying because it was true. But I wasn't sure which one of us it was referring to.

FIFTEEN

ABIGAIL

Our haggard bodies formed a circle around the camping stove as we slurped our half-portions of noodles from tin cups. I tipped the dish back as the diluted broth trickled from the corner of my mouth. My stomach grumbled, but my cup was empty. I noticed the same dissatisfied looks on the other faces in the group.

Liam leaned forward. "Sorry there isn't more for dinner. I wanted to make sure we have food for tomorrow."

Pete gave a nod. "It's all good."

"I've been meaning to lose a few pounds anyway," Kenny said, patting his hefty midsection.

Darla motioned toward the tents. "I have two energy crystals over there if anyone would like to hold one for a while."

Mom lowered her eyelids and chuckled in disbelief. "Are you serious? Maybe we should just eat moonbeams and stardust for dessert. That will really keep us going. What a bunch of nonsense!" As Mom threw her hands in the air, it was clear she'd done her best to play along, but her goodwill had reached its limit.

Darla lowered her cup, a tiny muscle twitching at the corner of her lips.

Kenny jabbed his index finger at Mom. "Hey! What's your problem, anyway? Don't *ever* talk to my wife like that! Unlike you, Darla's only trying to help."

The forcefulness of Kenny's voice made the rest of us sit up. Kenny's manner felt threatening, and I noticed how Dad edged forward as if preparing to defend Mom. But Mom refused to engage. She only grunted and looked away, pulling her knees into her chest.

"Okay, guys. Everyone, cool off." Liam stood, holding his hands out in opposite directions to create a buffer between my parents and Pete's parents. "I know we're all hungry, but how about we put aside our differences and switch gears?"

"Sounds good," Pete said, a little too loudly.

Liam exhaled. "We still have time to fit in a scavenger hunt before it gets dark. Three teams of two."

"John and I will be a team." Mom's steely voice stated the pairing as a fact, not a question. She scratched at her forearm, a little pink patch inflamed with insect bites.

Liam tucked a loose piece of hair behind his ear. "Okay. Each couple will be a team. That's a good idea."

Pete winked at me. "We got this."

Darla rubbed her hands together. "This sounds fun."

"Good." Liam nodded. "You guys can relax for five or ten minutes while I locate my pen and paper and put the lists together."

"Thanks for keeping us on track, Liam." Dad's chin lowered as he tossed a fleeting glance toward Darla and Kenny. "I'll wash the dishes tonight." Dad went around the circle and collected everyone's cups, then headed toward the pond to rinse them out.

I thought Mom might offer to help but she didn't. Instead, she leaned close to me, her tense body pressing against mine. "I'm going to rest inside the tent for a few minutes. Why don't you come with me?"

Again, the way Mom spoke was not really a question. I nodded and followed her to our tent, noticing what the others were doing before I ducked inside. Pete helped Dad over by the water's edge. Liam pulled a small notepad out of his backpack. Kenny and Darla sat on a boulder as Darla sifted through her crystals. I entered the tent, zipping the door closed behind me, and flopping on my back on top of the sleeping bag. "I'm sorry things aren't going that well."

Mom sat cross-legged next to me, eyes darting across the canvas walls, then back to me. A blue vein showed through the pale skin of her temple. "Abigail, I'm very concerned."

I heard the tightness, the trepidation, in her voice and sat up. "What is it?"

Mom reached for my hand and held it in both of hers, something she'd done every so often since I was a little girl whenever she was about to share bad news. "I'm worried about you marrying into this family. I'm seeing all sorts of red flags."

"But Pete—"

Mom held up her hand. "Pete is a wonderful young man in so many ways. But he lied to you—to us—about his family."

"He didn't really lie. He just never mentioned a bunch of things."

"Lying by omission is still lying. Other than that one quick dinner at Applebee's, he's basically kept his parents hidden until three months before your wedding. I find that troubling." She closed her eyes. "His dad is a thief and a gambling addict with a temper on top of it. His mom is a complete whacko."

My mouth had gone dry. I hadn't expected this extreme reaction from Mom after only two days with Pete's parents.

"And have you ever met Trent? What kind of person doesn't ask their own brother to stand up at his wedding? Is he a sociopath or something?"

"I've met Trent one time." I averted my eyes, remembering the awkward encounter on Pete's doorstep. "He's a little creepy, but he and Pete don't get along. They're not close. Pete is his own person."

"Yes," Mom nodded, lips pinched. "That's true, of course. But even if his family had no influence on him whatsoever—which I find hard to believe—are Darla and Kenny the people you want to spend every holiday with for the rest of your life?"

"It wouldn't be every holiday."

"Okay. Even if it's half of the holidays."

I wondered about the pureness of Mom's motives. Perhaps she was the one who didn't want to share Thanksgiving and birthdays with Darla and Kenny. But, regardless, she had a point. I remembered Betsy's complaints about her in-laws, how she dreaded the holiday season because of the constant conflict and the squabbling over who got the prime holidays with her and her husband.

A dire warning smoldered in Mom's eyes. "All I'm saying is that you don't need to rush into this. Marriage is difficult enough, even in the best of circumstances." Mom gulped and glanced away. "Your dad and I have had every advantage, every privilege. I'm a psychiatrist, for God's sake. And yet we've resorted to sleeping in separate bedrooms."

"You have?"

"Yes."

I pulled my hand from hers and crossed my arms in front of myself, remembering how they'd bickered during the car ride up here. The day before that, they'd been short with each other during our bike ride around the island.

Mom fluttered her fingers in the air. "It's not as bad as it sounds. Dad has back problems and he snores. He likes the firmer mattress in the other room. My point is that marriage is hard. It tests who you are. It forces you to give up parts of yourself and adopt parts of another person, which can be fine. But you need to make sure you're giving up the parts you can live without and gaining things that aren't contradictory to your core values."

I could feel my palms sweating, my heart thumping wildly inside my chest. "I'm not sure what to say."

"You can tell Pete you need more time. Maybe continue dating for another year, so you can get a true lay of the land."

Pete's face flashed in my mind. Mom's affection toward him had shifted in the wind, her words sweeping over me like an unexpected storm.

"But we already live together. We have a cat." I could feel the heat in my face, the tears building.

"That's not a reason to marry someone." She reached for me again, her thumb stroking the back of my hand. Even in the dim light, her skin appeared chalky. This trip had taken a toll on her. "Abigail, I know this is hard, but it's a mistake to rush into a commitment like this. Please don't marry Pete."

"I'm not sure what to say," I said again. I felt as if I'd fallen into a rushing river, carried away by the current. But Mom was there next to me, a broken branch for me to cling to.

Rocks crunched outside the tent, a shadow shifting. I froze, scared to even take a breath. Mom glanced toward the movement, a streak of terror in her eyes.

I wiped my tears with my hand and smoothed back my hair, trying to identify the person who lingered outside, and worried whoever it was may have overheard Mom's words. And mine.

"Who's there?" Mom only mouthed the question, but it was easy enough to read her lips.

I crawled forward and spied through a tiny gap in the zipper just as the shadow slipped away, a flurry of soft footsteps receding. Whoever had been there had taken a hard turn and was now gone. "I don't know. They left." I sat back down, again noting Mom's strained face. "Hopefully, they didn't hear us."

Mom leaned forward with the same desperate look. "You haven't seemed yourself lately, Abigail. I'm worried."

"Does Dad feel the same way?" I spoke barely above a whisper as I scanned the canvas walls, watching for the secretive shadow to return.

Mom lowered her gaze. "No. You know how Dad is. He thinks Pete is the best thing since sliced bread, the son he never had, the star employee, and all that. Pete could come from a family of cannibals and it probably wouldn't change his opinion." She gripped my hand. "But Dad's not the one marrying Pete. You are."

"Hey, guys. I've got the lists ready." Liam's voice bellowed from a distance. "Bring a ziplock bag from your pack. Two minutes until go time."

Mom hugged her arms around herself and shivered. "Please, think about what I've said. Successful relationships are built on honesty and trust."

I gave a nod even as my vision blurred, a flood of thoughts amassing in my head. "I heard everything you said, but I can't do this right now. There's too much going on. Too much to think about."

"I understand. You don't have to make any decisions until we're all back home."

The sleeve of my lavender polar fleece jacket peeked out from underneath my sleeping bag. I handed the fuzzy jacket to Mom. "Here. You look cold. Take this."

Mom nodded and put it on. I rubbed my eyes again to try to disguise my recent rush of emotions and waved Mom ahead of me. We exited the tent and walked toward Liam. The others already stood near him, waiting with repurposed plastic bags in their fingers. Their faces were expectant, smiling. There was no indication that anyone had overheard Mom's plea for me not to marry Pete.

"There's my teammate!" Pete stepped closer to me, holding a small piece of folded paper and a clear bag. I clutched his hand as guilt eroded my insides.

Darla peered at me, then looked at Mom. "Is everything okay?"

"Yes," Mom said.

I forced a smile, then angled my face away, hoping to hide my bleary eyes. "We're just a little tired. But I'm sure everyone is."

Liam paced in front of us. "Okay, so here's the deal. It's pretty simple. Each team has eight items that can be found in nature. Every team has the same items. Whichever team finds all the items and returns them to me first wins the challenge. Because I've done this a few times before, I recommend that you and your partner divide the list and split up."

Dad raised a fist in the air. "Divide and conquer!"

"It's okay to leave the campsite, but don't wander too far away from the trail. We don't want anyone getting lost."

"What do we win?" Pete asked.

"I don't know. Bragging rights." Liam twisted his lips to the side. "Maybe the winners can invite ten extra guests to the wedding?" He shrugged, eliciting a few uncomfortable giggles. "On the count of three, turn your lists over. One, two, three!"

Pete and I took a few steps away from the others. He flipped over our paper and read the items out loud. "A black rock the size of a golf ball, a green leaf bigger than your hand, something decaying, a pink flower petal (only the petal!), a crawling insect (don't kill it!), a white stone, a pine cone, a type of leaf you've never seen before."

"I don't want the crawling bug," I said.

"Okay. How about you take the first four and I'll do the insect, white stone, pine cone, and leaf?"

"Sounds good. Let's go."

"Here. You can use the bag. I don't need it." Pete handed me his empty ziplock bag and jogged to the trail opposite our campsite.

I started toward the woods but stopped when I realized

everyone except for Liam was scattering in different directions. I slipped behind a tree and waited until the others had disappeared. Then I crept back into the clearing where Liam was slouched by his backpack.

He looked up as I approached. "Hey."

"How do you think this is going?" I asked, keeping my voice low.

"There have been a few unexpected hiccups, but I think we're getting there."

I knelt beside him, struggling to keep the emotion from my voice. "My mom just told me to call off the wedding."

Liam faced me, eyes unblinking. "Really?"

I nodded. My fingers squeezed his rugged hand. Liam was the only one who knew my secret, that this camping trip had always been destined for disaster. "Yeah. Good work. Now I need you to get my dad on board."

He shook his head, smiling as if he couldn't believe what I'd told him. I glanced away, painfully aware of my dishonesty toward the rest of the group, my fake reasoning for planning this outing.

Because weeks ago, I'd come to the terrible realization that I no longer wanted to marry Pete. It was a reality I'd accepted even as the wedding planning sped forward like an asteroid hurtling toward earth. I didn't know how to stop it. Things were too far along. Everyone was so excited. Calling off the wedding would make me the villain in everyone's eyes.

But then Liam had given me an idea.

I looked around the empty campsite, my eyes snagging on the scraped section of soil where we'd discovered the unsettling message.

Someone is lying.

I still had no idea who wrote it, but they were right. Someone was lying.

And it was me.

SIXTEEN

LIAM

Wow. I closed my eyes, clutching my temples. This was seriously crazy. Our half-baked plan was actually working. I inhaled a breath and took a good look at Abigail, my former camper-client who'd become my lover but was now more like a friend. This whole deal was dirty and evil. But I had to admit there was also something exciting about the covert mission.

I loosened my jaw, trying to slow down my racing heart, my spinning mind. "I thought Kenny stealing your dad's pills would have been enough."

Abigail's mouth opened. "Wait. Was that you?"

"No!" I flung my arm toward Kenny's tent. "That dude swiped your dad's pills. Who does that?"

Abigail looked away. "Something really bad has to happen for Dad to change his mind about Pete." When she turned toward me, she chewed on her lip, eyes bulging. "But I don't know what."

"Don't worry. I got you." My voice was steady but I couldn't help wondering if Abigail was a special brand of psychopath. I removed my hand from hers, knowing that she didn't love Pete the way she'd hoped she would have by now, but that she was insecure and afraid of disappointing her parents and friends. She was way too deep into a situation that she felt she no longer controlled. The marriage cart had been driving the horse for months. One afternoon, I offered to help her put the brakes on the cart, to flip it around in a way that made calling off the wedding not her fault. I'd been half-joking when I first mentioned a Team Wilderness "unbonding" experience at a discounted rate. Only, Abigail hadn't interpreted it as a joke. That was a little over a month ago.

I gave Abigail a nudge. "Get out of here. Play along with the scavenger hunt."

She began to stand but paused. "Wait. Those creepy messages at our campsites. Was that you?"

"I didn't know anything about those." I returned her steady gaze because I was telling the truth. I hadn't known those messages were going to be there. But they'd been perfect. Absolutely spot on. And what was up with that scream from the woods? I couldn't have timed it better if I'd made the blood-curdling noise myself.

Kenny's cough echoed from nearby. Abigail's head jerked up, and I waved her away. We hadn't made it this far to blow our cover. She stood and trotted toward the woods, her purple shirt disappearing behind the trees.

I looked at Kenny, who nodded before bending down to sift through a clump of weeds at the base of a tree. I did a double-take at his empty bag, wondering how he hadn't located a single item yet.

It had been about eight months since I first met Abigail. The public relations company where she worked had scheduled a two-night workshop with Team Wilderness in the hopes of boosting morale and improving communication. There'd been another guide working with me then, but Abigail Cates had been on my team, and I'd noticed her right away, hadn't been able to stop staring, actually. I'd kept my distance, at first, nerves getting the better of me. I stuck to my role as wilderness leader, offering instructions and observing her interactions with her co-workers as they helped each other through a ropes course. Abigail was agreeable, quick to help, and had an easy laugh. And she was hot too. Long and slender with shiny, windswept hair and perfect lips. She had the look of someone who belonged outside in the sunlight, like a sapling blowing in the breeze. She'd caught me staring more than once, smiling each time but glancing away, bashful. So, when it came time to sit around the bonfire, I'd slid into a narrow opening next to her, the smoke snaking around our heads. As the others roasted marshmallows, she asked me questions about my experiences in the wilderness and I repeated only the most impressive stories, the ones that made me sound like a badass. Like the time I'd followed mountain lion tracks for over two miles while back-packing in Colorado. Or the time a guy in my group got his leg caught in a crevice and I had to chip away the rock to free him. Then I asked about her life, listening with every cell in my body.

She'd worked at Pegasus Public Relations for three years as a content writer. Her boyfriend—blah, blah, blah.

My mind had gone blank at the word *boyfriend*. Of course, Abigail had a boyfriend. Why wouldn't she? I hated the way my chest filled with despair, my shoulders slumped forward, and my eyes quit blinking away the smoke. But I reminded myself that just because she had a boyfriend, it didn't mean she was happy. Sure enough, as the night wore on, her hand brushed against mine more than once, sending a surge of something powerful through me. The third time it happened, she looked right at me and smiled. That's when I knew that she felt it too.

That night, I'd fallen asleep in my tent, thinking of her. The next day, I found a moment of courage, escorted her away from the group, and told her I hoped her boyfriend treated her well because that's what she deserved. When she stepped toward me, I kissed her. She seemed to like it when I snuck my hand up her shirt, had even leaned into it. But later, she pulled me aside and apologized, said she'd made a mistake.

We didn't contact each other for a week after the work outing. Then, one afternoon, she sent a text.

Want to grab a coffee?

We met at a Starbucks a couple of miles from her office and close to my apartment. The coffee was good, but frantic energy pulsed between us. We both seemed to know we weren't there to sip oat milk lattes. I told her I lived nearby, and we threw away our cardboard cups and left.

The sex was good—urgent and dangerous, almost like a drug. Abigail said I was so different from Pete, and she'd meant it in a good way. I could see she didn't know what to make of her attraction to me, a recovering addict, a laid-back nature boy with little to no future career aspirations. I glimpsed the confusion and guilt pulling across her face, the same expression I'd see dozens of times in the weeks to follow. Yet, Abigail kept coming back, usually after work on days she knew Pete was working late. She liked that I was authentic, comfortable in my own skin, that I stood for something—protecting the environment and preserving wilderness—no matter whose panties got in a wad as a result. Little by little, she opened up to me, telling me about her passion for traveling, the places she'd been, and her hopes for the future. She spoke highly of her parents—her dad, the real estate genius, and her mom, the sought-after psychiatrist. But their expectations for their daughter had been permanently set on the highest rung. A lifetime spent not disappointing them had taken its toll on Abigail. Lucky for me because somehow all that pressure to be perfect had led Abigail directly to my apartment for a series of illicit early-evening hookups.

It wasn't a huge surprise when our arrangement didn't last. About six weeks after that first rushed coffee date, Abigail showed up at my apartment, standing in the doorway and pulling her coat tightly around her body.

"Pete and I got engaged last night."

I laughed at first, assuming she was joking. But she only stood there like a statue, never cracking a smile. It took a few seconds to realize she was serious. "What the hell are you doing?" My voice had stretched to its breaking point. "You can't marry that guy."

"I'm sorry. It's complicated. I really do love Pete, despite everything here." She motioned between us. "I'm ending this thing with you. It was a big mistake. We never should have—" She paused. "I realize now that Pete is the man I'm supposed to marry."

"I'm not saying you have to choose between him or me." I almost laughed because I'd never had any desire to marry Abigail and I guessed she viewed me in the same light. "I'm only saying, don't marry him."

"I already said yes." She blinked rapidly as she held up her hand to display a glittering diamond on a silver band, hugging her slender finger. "Pete is everything I need."

I couldn't help chuckling at that statement because, obviously, Pete wasn't *everything* she needed. I didn't understand her decision, but I decided to keep my cool and stay on the periphery for when things changed, which I was confident they would.

I gave Abigail's arm a friendly punch. "Well, I don't agree with what you're doing. I really don't. But can you do me a favor?"

"Sure."

"Keep in touch, okay?"

"Yeah. I will." She pinned her lips together. "We can still be friends."

We kept our distance then, at least physically speaking, but we still communicated. Abigail texted once in a while, complaining about a few of her co-workers who I'd met at the wilderness outing. I sent her a funny GIF on her birthday, and occasional photos of scenes from my hikes. But I was still surprised to get her text with the same words she'd first sent me months earlier.

Want to meet for coffee?

We met at the same Starbucks we'd met before. But this time there was no lust-filled trip back to my apartment, only a frail and hollow-eyed Abigail crying and explaining that she didn't want to marry Pete, although she couldn't pinpoint the reason. Pete was perfect on paper—he was handsome, he treated her well, had a promising career, and had quickly been approved by her family and friends. But something in her gut knew he wasn't the right partner for her. A chance encounter with Pete's creepy brother and an awkward first meeting with Pete's parents at an Applebee's restaurant had unleashed a new flurry of questions. *Were these really the people he'd come from?* As much as she tried to push aside her apprehension and focus on the positives, the doubts consumed her. She couldn't sleep, could barely eat.

"Call it off," I said, for what must have been the hundredth time.

"No. You don't understand. I can't." Abigail's eyeballs bulged, her voice echoing with desperation. "My parents aren't used to me letting them down. And this would be the ultimate disappointment in their eyes. Pete is already like a son to my dad. I don't even have a good reason to give them. Or Pete. What am I supposed to say? You flatter me too much, agree with everything I say, and do whatever I want. I can't take it anymore?"

I could see that Abigail was the ultimate people-pleaser. She wasn't someone who rocked the boat, even if it meant she suffered as a result. She didn't want to be the bad guy, to let down her friends and family. She didn't want to hurt Pete. She'd let the relationship go way too far already. She and Pete had moved in together, adopted a cat, booked the wedding venue, and ordered the invitations. The more time that passed, the harder it was to stop the machine.

That's when I suggested a private wilderness outing led by yours truly. I described a rugged and twisted version of *Romeo and Juliet*, designed to fail, orchestrated to make sure the families didn't get along, that irreconcilable differences were exposed. Abigail didn't laugh at the idea. Instead, she sat up straighter in her chair, nodding vigorously. She believed the plan would work, that its success would remove the weight of the blame from her shoulders because at least her parents would be on her side. After spending three nights in the woods with Darla and Kenny, everyone would understand why she couldn't move forward. Maybe even Pete and his parents would see the writing on the wall. Amazingly, Abigail had managed to get Pete and both sets of parents to unwittingly sign on the dotted line under the guise of "relationship building." And now here we were.

A crow flew overhead, cawing. My eyes followed the bird as my tangled thoughts took a turn. *SOMEONE IS LYING!* Abigail wasn't the only one with secrets. I'd lied about some things too, had led her to believe we were on the same team, that we were working toward a common goal. She thought she knew everything about me, but she didn't. Not even close.

I'd stayed clean, more or less, for months. But now I dug the tiny bag of white powder out of an interior pocket of my pack. After scanning the surroundings and confirming I was alone, I poured the powder in a line onto a tin plate. My body curled forward as my index finger closed one nostril and I snorted the line with the other, waiting for the rush.

Even as I was doing it, a part of me knew it was a bad idea. But a bigger part of me didn't care. The chemical courage was necessary to do what I needed to do next.

SEVENTEEN

ABIGAIL

My hand quivered as I read through the items on the list, but I couldn't focus on the scavenger hunt. Mom's plea for me to call off the wedding cycled through me like adrenaline. It felt as if a small weight had lifted. Maybe I didn't have to bear this enormous burden on my own. I hoped she'd share the shift in her feelings with Dad, plant a seed of doubt in his mind as to whether Pete and his family were really the best fit for me. Still, whenever I pictured Pete—his hopeful eyes, the way he winked at me when he made a bad joke—my stomach folded. He'd participated in this camping trip for my sake. He'd told me many times that he'd lay down his life for me without a second thought. He'd even given me his ziplock bag for this ridiculous scavenger hunt when he was the one collecting a crawling insect. He always put me first. It would be devastating to hurt him. Breaking his heart was the thing I dreaded the most because he'd been nothing but good to me. I feared our breakup might destroy both of us. It was the main reason we were still together.

Our relationship was a decent one most of the time. And because things had never been too bad, I'd skated along, avoiding conflict. I'd allowed our plans for the future to snow-ball, growing bigger, more complicated, and more serious the faster it rolled forward. Once the diamond ring and wedding planning had been added to the mix, I couldn't stop the ball from toppling over me and carrying me with it, picking up speed. Maybe someone else would have been strong enough to stand up and slam on the brakes and smash that ball to pieces, but that person hadn't been me. I needed help to escape the tangled mess I'd created.

I spotted a figure in the distance, darting past the trees, someone on a mission. "Pete?" I yelled, but the person didn't respond. "Dad?" I tried again, but still no response.

A stick cracked somewhere within earshot, and I flinched. My nerves were all over the place. The forest was dense off the trail, and it was nearly impossible to get a decent view of anything more than a few feet away. I thought about what Liam had said about those messages in the dirt. *WATCH YOUR BACK!* and *SOMEONE IS LYING!* He'd sounded sincere when he said he hadn't known about them. Yet such a coinci-dental message—much less, two—seemed unlikely. I couldn't shake the feeling that someone else knew about us. About me, in particular.

I wondered again if Trent could have followed us here. But Pete hadn't thought it likely, had discounted the idea almost as soon as I'd mentioned it. Even if he was correct, there were plenty of other troubling possibilities. That creepy hiker in the woods refused to exit my thoughts. Although the others in the group didn't seem to think so, I suspected he'd been following us. I peered between the gaps in the trees again, fearing the strange man was out there. Anyone in our group probably would have responded to my calls just now, even if I'd yelled the wrong name. And why had that other hiker looked so famil-iar? I'd sorted through a hundred possible connections in my mind and still couldn't figure it out.

After waiting for a solid minute and hearing and seeing nothing, I forced my feet forward, realizing my imagination was in overdrive. No one except Liam was aware of my ulterior motive, and he had no reason to harm me. Up ahead, a rotting piece of wood sat nestled beneath a bed of needles. *Something decaying.* It was one of the items on my list, so I broke off a loose piece of the spongy log, flicking away the ants and placing it in my bag. I reread the remaining items. *A black rock the size of a golf ball, a green leaf bigger than your hand, a pink flower petal.* I scanned the immediate area for anything else, coming up empty. I remembered the black stones lining the creek bed at the last campsite and headed toward our new watering hole, hoping to locate something similar.

Once back on the trail, I turned in the direction of the camp. Footsteps plodded toward me, disturbing the relative silence. Kenny's sturdy frame and wiry beard appeared from around the bend, his white knee socks looking ridiculous beneath his sandals. He raised his flimsy bag, which contained a single pine cone.

"Not doing so great here. How about you?"

"Me neither." I pointed to the chunk of rotten wood in my bag.

"Well, good luck." He shrugged and continued past me.

I watched him disappear, hating that Kenny seemed like a good guy deep down, except for his apparent inclination to steal things. I couldn't help wondering if he'd swiped Liam's bear spray too. Still, there was no denying that I was the evil one in this group. I blinked away thoughts of my traitorous behavior as I forged ahead.

Beyond a row of maple and hemlock trees, the smooth, light bark of a single tree stood out from the others. I couldn't identify the type, but its oversized green leaves flapped in the wind. I scooted off the trail and plucked a fallen leaf from the ground, slipping it into my bag.

Two minutes later, I returned to the campsite, surprised to find no one there. Even Liam had wandered off somewhere. The sky had dimmed in the last few minutes, the sun sinking below the trees. I moved toward the edge of the pond, peering into the stagnant and murky water. It wasn't at all like the clear, rushing creek from yesterday and I was amazed our water filters had cut through the muck, and thankful that Liam had taken the extra step of boiling the already-filtered water when he'd cooked our noodles. A few grayish stones sat around the water's edge, but none were black and the size of a golf ball.

Something howled in the distance, high-pitched and trailing off at the end. My head jerked up at the haunting noise, a slightly higher pitch than the one we'd heard the night before. A coyote? Once again, the eerie scream had almost sounded human, but I'd heard coyotes were active at dusk. The thought of wild dogs circling our campsite instilled a new fear in me.

Mosquitos swarmed the shoreline and I batted them away from my face and gave up on locating the rock here. I remembered the pink flowers called lady slippers that Mom had spotted near the edge of Norton's Gulch. Nobody else was back at the campsite yet, but they were likely to return soon. I craved a few more minutes alone, a few moments to not have to listen to Kenny and Darla's constant chatter, Pete and Dad's work talk, and Mom's elongated sighs. A few minutes to gather myself. I still had time to collect the flower petal if I hurried.

I jogged along the path, backtracking along our route from earlier in the day and hoping not to run into anyone else from the group. Just as I had the thought, Darla plodded around a turn in the trail.

She huffed out a breath and squared her stocky shoulders as if to stop me. "We better head back. It's getting dark."

I lifted my bag. "I only need a couple more things."

Darla frowned. "Look at the sky."

My face angled upward. The sun had already set. Above

the blackened tree branches, the sky had taken on a purplish hue. "It'll just take a minute." I stepped to the side to edge around her.

"Don't go!" Darla lunged in front of me, blocking my path. She gripped her bag so tightly, that I could barely see the corner of a pink flower petal inside. "Forget about the game. It's not worth getting lost out there."

I widened my stance, looking further down the trail, then back toward camp. She was being more forceful about my safety than I expected, but she was probably right. As much as I wanted to be alone for a few more minutes, the night was descending on us, the faint call of the coyote still sounding in my ears. The scavenger hunt wasn't worth it, especially considering the entire wilderness outing was a hoax of my own making. I nodded and turned around with Darla leading the way back to camp. Her long braid swayed back and forth across her back as she walked. As we made our way back to the campsite, I couldn't help wondering how much of my mind she'd been able to glimpse with her cards and palm readings.

I released my breath when other voices reached my ears. Dad and Pete sat in the clearing, laughing about something funny that had happened at work.

"There they are." Pete raised his chin toward me. "I was about to go look for you."

"You're going to be disappointed in me." I realized my comment could refer to something much bigger, but I held up the bag, containing only two of the four items.

Pete patted a space on the log, and I sat next to him. "Don't worry. I got some of your items too." He reached into his pocket and pulled out a round, black rock and a partially crushed petal from a pink lady slipper. They were the same flowers I'd just been searching for. Pete had saved me again.

My back slouched. "Thanks."

Dad held up his bag. "I found the same kind. They're the flowers Mom liked. Remember?"

"Yeah." I looked back at Dad, noticing how his usually neat hair stuck up on top. Three thin lines of blood beaded across his cheek. "Dad. Your face is bleeding." I pointed below his eye.

He touched it. "Oh. I ran into some nasty thorns when I was reaching for the flowers. I didn't realize they drew blood."

Darla plopped onto the ground across from us. "I made Abigail turn around. It was getting too dark out there."

Kenny coughed from the perimeter of the woods, appearing a second later and pointing at Darla. "Mission accomplished."

"Where's Liam?" I asked. "And Mom?"

Pete looked toward Liam's empty spot. "I don't know."

We peered around the campsite and toward the shadowy forest. A moment later, an upbeat whistling tune cut through the silence. Liam popped his head out of the nearby trees and jumped into the clearing. "Sorry, guys. Nature called." He rubbed his hands together. "How'd everyone do?"

"Good," Kenny and Pete said at the same time.

Dad leaned back, looking toward the closest trail. "Kristen isn't back yet."

"Did anyone see her out there?" I scanned the faces around me as everyone shook their heads. Our vacant tent caught my eye, causing a fresh wave of dread to seep through me.

The whites of Darla's eyes practically glowed in the dwindling light. "Kristin shouldn't be alone out there. We're losing daylight."

Dad held up a hand. "Let's not panic. Kristen isn't reckless. I bet she's on her way back to us right now."

Dad was right. Of all the people unlikely to wander too far from the trail, Mom was at the top of the list. She played by the rules. Wasn't a risk-taker. Still, people made mistakes. Things changed in the woods. Even a sensible person could get turned around. And once it was dark out, the odds of navigating the unfamiliar surroundings dwindled further.

Liam twitched and fidgeted, unable to make eye contact. I wondered what was going on with him.

"Are you okay?"

He nodded, rubbing his eyes, which looked different in the fading light. "Yeah. Let's give her a few more minutes."

We waited for a minute, listening to the impatient tapping of Liam's foot. I scanned over each person in the group, everyone fidgeting, frowning, and glancing toward the surrounding forest. My gaze landed on Dad, who placed his palms on his knees and attempted to smile. But his calm exterior was a poor mask for the anxiety that clearly brewed directly below the surface. Worry creased his face, and the fresh scratch marks made him look vulnerable.

I stood and cupped my hands to my mouth, facing the woods. "MOM!" I turned in the other direction, aware of the panic straining my voice. "MOM!!!"

Everyone slid forward, listening. The only response was the creaking of the trees, the chatter of a squirrel.

Kenny sat up. "We should wander down the trail each way and see if we can find her."

"Yeah. Let's do that." Liam popped up as the rest followed.

Dad was already standing, striding toward the trail as Pete and I jogged to catch up. "Wait. We need flashlights." I sprinted to my pack and removed the handheld light, then returned to the group. Kenny had done the same.

"Let's split into two groups," Liam said. "Everyone stay with your group."

Now Darla, Kenny, and Liam headed in the opposite direction, while Dad, Pete, and I followed the trail beyond the pond. Calls of "Mom" and "Kristen" and even "Dr. Cates" echoed through the trees.

My legs grew shakier with each passing minute, my insides

hollow as if eaten away by a thousand termites. "Where is she?" Tears burned the corners of my eyes as I imagined Mom lost and scared somewhere in the dark forest.

Pete gripped my hand. Dad turned to me. "We'll find her. Keep your wits about you."

I nodded, reminding myself to remain calm. Maybe we'd locate Mom around the next turn, and we'd all be laughing about this in a couple of hours.

A high-pitched yipping sound echoed in the distance, followed by another similar call.

Pete looked at me. "Those are coyotes."

A breath of fear prickled the back of my neck. These cries sounded different than the one I'd heard earlier and the one we'd all heard last night. There'd been no response from the pack members before. I couldn't stop my thoughts from tumbling downward as a storm of images bombarded my mind. The pink lady slippers growing near the edge of Norton's Gulch. The ghost story Liam had told us. The disruption Darla had observed in the Line of Life on Mom's palm. Still, I had to get a grip, to not let myself believe the worst. Dad had found the flowers for his team. Maybe Mom hadn't even gone near the gulch.

"Dad, you were in charge of finding the pink flower petal, right?"

His feet stopped moving. "I found them, but Mom and I didn't divide our list like everyone else. We agreed to collect whatever we came across and hoped we'd have everything when we met up again."

I gasped. Pete and Dad turned to face me. "What if Mom went back to the gulch to pick the flowers? What if she slipped?" My hand flew to my mouth. I remembered the way Mom had crept too close to the edge earlier and felt as if I might vomit.

Pete looped his arm around me. "Abigail. You're freaking

out. She probably just turned the wrong way on this trail." He rubbed my back. "We're going to find her."

I raised my head, glancing at Dad whose pallor had increased. He gave a subtle nod and we continued forward, yelling her name in all directions. My hope dwindled further as our calls went unanswered.

Thirty minutes later, my throat had turned raw and the sky black. We'd covered some ground, a couple of miles at least. But there was no sign of Mom.

"Maybe we should turn around." Pete held me close to him, his face barely visible behind the glow of the flashlight.

Dad slumped forward, breathing through his mouth. He repeatedly tugged at his collar and I could tell he was worried. "You're probably right. I think we should head back. Hopefully, the other group has already found her."

I struggled to pull the night air into my lungs, to keep the panic from overtaking my body. "I hope so."

We turned and walked back along the trail, our cries into the woods less frequent and more subdued. I clung to the spark of hope that Liam, Darla, and Kenny had located Mom, that they waited back at camp for us at this very moment. Convincing myself of the happy outcome was the only way to get my legs to move forward. I could sense from Dad's strained breathing as he walked behind me that he was using the same mind trick.

"We'll find her, guys," Pete said from the back, but there was a crack in his voice.

We traveled faster on the way back to camp, covering our tracks in almost half the time. But the trail was dark and one of my steps didn't land right, my toe catching on a rock or a root as my ankle twisted backward. Something popped and an agonizing pain radiated up my leg.

"AHH!" I tried to set down my foot, but it refused to support my weight. "My ankle!"

Dad and Pete huddled around me, shining flashlights on my leg and instructing me to sit down. I clutched my ankle, as Pete gently prodded it with his fingers. "Does that hurt?"

"Yes."

"Take off your shoe."

I winced as I removed the hiking boot and the sock underneath, revealing my tender and swollen ankle.

"Can you wiggle your toes?" Dad asked.

I managed to wiggle them, but I wasn't sure what that proved. We sat there for a moment, not speaking. Mom was the only one of us with a medical background.

Dad scratched his head. "We're almost back to camp. Do you think you can make it?"

I tried to rotate my foot, but the muscles above it throbbed. I bit my lip to keep from screaming.

Pete scanned the woods as if looking out for predators. Then he refocused on me. "We shouldn't stay out here. I'll help you up. Put your arms around us so you can walk on one foot."

I picked up my hiking boot and sock and grasped his hand, digging the heel of my good foot into the ground and lunging myself upward. Dad and Pete supported my weight, moving ahead at a slower pace so I could hop along between them. We continued that way for another fifteen or twenty minutes, making slow and steady progress.

Kenny's voice mumbled from somewhere in the distance and I realized we were almost at the campsite. I forgot about my injury for a second, my thoughts shifting back to Mom. But as I reached the clearing, I registered the three bodies sitting in a semi-circle around a camping lantern—Liam, Darla, and Kenny. They peered up when they saw me.

"What happened?" Darla asked.

When I didn't answer, Pete said, "She twisted her ankle."

Liam popped up to get a closer look as the others grimaced from their seats.

"Did you find Kristen?" Kenny asked.

His question only confirmed what I'd just realized—that Mom wasn't with them. I had the sensation of toppling over, like a tree whacked at its base with an axe and landing with a deadening thump. Only when Dad and Pete reached me did I realize I'd collapsed to my knees, my hands outstretched, my forehead touching the cold, damp ground. I began to sob.

Dad tried to say something, but his voice hitched in his throat.

The tighter I squeezed my eyelids, the less I could stop the flood of tears, the crippling thoughts. My ankle didn't matter anymore.

Mom was missing. And it was all my fault.

EIGHTEEN

ABIGAIL

I wasn't sure how long I lay there like that, sobbing on the forest floor. But when my agony had finally dried up, I felt a hand supporting me from behind. I forced myself to sit up, my insides hollow and shaky, ankle aching. Pete rubbed my back, whispering in soothing tones that everything was going to be okay. I rested my head on his shoulder, finding it solid and warm. Even though I'd detected a quake of fear in his voice, his presence comforted me. This trip I'd concocted hadn't been easy on him either, but he was putting me first. I realized he'd always been there to pick me up when I fell. After a hard day at work or whenever I had a disagreement with a friend, Pete was quick to take my side, to stand in my corner. I'd taken his loyalty for granted. In so many ways, he was just like Dad.

A panicky realization jolted through me. What if I'd made the most royal of royal mess-ups? What if I had gotten this whole thing wrong? Perhaps my nervous instincts and cold feet about the wedding had been nothing more than that—nerves. The same nerves that every bride and groom around the world experienced every day. Romantic feelings ebbed and flowed in all relationships, didn't they? Maybe my meaningless fling with

Liam had merely been a selfish, short-sighted decision. One which I now regretted and wished I could take back. My rational mind knew that men like Pete were exceedingly rare. Pete couldn't help what family he'd been born into. He'd done everything in his power to create the life he wanted for himself. Lately, my heart had been lagging behind, slow to catch up to what my brain recognized—that Pete was the perfect partner for me. But now as Pete held me, preventing me from completely falling apart, my emotions pulled me toward him, my heart warming once again to the man who'd been so loving and loyal, the handsome stranger who'd taken my breath away when I'd first met him as he stood next to Dad's desk two years ago. What if it had taken the current crisis for me to see things clearly? How could I have been so blind? So stupid?

At last, I straightened up, shoulders trembling, and looked around. Dad sat on my other side, eyes glassy. Concern pulled down the faces of the others who sat nearby.

"I'm sorry." I blinked my wet eyes, looking at Pete, then Dad. "This is all my fault. Mom is missing because of me. We're all out here because of me. This was such a stupid idea. I made a huge mistake."

"Stop talking like that." The sharpness of Liam's voice cut through my lame attempt at a confession. He sniffed, wiping the back of his hand underneath his nose. "Nothing like this has ever happened on any of my camping trips before."

Dad's chin dipped toward me. "This isn't your fault, Abigail. No one could have foreseen your mom getting lost."

Darla's eyebrows lifted, her throat clearing as if she begged to differ, as if she'd somehow known all along that a horrible fate waited for Mom. At least she had the sense not to speak. The stars pulled Darla's gaze upward as she muttered some sort of mantra under her breath. I wondered what she thought she'd discerned from looking at the lines on Mom's palm, the images on her Tarot cards, or the alignment of the stars.

Kenny picked at his teeth, then motioned toward the woods. "You're all acting like Kristen is dead. She probably just took a wrong turn and is hunkering down for the night until she can get her bearings in the daylight."

Darla's pale face glowed in the moonlight. "The moon is nearly full. It's likely it led her astray. That's a very common phenomenon."

Pete threw up his hands. "Mom! You're not helping."

Liam's knee bobbed up and down as he ignored Darla and Pete's squabble. "Kenny's right. Kristen might be a little cold and scared tonight, but she'll be okay until we find her." He held his phone in his hand, raising it to the sky. "I don't have any reception here, but I'll hike to a better spot as soon as the sun rises to call the Park Service and submit a missing persons report."

I crawled over to my pack, digging the phone out of a water-proof bag I'd buried in an interior pocket. "Maybe one of us has reception." I powered it up, finding zero bars. Pete and Dad did the same, discovering the same discouraging result. Darla and Kenny didn't have phones to check, having left theirs in the lockers back at the visitors' center.

I put my useless phone away and hoisted myself onto a log next to Pete.

Liam stared at my enlarged ankle. "I have a bandage in my first-aid kit. I'll get it." He retrieved the bandage and crouched in front of me, wrapping it tightly around my ankle. I tried not to think of Mom with a similar injury as an imaginary pack of ravenous coyotes prowled its way into my mind. But I reminded myself that coyotes didn't eat humans, only rodents and small mammals. Still, there could be a cougar out there. A bear. Mom had no defense.

A vision of the half-starved man we'd encountered in the woods and the strange messages awaiting us at the campsites replaced the thoughts of wild animals. I might have glimpsed the man a few hours earlier, but maybe I'd been mistaken. More questions swarmed my mind. Was Mom merely lost, or did that rogue hiker have something to do with her disappearance? Were the ominous messages at the campsites somehow related? Did someone besides Liam know about my ulterior motive? I considered voicing my worries, but I didn't want to make things even more difficult for Dad, who rubbed his eyes.

I scooted closer to him, hugging his warm body. "We should go to bed soon, so we can get up at sunrise and start searching again."

Dad nodded. "Thanks, honey. I might lie down for a couple of hours, but I don't know if I'll be able to sleep tonight. I hope your ankle feels better soon." His arms hung limply at his sides. He appeared to have aged ten years in the span of a few hours. He squeezed my shoulder and turned away, crawling into his tent.

Pete turned toward the tent Dad had just entered. "I got him," he said, looking back at me. "We'll find your mom in the morning." He nodded at my leg. "And then we'll get you to a doctor ASAP."

"The bandage is helping a little bit."

He leaned close to me. "I love you."

"I love you too." The phrase popped out of my mouth easily, and I realized for the first time in a while that I meant it. The sentiment was true, not merely something I wanted myself to feel, which had been the way it was for many weeks prior. I'd never been more grateful for Pete's calming presence, for his steadfast love. I wondered, again, how I could have taken that for granted.

Pete followed Dad into their tent as Darla and Kenny fumbled with their packs, and Darla removed her bag of crystals. I stood up and hobbled toward Liam's shadowy figure, pacing back and forth near the tree line on the opposite side of camp. I'd told him earlier that something big needed to happen for Dad to change his mind about Pete. Was this what he'd done? What he'd thought I meant? Liam brushed right past me as I approached. He stopped and turned, and so did I. I glared at him and obstructed his path as he headed back in my direction.

"What did you do?" My voice hissed out in a loud whisper. "Did you tell her to hide or something?"

Liam paused in front of me, blinking and sniffing. "No. I didn't do anything. I swear."

I cocked my head, studying him in the dim glow of my flashlight, the dilated pupils and sweat-covered skin. "Are you high?"

"No. I'm just..." He paused, head jerking toward his shoulder.

"Oh my God." I buried my face in my hands, remembering how Liam had confided in me about his cocaine addiction. I'd never seen any sign of it before, but there was no mistaking his sniffling, twitching, sweating, and nervous pacing. He'd relapsed at the worst possible moment—during our wilderness outing.

He kicked at the dirt. "I can't believe your mom is missing. *Shit.* And now this." He motioned toward my ankle.

"Why did you send us out so late? And tell us to split up?"

"I don't know. I thought everyone would be back within twenty or thirty minutes. That list of items was insanely easy to find." His face zeroed in on me. "I didn't do this. Okay? Whatever happened here, it wasn't me."

I stared at Liam's crazed eyes and rigid spine, unable to believe I'd ever been attracted to him. He was freaked out for sure. As much as I was annoyed with his recklessness, I believed him.

He scratched at his hair, which had come undone from its usual ponytail and hung in limp sections around his face.

I grabbed Liam's arm, forcing him to look at me. "I think that guy we passed in the woods yesterday—the one who took our granola bars—is following us. I saw someone out there earlier. It might have been him. What if he kidnapped my mom?"

Liam shook his head. "Why would some random hiker in the woods kidnap your mom?"

"Sometimes there isn't a reason. Maybe he's mentally ill. Maybe he needed more food and she didn't have any left."

Liam waved his hands in the air. "Your mom's a psychiatrist. She, of all people, would know how to talk him down. It seems more likely that he's a guy who prefers living in the forest and your mom got lost looking for a rock or a flower. We'll locate her tomorrow as soon as the sun comes up." Liam's voice had grown loud enough that Kenny looked over from across the clearing.

"Everything okay over there?" Kenny yelled.

"We're fine," I said in Kenny's direction, although I was anything but. I angled my body away from the others and motioned for Liam to do the same. We needed to hide his impaired state.

Liam picked at his thumb, lowering his voice. "I'm not going down for this mess you created. Remember, we both did this. We've got to stick together."

I stared at the ground as I nodded.

Liam gestured toward the tents, his face softening. "Why don't you get some rest? I'll stay up for a while and sit by the lantern in case your mom is still making her way back to us."

"Okay." I began to step away but turned back. "Lay off the drugs until we all get out of here." Without giving Liam a chance to respond, I limped over to my tent, every other step bringing with it a barb of agony. Darla had, once again, arranged a colorful array of crystals around the perimeter of the tent and had even placed a few around the other two tents. I didn't comment on her ritual in case whatever she was doing actually helped bring Mom back. Behind me, Liam wrestled the bag of our remaining food and a separate bag of trash, which he strung up from the limb of a tree.

"C'mon, honey." Darla placed a hand on my shoulder, eyeing the surrounding trees again as she led me to the tent's opening. "Let's lie down and get some rest so we have the energy to find your mom in the morning."

I let her guide me, aware of my weak and broken body. It would be good to lie down for a while. She zipped us inside the tent, where I stared at Mom's vacant sleeping bag, tears stinging my eyes. My heavy head landed on the pillow, and I forced my eyelids closed as Darla mumbled nonsensical phrases so quietly that I couldn't make out the words. I fell asleep, wondering what had happened to my mom.

NINETEEN

DARLA

The sleeping bag shifted across Darla's feet as her fingers tightened around the crystals—onyx for strength and black tourmaline for protection. Abigail tossed and turned beside her. Darla couldn't see much more than the shadowy outline of Abigail's head, but she didn't need to because the young woman's desperate and hopeless energy radiated from her. No one could get a restful sleep with energy like that. It took all of Darla's resolve not to hug Abigail, to tell her the horrible thing she'd seen in the cards. But that could ruin everything. She sealed her lips closed and focused on her breathing.

Over the last two days, Darla had grown fond of her son's fiancée. There was something about Abigail's quiet nature and her openness to new experiences that made her easy to be around. Even so, Darla wasn't sure she completely trusted the young woman. Geminis could be like that. Duplicitous. One way on the outside, while something altogether different bubbled on the inside. Still, Abigail seemed as good a pairing as any for Pete. His standards had always been set so high, his eyes focused on a brighter future he believed existed somewhere over the horizon, far away from her and Kenny and Trent. She was happy that Pete had finally found what he'd been searching for.

Darla's stomach grumbled with hunger and her lower back ached. She flipped onto her right side, facing the wall of the tent, which smelled faintly of mildew and sweat. A tapping sound echoed from outside, and she knew it was Liam keeping a hyper-alert vigil in the light of the lantern.

She closed her eyes, struggling to tune out the noises around her. Colorful images shuffled through her mind, and she wished she could go back and place the Tarot cards in a different order, both for Abigail's reading and the reading she'd done the morning of the trip. But, of course, Tarot didn't work like that. She smiled at the absurdity of the idea. Darla couldn't reshuffle a reading any more than she could travel back in time and be born under a different sun sign. Tarot had shown her several truths before they'd left—a renewed spark of love between a couple, a disruption in a journey, a conflict or hardship to overcome. Admittedly, she hadn't interpreted everything correctly at the time. She'd envisioned the hardship as being more of a "steep hill" or "rapid river crossing" type of scenario, not Kenny swiping John's pills or their tour guide being more hopped up on cocaine than a 1980s Wall Street stockbroker. And now Kristen was gone.

Kristen wasn't Darla's favorite person. She was uptight and a bit of a snob. But Darla hadn't wished for this outcome. She ran her fingertip over the edge of the crystals, retracing in her mind the palm reading she'd done on the reluctant woman. There'd been a clean break in her Line of Life, a kind she'd never seen before—until she spotted the identically defined break again on Abigail's hand a few minutes later. She'd told them the marking had likely represented a disruption to their well-being or health. But now Darla wondered if the broken line on Kristen's palm had indicated something more sudden and violent, the kind of severe disruption that led to death.

Darla knew palm lines didn't predict the future, but they did offer clues, especially to those who were more intuitive like herself.

The energy around the gulch had been thick and harrowing for such a beautiful place. Darla had sensed the spirits surrounding her there as she slunk along the path. She perceived the windswept whispers of the dead latching on to the group's negative energy, luring them all a little too close to the edge. Kristen had been so easily drawn to those pink flowers. The restless spirits had been known to cause people to do things they normally wouldn't have done—tell a lie, give a push —even good people. Darla had never been one to argue with the cards, even when she didn't like what she saw.

They weren't alone in the forest. That was obvious from the messages at the campsites. But even without the messages, Darla perceived someone else out there, lurking in the woods. Her senses had alerted her to a presence. They'd passed that other hiker with the negative aura, but Darla worried the person hiding beyond the trees could be someone else altogether. Someone closer to home. Kenny claimed he didn't know anything about those messages at the campsites. He insisted Trent was back home in a bowling tournament this weekend, and he hadn't given Trent their route. Maybe he was being truthful. But Kenny and Trent were similar. They had a habit of acting without thinking things through, of brewing up trouble. Kenny had never mentioned his plan to steal that car either. Darla hadn't learned of that previous misdeed until she'd received a call from the police station, informing her that her husband had been arrested. Desperate to pay his debts and achieve some sort of vigilante justice in one fell swoop, Kenny and his friend had targeted the car of a woman who'd left a one-star review for Darla's palm reading business on Yelp. And now Kristen, equally skeptical and just as critical of Darla's abilities, was missing. As Darla contemplated the depths of Kenny's loyalty, she didn't want to believe her husband would make the same mistake twice, not after what he'd been through in prison. She wouldn't let him go back.

Darla squeezed her eyes shut, traveling further inside the dark hollows of her mind. Her older son's disappointment at being cut from the wedding party needled through her. Even if Kenny wasn't involved, she feared Trent could have followed them out here on his own if only to feel included. Or maybe to mess things up for his brother. If that was the case, Darla wondered how much he had witnessed. And what was his endgame?

Darla held a breath of musty air in her lungs, grounding herself. Sometimes her thoughts ran away with her, creating wild truths to match what the cards had revealed instead of the other way around. Maybe she was doing that now because she couldn't shake the memory of Abigail's reading this morning. She couldn't forget the flash of fear and the taste of dread that had filled her mouth when she flipped over the last two cards. The Ten of Swords with the Two of Cups reversed had presented themselves as the best-case scenario for their marriage, with the Two of Cups somehow stuck to the bottom when Darla had only meant to deal one card. Those two cards, when taken together, were often believed to indicate an intentional death. A murder. But how could murder be the best-case scenario? It hadn't made any sense. They were the identical cards Darla's client, Lydia, had drawn last year. Darla had experienced the same taste of dread in her mouth at the sight of them, had felt the same hot fear running through her veins. She'd warned Lydia to be careful and to avoid high-risk situations, such as returning to her isolated office at the rental car company where Lydia worked and had mentioned feeling increasingly unsafe. After the reading, Darla had even shared her fears about Lydia's life being in danger with Kenny. Three weeks later, Lydia was shot and killed at her desk by a disgruntled ex-co-worker. That's why Darla had gotten flustered and hidden the images to avoid upsetting Abigail.

She pulled in a breath and reminded herself that just as the lines on one's hand could have many meanings, so could the cards. Maybe the two cards had represented two alternate paths and had not been meant to be taken together. No one's fate was set in stone. Still, it was better to hedge one's bets and prepare for multiple scenarios. Darla had failed to predict things in the past, vital events that had altered their lives. But she hadn't had her Tarot cards back then. Sometimes the cards offered glimpses of possible things to come. Other times they hinted at actions to be taken. Despite Pete's complaints about Darla's mystic practices, her main goal had always been to protect her family. And so, as she listened to Abigail's haggard breath, her kicking feet, and sniffling nose, she could feel with every cell of her body that Abigail was a daughter who loved her mother, a woman who hadn't fully grown into herself yet, but whose fate had collided with hers.

Darla loosened her grip on the crystals and placed them under her meager camping pillow, hugging the scratchy fabric to her face. Clearly, some of the others didn't approve of her techniques, but Darla had always let her findings guide her. There was only one clear path for best protecting her family, a path that was leading her deeper into the dark and tangled forest, indeed. But she didn't have a choice.

TWENTY

ABIGAIL

Darla's face was inches from mine. "I had a dream about the pink flowers near the gulch."

My eyes popped open and it took a second to get my bearings. I was inside the tent, a hint of purplish light glowing outside. It was morning. My ankle pulsed, suffocating beneath the tight bandage. The terrible events of the night before tumbled through me as I rolled closer to the empty sleeping bag next to me.

"Vivid dreams should never be ignored." Now Darla's fingers gripped my wrist, her eyes imploring me through the morning shadows. "Our subconscious minds know things that our conscious minds can't acknowledge. Never forget that."

My tongue felt thick in my mouth, and I couldn't respond. Darla was eccentric, but usually seemed pretty accurate in her assessment of things. The truth was that I hadn't been able to discount most of her intuitions. Her Tarot cards had revealed that I'd been feeling trapped, that there an event—a wedding—holding Pete and me together. I'd been thinking about those stupid flowers too. Mom had been attracted to them, giddy at the sight of them. What if she *had* gone back to collect them, eager to knock one item off her list? I managed a nod at Darla, who finally released her grip.

A cough came from outside the tent. Dad was awake. I clawed out of my sleeping bag and exited the tent, gulping in the cool, damp air and eager to put some space between me and Darla. Dad crouched forward, cradling his head in his hands. Pete, Kenny, and Liam weren't with him. The other tents were quiet, and I guessed they were still sleeping. Dad looked up when I approached, his face haggard. I could see he hadn't had the luxury of the few hours of sleep I'd gotten.

"No sign of your mom." His lips pulled down and I thought he might cry.

I sat next to him. "It's getting lighter now. We have a better chance of locating her."

He didn't respond at first. "How's your ankle?"

"It still hurts, but I'll live. I think we should go back to Norton's Gulch. That's where those pink flowers were. She might have—" A surge of nausea rose in my stomach, and I couldn't complete the thought. Instead, I said, "She might have turned in the wrong direction from there."

Dad rubbed his forehead. "I would feel better just knowing she wasn't there."

Darla emerged from our tent, wearing a different shirt than the one she'd slept in. She dug through her pack, removing four granola bars and holding them above her head. "We can each have half a bar. Everyone needs to eat something, even if you're not hungry." She rustled the side of the men's tent. "Kenny. Pete. Time to get up."

I looked toward Liam's tent, then strode over to it and unzipped the door, hoping he'd slept off the effects of the drugs. "Get up. We're heading out to look for my mom." My voice held an edge because I blamed him more than anyone for this turn of events. Liam was the one who'd made up the pointless scavenger hunt, had told us to separate so late in the day, and had listed pink flower petals as one of the items. As if that hadn't been reckless enough, he'd snorted a line of cocaine just as Mom went missing. I might have been the one who'd brought us all here, but our trusted guide had gotten us into this terrifying situation, and now he needed to do something to fix it.

Liam groaned but sat up, squinting. "Yeah. Okay. Sorry, I was up really late."

I turned away from him, and took half a granola bar from Darla, choking it down. A few minutes later, Liam and Kenny pumped murky water through purifiers and filled everyone's water bottles. The group had never been so quiet. Pete rubbed my shoulder and whispered that Dad had had a tough night. "Did you get any sleep?" he asked.

"Maybe three or four hours." My eyelids blinked rapidly as tears filled my eyes. Pete hugged me, resting his chin on the crown of my head. "Don't worry. We'll find her. We'll send for outside help today." His words comforted me, loosening everything that had been wound so tightly inside. I could feel the pulse in his neck beating in my ear in a steady rhythm. Mom's disappearance had altered my perspective. More than anything, I wanted everyone to be safe. Pete had been my rock these last two years. This horrible ordeal reminded me how lucky I was to have him as my partner. And now, folded into his arms, I couldn't envision getting through this without him. His mere presence seemed to be saving me from falling into a bottomless abyss. The doubts invading my psyche over the last couple of months had been confused and misplaced. I'd been over-thinking things, creating issues where none existed. I didn't care whether our parents got along anymore. It no longer seemed important. Pete and I could figure it out. We could trade off holidays like so many other couples did. I breathed in Pete's scent, fighting the urge to confess to everything—my apprehension about the wedding, my fling with Liam, this sham of an outing that had never been meant for bonding at all but was somehow steering me back into the arms of my fiancé. I swallowed the words, reminding myself that no one needed to know what I'd done. Liam's lips were sealed, and a confession from me would only cause more damage. When I finally moved away to tie on my hiking boots, Pete repositioned himself next to Dad, offering a pep talk, reassuring him that we'd find Mom today, that he'd take us all out to dinner to celebrate once we got back home.

With my chest heavy and my water bottle filled, I followed Liam and the others along the trail leading to Norton's Gulch, Pete supporting me on one side. Each laborious step felt like a move closer to an invisible monster, a march toward an execution. I silently scolded myself. *Stop imagining the worst! Mom is fine. She's probably waking up in a butterfly-filled meadow somewhere close by.* Still, a turning in my gut didn't quite believe my upbeat sales pitch.

At last, we rounded the bend where the earth descended, the rocky cliff cascading downward. Liam was at the front with me right behind him, but when we arrived at the gulch he paused and stepped back like he was afraid to look. I was the first one to inch toward the edge of the gulch, to peer over the ledge with my heart in my throat. My eyes scanned over the ridge. I looked down across the rugged and barren terrain. A pop of color caught my eye—the purple fleece jacket I'd lent to Mom last night. I gasped, hands flying to my mouth as my brain slowly processed the sight below.

Mom's body lay motionless, torso twisted one way, the head facing the other direction. A leg splayed sideways at a severe angle. She was almost unrecognizable with streaks of blood slashed across her pale face, her skin a grayish hue. More blood bloomed across her stomach, which had been impaled by something. It was like a scene from a horror movie. I didn't want it to be her. I couldn't let it be her.

"Mom!" I yelled. "Mom!"

There was no response. No movement, not even the slightest rise and fall of her chest.

The rest of the group edged beside me, toes inching forward, eyes pulling downward. Darla whimpered. Dad turned away and collapsed to the ground, his legs no longer able to support him. Pete released a guttural groan, hands on his head. Liam kicked a rock, his mouth reciting a string of unintelligible swear words. My mind still refused to accept the sight that lay two hundred feet below; it was too gruesome, too unbelievable to be real. I had to take another look if only to make sure my eyes hadn't played tricks on me. But when I did, I recognized Mom's face, the hair that looked so much like mine, the glint from the watch on her wrist I'd given her for her birthday, the lips that had kissed my forehead every night before bed for nearly eighteen years. Even from up here, it was obvious we were too late, that her injuries were too severe. All signs of life had vanished.

Dad attempted to stand but immediately doubled over, heaving for breath. I wanted to comfort him, but the granola bar I'd forced down earlier reversed course, hot liquid making its way back up my esophagus. I lurched toward a spindly pine tree and vomited beneath it. When I turned around a minute later, wiping my mouth, my limbs felt heavy, my thoughts amassing like thick mud.

"We need to help her." Dad's eyes were wild as he got low and dipped his toe below the edge of the trail.

"Dad!" I screamed, worried he might topple down into the deadly gulch too.

"No! Don't!" Liam yanked Dad backward by his arm. "We're too late, John. I'm sorry. No one could survive that fall. And the gulch isn't hikeable. We need to call for outside help."

Pete's hand was on Dad's shoulder, and he was saying something to him. But when he saw me, he left Dad's side and enveloped me in his arms. "We'll get through this,

Abigail. I promise. I'm here for you and we'll get through this."

I let Pete's solid body support me as I leaned my weight into him, too stunned to cry. My mind couldn't process what had happened, wouldn't let me believe Mom was lying dead at the bottom of the cliff, despite what I'd seen. Mom probably would have explained my denial by citing some decades-old study about how the human mind created defense mechanisms to protect itself from experiencing extreme trauma. This was my brain protecting me from the most traumatic event in my life.

As I leaned my chin into Pete's shoulder, my lifeless stare snagged on something out of place—a tiny, gleaming object with a familiar pale-pink color. I recognized it as one of Mom's acrylic nails, the ones she'd had applied and painted at the salon last week. I limped away from Pete and toward the nail, which lay near a bed of weeds about two feet from the cliff's edge. Pinching it in my fingers, I lifted it to eye level, noting the jagged edge. The nail was broken.

"This... It's Mom's nail."

Dad stopped heaving and peered at me. My eyes gravitated to the scratches on his face, the ones that he said were from the brambles. Mom had told me there'd been tension between them, that they'd been sleeping in separate bedrooms, that she'd be happy for the change of scenery. I remembered the pink flower petal in his bag. He must have been here. Was it possible things between them had been worse than she'd let on?

No. No. No. I spun away from Dad. My mind was reeling, kicking up wild thoughts. I wasn't thinking clearly. Dad sat hunched on the ground, body jerking as he choked on his tears. His emotion was real. He loved Mom with all his heart, had never once been violent toward her, and now he was devastated.

Pete and Liam stepped in my direction, eyes fixed on the object pinched between my fingers. The stunned looks on their faces as they studied the nail told me they were thinking along the same lines. That maybe Mom had tried to fight. That maybe she hadn't merely slipped on her own.

Darla and Kenny hovered a few feet away, and I noticed a strange look pass between them, something secretive, ominous. But just as quickly, Darla broke her gaze with Kenny and locked eyes with me instead. Her mouth pulled down as she gently shook her head. I could see now that she was upset, maybe even frightened. But I wondered why she'd stared at her husband like that.

All at once, I remembered what she'd said this morning about the pink flowers, the gulch. How had Darla known Mom was here? None of it made sense. Suddenly, I didn't believe the vision from her dream or any of her other mystic bullshit. She'd been playing me.

I squeezed Mom's broken nail in my palm. *Leave no trace.* Except she had. Mom had left this clue for me to find. My head jerked toward Darla. "How did you know she was here?"

"Huh?"

"This morning. You said we needed to go to Norton's Gulch. You knew my mom was here. How did you know?"

"I told you, sweetie. I had a vivid dream about the pink flowers. This is where they grow."

My molars ground together as I tried not to scream. "No. I think there's more to it. Last night, I was heading this way, toward the gulch, and you wouldn't let me pass you. Was that because you knew she was here? You didn't want me to see her!"

"Of course not! That's ridiculous." Darla frowned as she waved her hands in the air. "It was getting dark, and I didn't want you out here alone. That's all there was to it."

Kenny stepped beside his wife, narrowing his eyes. "I know you're in a bad spot, Abigail. But don't accuse my wife of something she didn't do."

"Or what? Should I watch my back?" I squared my shoulders at him, a mixture of rage and anguish pulsing through me.

Kenny stood there glaring back at me, shifting his weight from foot to foot. I took in his scraggly beard, the eyes that sat slightly too close together, and the thick fingers clenched into fists. The endearment I'd cloaked him with earlier had fallen away, leaving me with an unfiltered view of the real Kenny—a quick-tempered and simple-minded criminal who was overprotective of his wife, a man who, quite frankly, had very little to lose. The secretive look Kenny and Darla had shared a minute earlier again flashed in my mind, along with Pete's statement that his parents couldn't be trusted. I got a sickening feeling they'd done something to Mom, that they'd worked together.

Before I could respond, Pete took a half-step in front of me, blocking me from his parents. "Abigail didn't mean anything by it. We're all in shock." He motioned at Kenny. "So just back off."

Darla lifted her chin, whisking away a fresh stream of tears with the back of her hand as her husband turned toward her and pulled her into his arms. "How could she think that?" Darla muttered into Kenny's chest.

I bit my lip, feeling my cheeks burn. My accusation had offended Darla, assuming her emotion wasn't part of her act. It was true that, other than the broken nail, I had no real proof of foul play at all. But something dark and troubling churned in my gut. Mom was so cautious, had never been a risk-taker. I couldn't imagine her gambling on her life to pick a flower. I remembered how the campsite had been empty when I'd returned from my trek into the woods to search the watering hole for rocks. Everyone had been out hiking separately from one another to complete the scavenger hunt. Then that haunting scream—the one that had sounded different from the lower-pitched scream we'd heard the night before—had pierced the air. I'd convinced myself it had been a coyote. Now it struck me that I might have heard Mom's final cry.

My gaze hovered on Darla and Kenny, then slid over to Liam, and even paused on Dad, and then Pete. Everyone appeared grief-stricken, stunned into inaction. They were red-faced, mumbling, not sure what to do with their hands and legs. But my gut told me something wasn't right, that maybe Mom had been shoved to her death like the people in that ghost story. And if that was the case, anyone in this group would have had the opportunity.

TWENTY-ONE

ABIGAIL

Pete helped me wobble toward Dad, who hunched over his knees, hands covering his face and body shaking. Dad had always been my superhero, someone who seemed invincible. The sight of him broken cracked something open in me, and I couldn't stop the tears from brimming over and streaming down my face. "I'm sorry. I'm sorry." I repeated the phrase over and over as Dad sucked in an occasional breath and hugged me.

The others stood at a distance, giving us space. Darla continued to cry quietly as Kenny comforted her. In my peripheral vision, Liam fumbled with his phone, tipping his head back in frustration. Pete paced nearby, a grimace forming amid his five o'clock shadow. Then Liam motioned to Pete, and they discussed something, voices low. A minute later, Pete approached me and Dad.

"I'm sorry, guys. Liam thinks we should head back to the campsite. He'll hike out and get help. He can do it faster without us."

I looked up at him, then turned my head to the cliff's edge. "What about Mom? We can't just leave her here!"

"We need to wait for help. The gulch can't be hiked. At

least, not by any of us." Pete waited but neither Dad nor I responded as we eyed the severe drop-off. We knew he was right. "Come on. The faster we get back to camp, the sooner Liam can leave. I'll help you up."

It took a minute, but Dad and I eventually raised ourselves off the ground. The others surrounded us, pale-faced and tear-stained. Pete supported me with his arm, while Kenny placed a hand on Dad's back. "Let's get you back to camp."

I watched Kenny help Dad, catching another fleeting glimpse of his goodness. His kind gestures were so at odds with the threats he'd made to defend his wife, the wild eyes and bared teeth he'd shown a few minutes earlier. How could someone be so changeable? I didn't trust him.

Liam turned to look at us. "Our top priority is keeping everyone safe until I get back with help. My phone doesn't have any reception, but I can get back to the visitors' center in four or five hours if I don't have a pack and run the whole way. So, I'm going to do that and return with help before nightfall." His body twitched and I couldn't tell if it was because the cocaine still lingered in his system or because he was itching for more of it.

I glared at Liam. I hated myself for having trusted him, for leaving this camping trip in his jittery, incompetent hands. I wanted to strangle him. If Pete's arm hadn't been looped around me, I might have lunged at our reckless tour guide and pushed him toward the deadly cliff. He was the one who sent us out at night, who chose pink flower petals as one of the items on the list, knowing Mom's attraction to the lady slippers that grew near the gulch. If Mom *had* accidentally slipped and fallen to her death, I was sure of one thing—it was Liam's fault. But I wasn't convinced it had been an accident. And I could see by the way Liam's lips pulled back and his eyelids fluttered that he was barely holding it together, that the others would come to his defense just as they had when I'd confronted Darla. So, I bit my tongue and decided to save my accusations for another time.

With no discussion, we followed Liam back to camp. My head was dizzy and the woods seemed to spin around me, but Pete kept me upright and moving in the right direction. In a matter of minutes, Dad, Pete, and I sat in the clearing near the tents with Darla and Kenny hovering nearby. Liam filled his water bottle, tossed us what was left of the meager stash of food, and instructed us not to leave the campsite for any reason until he returned, all the while refusing to make eye contact with me. I wondered if he'd have to spill my ugly secret to the authorities. Maybe this was karma coming back to bite me in the most horrific way possible. But I hoped my real motive for this wilderness outing wasn't relevant to Mom's death. I prayed Pete and Dad would never find out what I'd been trying to do when I'd set up this trip.

I grabbed Liam's arm, forcing him to look at me.

When his eyes locked with mine, they were clear again, a sheen of understanding in them. Liam lowered his voice as if speaking only to me. "Don't worry. I'll handle it."

I gave a slight nod and released his arm.

Kenny cleared his throat. "I'll make sure everyone stays put."

"Good luck, Liam." Darla stepped next to him and forced him to take one of her crystals. Liam tucked it into his pocket and high-tailed it around the bend.

I stood, frozen in shock as Darla helped Dad into his tent and told him to lie down. Pete asked if I wanted to rest too, and I nodded, tugging his shirt. "Come with me."

A minute later, we were lying side by side inside the tent, its canvas walls fluttering in the wind. I stayed still, trying not to let the darkness of my thoughts consume me.

"I'm so sorry this happened. It doesn't seem real." Pete squeezed my hand. "I'm here for you no matter what."

I sat up, staring at Pete through my tears. "What if Mom didn't just slip and fall by accident?"

Pete cocked his head. "What do you mean?"

"The broken nail. I think she fought someone off." My voice cracked. "Or tried to."

Pete ran his hands through his hair, listening.

I dug into my pocket, feeling Mom's acrylic nail between my fingertips. "She wouldn't have gone that close to the edge on her own."

"But she did, remember? You called her back from the edge when she first spotted the flowers."

I dipped my head because Pete was right. Mom had wandered dangerously close to the gulch. Still, I shook my head because Pete had left out an important piece of information. "That was before she realized where the drop-off started. Once she knew, she wouldn't have gotten that close again. Mom was so overly cautious all the time. She wouldn't even cross a street unless she was at a crosswalk with a signal. I just can't see her leaning over the edge of a deadly cliff to pick some flowers. It doesn't make any sense."

"Look, my mom and dad have a lot of issues." Pete paused, lifting his chin. "And they may have had a mild dislike for your mom, but I've known them my whole life. They're not murderers."

"I'm not saying that they..." I plucked at the edge of my sleeping bag as my voice trailed off. The shadow that had lurked outside the tent just as Mom told me not to marry Pete entered my thoughts. "Your dad spent time in prison recently. Maybe that changed him. I mean, for the worse."

Pete stared straight ahead, not responding.

I thought of the way Darla had prevented me from walking toward the gulch last night, almost as if she'd known Mom was there and hadn't wanted me to see. "Your mom and her visions. It's all kind of creepy." I paused, picking at the skin around my thumbnail. "She didn't like that my mom was so skeptical.

What if your mom wanted to make one of her prophecies come true? You know, to prove a point."

Pete shook his head, interrupting me. "I don't know. Killing people has never been part of her act." His breath was labored now.

"You don't exactly spend much time with them."

Pete lowered his eyelids but didn't respond.

I could see that I'd poked too close to an open wound, so I stopped talking. I shifted my legs as a branch cracked somewhere outside. My thoughts turned to the shadowy figure in the woods and Darla's complaints about Trent not being included in the wedding party. "And you're sure Trent's not out here?"

"No. I mean, I'm not a hundred percent sure. But he's supposedly in some bowling tournament this weekend, remember? Besides, he's never even met your mom before."

I chewed on my lips, realizing Pete was right about Trent not knowing my mom.

"What about that weird guy in the woods? He was probably the one who left those strange messages for us at the campsites. Maybe he encountered Mom on the trail and pushed her."

Pete sat up straighter, breathing deliberately. "That guy was strange, for sure. But you're getting a little ahead of yourself, don't you think? We haven't seen him in two days. And he doesn't even know us. Your mom gave him food!"

I heard what Pete was saying and knew his words made sense, but I still couldn't drop the feeling that Mom's fall hadn't been accidental. "Liam said he didn't have anything to do with it. I mean, with... what happened to Mom. But I'm not sure if I trust him."

"Abigail, Liam had nothing to gain. He's probably going to lose his job after this, and that's the best-case scenario."

I pulled at a loose thread near the zipper of my bag. It was true that Mom's tragedy could be devastating for Liam. Yet Liam was a wild card, a person who I knew well in some respects and not at all in others. I wondered if our interests were as aligned as I'd initially believed.

"And you were with Dad the whole time during the scavenger hunt?" I asked.

"Huh?" Pete flashed a suspicious look. "Yes, I was near him at least three-quarters of the time we were out there."

"Did you see him scratch his face on the brambles?"

Pete leaned away from me, biting his lip. "Oh my God, Abigail. This is crazy. No. I didn't see him scratch his face. But I've never seen a man love someone as much as your dad loved your mom. You know that as well as I do."

I grabbed my elbow with my opposite hand, uncomfortable with my thoughts. "Did you know they've been having problems?"

Pete hesitated, angling his face away from me for a moment.

"What is it?" I asked.

"Your dad never said anything about marital problems to me —" Pete stopped himself again, and I got the feeling there was something he wasn't telling me, that he was lying.

I remembered a day I'd stopped by his office to meet Pete for lunch. There'd been a woman standing in the parking lot near Dad. Too near. At first, I thought it was Mom because she had a similar build and the same hair color. But as she'd touched his arm and Dad had thrown his head back in dramatic laughter, I realized it was someone else. I'd discounted it at the time but remembered thinking, *Mom wouldn't like that.*

Mom's comments played an ugly loop in my mind. *We don't have much fun anymore... Marriage is hard enough, even in the best of circumstances... We sleep in separate bedrooms now.*

Now I locked my stare on Pete. "I saw Dad with an attractive older woman in the parking lot once. He didn't know I was there." It took a second to process my thoughts. Mom and Dad's bickering. The scratches on Dad's face. The mangled flower petal in his bag. Mom's broken nail. Dad's refusal to turn back even after his medication went missing. Had things been much worse than I'd ever imagined? Had Dad been having an affair? Had Liam's stupid ghost story given him a horrible idea? My body felt numb. "What if he..."

Pete held up his hand. "Let me stop you right there."

"There's someone else. Isn't there?"

"What? No!"

I gripped Pete's hands in mine. "Please don't lie to me. I know what I saw."

Pete sighed. "Okay. There's a woman who comes by the office sometimes. Janie Metz. That's probably who you saw, but you've got it wrong. She's an accountant who gives him tax advice. They meet for lunch maybe once every month or two, but it's nothing more than that. He writes it off as a business lunch. I'm sure they're only talking about financials."

"Once every month or two?"

"Yeah. He's allowed to have female colleagues, isn't he?"

"I guess," I said, but my mouth had gone dry.

"I promise you, it's nothing. Your dad is faithful to your mom. That's what I've witnessed. And even if they weren't getting along, do you honestly think this is how he would resolve things?"

I buried my face in my hands, ashamed for thinking the worst. My parents had had their ups and downs lately, but what marriage didn't? Pete was right. Dad would never hurt Mom, much less kill her. But I couldn't get Mom's desperate words out of my head. *Please don't marry Pete.* I wondered if she'd told Dad what she'd told me—that I should call off the wedding. Dad had been waiting his whole life for a son like Pete. He would have been pissed at her for intervening and ruining things. Still, I'd never known Dad to be violent. Of all the possible scenarios spinning through my head, this one seemed the least likely.

"Mom was talking to me inside our tent right before the

scavenger hunt. She wasn't herself. She was out of sorts because of this stupid camping trip."

Pete stared at me, confused.

"There was a shadow outside the tent. I'm worried someone might have overheard her saying some not-so-nice things about your family." I squeezed his hand tighter "It wasn't you out there, was it?"

"What? No. I was with your dad over by the water until we met up with Liam to get the lists."

I remembered Pete standing near the water with Dad when I'd entered the tent and when I'd exited with Mom, and knew he was telling the truth.

He cocked his head. "What was your mom saying?"

I loosened my grip on his, feeling a shred of relief. "It doesn't matter. Just a couple of things about what she thought of your mom's palm-reading abilities. She wasn't even making sense." I rolled onto my shoulder. "Did you see my mom at all later? When you picked the flowers by the gulch?"

"No. I wish I had. I'd already split from your dad when I spotted the flowers in a crevice in the rocks. It was right before I rounded the bend to Norton's Gulch. Then I ran into my mom for a second. I'm sorry. I never made it over there."

I could feel my lips pulling down, the tears building behind my eyes.

"It's human nature to want to blame someone else when something terrible happens. Your mom told us that, remember?"

I nodded again because I did remember Mom telling us exactly that a few months ago. We'd been discussing a lawsuit filed by the tenants of an apartment building that had burned down. Mom said the residents of the building needed someone to blame after having lost their home and all their earthly belongings, even though one of the tenants had admitted to passing out while smoking and was likely the one who'd started the fire. Now here I was doing the same thing, trying to place blame on everyone else for losing my beloved mother when I was the one who'd dragged us all out here under false pretenses. I was traumatized, sleep-deprived, and hungry, and I realized my thoughts were anything but clear. My heavy head rested on Pete's chest as I closed my eyes. I pulled in a long breath and tried to convince myself that Mom's death had been an accident.

TWENTY-TWO

LIAM

Shit! Shit! Shit! I couldn't believe this was happening. None of my campers had ever been seriously injured, much less died, on any of my wilderness outings. I couldn't wrap my head around this morning's discovery, even though I'd seen Abigail's mom lying dead at the bottom of the gulch.

Now I forced my feet to move faster along the narrow trail, my mind kicking up a dust storm of troubling thoughts. All this time, Abigail thought she'd been the one playing everyone on this fake "team-building" journey, but she'd never known the whole story. Not even close. I'd been the one playing her from the start. But now my elaborate scheme, nearly a year in the making, had taken a downward tumble, so to speak.

I squeezed my hands into fists as I hopped over a rock, admitting the truth to myself. I'd wanted Dr. Kristen Cates to die. I'd dreamed about her death, actually. I wasn't lying when I said my mom passed away three years ago, that her death messed me up, ultimately leading to my drug addiction. But it wasn't cancer that ended my mom's life. It was suicide. Mom had endured a years-long battle with depression. A few vague memories from when I was young clung to my psyche—Mom crying at the kitchen sink as hot water streamed from the faucet over a pile of dirty dishes, Mom lying in bed all day as I walked myself to and from the bus stop, the house so messy that I'd been embarrassed to invite friends over, and Dad cooking up a watery version of mac 'n' cheese when he returned from work so we'd have something to eat for dinner. But Mom must have gotten help soon after because, by the time I reached middle school, things were better. The depression was something she'd managed with medication and routine visits with her psychiatrist.

But four years ago, her long-time psychiatrist retired, and Mom started seeing someone new. Her name was Dr. Kristen Cates. As far as I knew, things had been fine at first. Maybe too good. Because I later learned that Dr. Cates had told my mom to stop taking her pills. A respected psychiatrist, of all people, should have known not to mess with something that was working. A trained mental health professional didn't tell a patient with a chemical imbalance in their brain that she's suddenly all better. And I'd never heard of a competent psychiatrist who refused to refill the prescription of a struggling patient. But that's what Dr. Cates did to my mom, and one week before I'd graduated college, I learned my mom had thrown herself in front of a speeding commuter bus. She'd stopped taking her pills a month earlier. The authorities had ruled her death as an accident, but Dad had confided in me about Mom's change in meds. The dark memories stirred inside me, and I'd known instantly that it hadn't been an accident.

Now my breath heaved, and I stopped running. I dug into my pocket, removing a tiny plastic bag. A few pinches of white powder remained, more than enough to take the edge off my pain and give me a boost of energy to make it back to the base quickly. I took a few sips of water, then snorted the powder, waiting for the rush which came immediately. But even in my altered state, my thoughts plummeted backward, following the winding, treacherous path that had led us all to this point.

A little over a year ago, a few months out of rehab and clean at last, I'd landed my dream job as a guide at Team Wilderness. Around the same time, I began researching Dr. Kristen Cates. Despite an inquiry filed by my dad, Dr. Cates had never accepted any responsibility for Mom's death. I'd been hoping to find a slew of malpractice lawsuits pending against Dr. Cates, but I'd found just the opposite. High-profile awards decorated her page on the clinic's website. More searches led me to her Facebook page, which lacked all privacy settings. After flipping through a few posts about a charity golf event and vacation photos, I discovered my mom's negligent psychiatrist had a daughter about my age named Abigail who—judging by all the images posted of brunches, shopping trips, and dinner dates— was the apple of Dr. Cates's eye.

It occurred to me that the best way to get close to Dr. Cates, to mess up her perfect existence the way she'd destroyed mine, was to harm her daughter. *Keep your friends close and your enemies closer.* Abigail could lead me directly into Kristen Cates's life. I envisioned myself accompanying Abigail to her parents' house one day for dinner, sneaking into their bathroom to swap out Dr. Cates's pills with different ones. I dreamed of taking away the doctor's meds the same way she'd done to my mom. That was only the first of so many ideas to get revenge.

My scheme to befriend Abigail started as a long shot, nothing more than a crazy idea. But I had to try. I began advertising the "Team Wilderness Team-Building Experience" to Pegasus, the PR firm where Abigail worked. I peppered the company with enough emails and postcards that they might eventually take notice. And when I called Abigail's boss one day, offering a twenty-five percent discount on our two-night local excursion, she took the bait.

Three weeks later, twenty Pegasus employees arrived at the

state park on the outskirts of metro Detroit. I spotted Abigail right away, making sure she was assigned to my group. Like I said before, Abigail was even prettier in person with long limbs and wheat-colored hair that shone in the sunshine. The photos on Facebook hadn't done her justice. When I saw the way her smile lingered on me a beat too long, I doubled down on my plan to get involved with Abigail and mess up her life, mess up her mom's life by extension. Abigail's revelation that she already had a boyfriend hit me like a gut punch. But I was determined not to let that stop me. Instead, I decided ruining her relationship was a bonus.

And—*holy shit*—my plan worked! It had only taken a half-day of mild flirtation before we were making out behind a tree, my hand halfway up her shirt. It seemed Abigail's perfect relationship with her clean-cut, confident, and successful boyfriend wasn't so great after all. And, yeah, she'd tried to cut it off the next day, to tell me she'd made a mistake. But I recognized the attraction between us and knew it was too powerful for her to simply walk away.

A week later, Abigail asked to meet for coffee, leading to a rushed and slightly awkward lust-filled encounter back at my apartment. That was the first of several weeks of illicit and passionate meetups. She was close to breaking up with Pete, she told me. It would be difficult, but she'd seen the writing on the wall. I felt a natural high whenever I envisioned Dr. Cates's disappointment at Abigail ending such a promising relationship.

But when Abigail showed up at my apartment one day announcing that she and Pete had gotten engaged and that she was ending things with me, I was devastated. Not because I seriously believed Abigail and I had any kind of future together, only because I'd been so close to executing my plan, so close to destroying her relationship with Pete and becoming Abigail's new date at family dinners. My plan to get inside Dr. Cates' house and shatter her happy life had imploded. Suddenly, I was back to square one. That's why I kept in touch with Abigail after she left me cold. I insisted we could still be friends, and she accepted the idea. Her response wasn't surprising, considering I'd never met anyone who'd gone to such extremes to avoid even the slightest bit of conflict or confrontation. Our friendship offered an easy out for her.

Abigail came around a few months later, having finally decided she couldn't marry Pete. I joked about leading a special wilderness "unbonding" experience with her parents and future in-laws for a reduced price. She was quiet for a few minutes, then something flickered in her eyes. She liked the idea.

I'd almost laughed, realizing the scheme was batshit crazy and brilliant all at once. I told Abigail I'd help her because she was my friend; I cared about her and wanted her to be happy. In reality, three nights with Dr. Cates was more than I'd ever hoped for. I couldn't wait to witness that bitch's suffering first-hand, to watch as her dream for her daughter's perfect life disintegrated before her.

My anxiety had grown during the days leading up to our first meeting at the Hiawana National Forest Visitors' Center. But things seemed easier than ever once everyone arrived. I mean, were Darla and Kenny for real? Darla, a mystic who ruled her life by Tarot cards and palm lines, and Kenny, an ex-con who filled his day stealing things to pay off his gambling debts and watching trashy reality TV. I couldn't have imagined people more different than Abigail's strait-laced and highly educated parents. Even if I hadn't done anything to instigate conflict, the outing was guaranteed to fail.

Don't get me wrong, I still moved things along. I swiped John's pills in the middle of the night and hid them inside my pack. In retrospect, that had been a dumb move. I hadn't expected the group to want to bail out and head back because of it. But thankfully John kept us on track, insisting a couple of missed pills wouldn't harm him. Realizing he was probably correct, I later slipped the pills into the side pocket of Kenny's pack to make the others think he'd stolen them and lied about it. Another black mark against the Mitchells. I'd also paid my buddy and fellow wilderness guide, Ben, to hike nearby and cross paths with us once or twice. He'd been at the check-in counter before the outing with Pegasus, and I hoped Abigail wouldn't recognize him from their brief interaction many months earlier. But she hadn't. Ben had been training for a marathon and had lost weight since then. And, man, he'd done a good job acting creepy. Ben had even scared *me* a little bit with his Oscar-worthy performance. I hadn't told him to leave the written messages at the campsites but had been impressed with his creativity. The all-caps had been a nice touch. So had the midnight scream from the woods. I would have thought warnings like those would send Darla running for the hills, but she'd only acted slightly weirder than usual. Still, the vague threats had touched a nerve. Oh yeah. And I hadn't really slipped on that log at the river crossing. I'd fallen into the water on purpose, knowing I hadn't sealed the food bag all the way. Hungry people were angry people. Everyone knew that. It would have only been a matter of time before everyone started turning on each other.

I stopped to rest for a second, feeling light-headed and thinking about the pink flowers I'd added to the scavenger hunt list. Abigail said I'd been reckless to add those flowers that grew near the edge of the gulch, even more reckless to send everyone out at night and tell them to separate as I'd stayed back to snort a line of cocaine. None of it would look good for me when the facts came out. That's why I needed my true connection to Dr. Cates to remain hidden. My last name—Johnson—was common enough that I hoped no one would take notice of Dr. Cates's former patient, Margaret Johnson, now three years dead. Margaret, who had the same last name, and who'd left behind a son named William, who'd started going by Liam a year after her death.

My feet slowed as I reached a fork in the trail. Neither option looked familiar, and I wasn't sure which way to go. I pulled the map from my back pocket and studied it, my thoughts straying toward Dr. Cates and those flowers. I didn't know why she was so hopped up when she saw the lady slippers, but I noticed their ideal location. They were the perfect way to lure her to the isolated overlook. And, yes, I followed her through the woods high out of my mind, hoping to catch her alone to threaten or scare her. Maybe I thought about pushing her over the cliff's edge and watching her die. But I didn't do it. That's the thing. I didn't push her to the same kind of violent end my mom had met. Because when I got to where Dr. Cates had been standing near the deadly drop-off, someone else had beaten me to it.

TWENTY-THREE

ABIGAIL

I hid inside my tent for the first few hours after Liam sprinted away for help. Tears sprung in my eyes every few minutes until they dried up again, my insides hollow. It didn't seem real that Mom was gone. Memories I'd tucked away from years earlier began to surface—Mom squeezing my hand as she walked me into my first day in Mrs. Montgomery's Kindergarten classroom, Mom teaching me how to do an underwater somersault in our backyard pool, Mom preparing a tray of her famous veggie lasagna as she took a rare call from a patient at home, winking at me and making a face as she talked. It was funny, the things I remembered now. Not the grand gestures, but little moments of love that stuck with me.

Pete remained inside the tent for a long time as I cried, supporting my head with his arm. A lifetime of memories rushed through me, and it was almost too much to bear. After an hour or so, Pete said he was going to check on his parents and my dad. I was thankful he was there because I didn't think I could muster the strength to stand, much less move outside. All the while I was holed up inside the tent, I wondered where Liam was, how far he'd traveled, and if he'd reached the visitors' center or been able to call out for help. I tried not to think of Mom's current location at the bottom of the gulch, the jagged rocks that had broken her bones and speared through her soft flesh. But of course, the more I tried not to think about it, the more the horrific scene carved itself into my mind.

I wasn't sure how much more time had passed when Darla ducked her head into the tent and touched my leg.

"Hi, honey." She looked different with her unbraided hair hanging in clumps around her face. "Kenny's making some ramen noodles. What's left of them, anyway. I think a little bit of food would do you good. Your dad too."

"I'm not hungry." I raised myself up on my elbows, staring beyond Darla to the opening in the tent above her shoulder. "Is Dad out there?"

"He will be in a second. He just woke up."

"Dad fell asleep?"

"Yes. He sure needed the rest."

I wondered how Dad could have slept at a time like this, but then remembered he was thirty years older than me and hadn't gotten any sleep the night before. I'd at least slept for three or four hours last night. I shook away unwanted thoughts of him meeting another woman behind Mom's back. Pete had assured me she was only the accountant.

"I'm sorry this wilderness outing didn't go the way you planned." Darla paused, staring as something indiscernible shone in her eyes.

I sat up taller, rubbing the back of my neck. Had there been a hint of hostility in Darla's voice? It sounded almost as if she was threatening me. I suddenly wondered if she knew about my backhanded plan to create a wedge between the families. But that was impossible. She couldn't have known. Liam was the only one who'd been aware of my true motives when the seven of us had set out together.

Darla squared her shoulders, blocking the opening in the

tent. "You're going to marry Pete, aren't you? Despite every-thing that's happened."

My eyes flickered away from her, my throat dry. I remem-bered the shadow lurking outside the tent as Mom begged me not to marry Pete. Judging by Darla's question and the way her eyes pierced directly through my soul, I realized it must have been her out there. But, short of asking her, there was no way to know for sure. It had taken this disastrous trip to make me see things clearly, but I'd come to my senses and changed my mind. I wanted to marry Pete. In fact, I realized, I wanted him to be my husband more than anything in the world, even despite his family. He was the person who kept me grounded, who supported me, and made me laugh. I refocused on Darla. "Yes. I'm going to marry Pete. I just don't know about the timing because of..." I couldn't finish the sentence. "We're going to have to arrange the funeral first."

Darla nodded. "Pete will wait for you. And we're all here to help you through this, the funeral planning, and whatever else you need."

"Thank you, Darla." Pete had already said as much to me. I had no idea how I could tackle any of what was to come on my own. The process would be just as difficult for Dad.

Darla dipped her chin and motioned at the opening behind her. "I'll be out there when you're ready."

I grabbed her arm. "Wait. I have to ask you something."

She turned to face me.

"What did you see on my mom's palm? You knew some-thing bad was going to happen, didn't you?"

"Oh, honey." Darla bit her lip, pulled me into a brief hug, then released me. "I noticed an unusual break indicating a disruption or the end of something. But if you're asking if I knew that your mom was going to die or fall off a cliff on this camping trip then, no. I didn't know that. Palm reading doesn't work that way."

I held my palm up, arm trembling. "And I have the same unusual break in my Line of Life?"

Darla pursed her lips. "Yes, but it doesn't necessarily hold the same meaning for you. Palm lines can be interpreted in many ways. That line generally relates to health or well-being, but some construe it more broadly. The break in your line could represent the end of life with your mom and the start of a new life with Pete. You see what I mean?"

I nodded because I did understand. Still, Mom's observation about how people could assign any meaning they wanted to the palm readings or the Tarot cards circled in my head.

"There was something bothering me about the—" Darla stopped talking abruptly and angled her head toward the tent opening.

"What?" I leaned toward her. "What were you going to say?"

She sighed and pinched the bridge of her nose. "Nothing. I don't know. I'm sorry, honey. It's been a long day and I lost my train of thought." Darla threw her hands up. "That's what happens when you get old. Let's go outside and sit with everyone."

An unsettling feeling weighed in the pit of my gut. It seemed Darla had more to say but didn't want to tell me. I still had so many questions about Mom's death, but my energy was drained, and I'd have to let them sit for now. I managed to crawl out behind Darla, while avoiding putting weight on my swollen ankle. My eyes blinked against the light. Clouds layered the sky, the sun struggling to burn through. Kenny hurried over from his post near the stove and helped me to my feet. At the same time, Pete emerged from the other tent, followed by Dad, who appeared like a meeker version of his former self. He slumped forward as I made my way to his side, hugging him. Pete and I guided him to the sturdiest log. I lowered myself next to him if only to make sure he didn't fall over.

Kenny stirred the pot that sat on the camping stove. "It's been a hell of a day, I know. But I thought some soup might make you feel better."

Dad managed a nod.

"Thank you," I said.

Kenny explained how he'd filtered the water first, then boiled it for the ramen. He lined up five tin bowls and poured a little broth into each one, rationed out the noodles, and handed a bowl to each of us.

I wasn't sure if I could stomach it, but I took a tiny sip of the salty broth, then set down the bowl, afraid the soup might come back up. Dad slurped his soup next to me. I turned to look at him, noticing the scratches on his face appeared darker. They were already healing.

Pete lowered his bowl and cleared his throat. "John, I'd love to know how you and Kristen met? Can you tell us?"

A tug of a smile played at Dad's lips, despite the deadened look in his eyes. He sat up a little straighter. "That seems like a hundred years ago. I met her at a Halloween party my junior year of college. She was dressed as Snow White. I couldn't take my eyes off her." Dad chuckled, but it sounded sad. "And when she took off her wig when we were dancing and her long, wavy hair fell out, I could see she was even more beautiful beneath her costume. And that was before I even found out how smart and kind she was." Dad gave Pete a solemn look. "I remember I went back to my apartment that night and told my roommate that I'd just met the woman I was going to marry."

I felt new tears burning my eyes as I watched Dad reminisce.

Darla clasped her hands together. "That's such a sweet story. You'll always have those precious memories."

Pete nodded. "I knew right away when I met Abigail too."

"Me too," I said, but my voice was weak and guilt gnawed at

my insides because my feelings toward him hadn't always been as steadfast. I vowed to be a better partner going forward.

"How did you and Kenny meet, Darla?" Dad asked.

We listened as Pete's parents took turns telling a tale of meeting at an outdoor bar near the shores of Lake Michigan thirty-two summers earlier. The conversation continued for over an hour, with one story leading into the next. I shared some of my favorite memories of Mom, my throat hitching at some and laughing at others. Finally, the anecdotes lulled as we stared across at each other, remembering our current circumstances. Mom was dead and our guide had left us here to fend for ourselves. Help should have arrived by now, but it hadn't.

Pete shifted on the log beside me. Darla and Kenny exchanged another glance, the kind that seemed to ask and answer a question in an instant. I wondered again if those two were hiding something. I scanned the surrounding woods, my senses alert for any outside threats—a glimpse of that strange man in the woods or the yip of wild animals. Perhaps noticing the fear in my eyes, Pete took my hand. "Are you doing okay?"

I nodded, even though I was far from it.

He leaned into me. "I bet it won't be much longer now. Then we'll be safely back home."

I looked at Pete's face, registering earnestness in his eyes. I so wanted to believe him.

TWENTY-FOUR

ABIGAIL

We sat in our haggard group, waiting for help to arrive. I wasn't sure how many hours passed. My phone battery had long since died and I measured time only by the movement of the clouds across the sky and the height of the sun above the trees. The later it got, the weaker and more unstable my body became, the heavier my eyelids felt, the more my stomach twisted with hunger, and my ankle throbbed with pain. I felt like death, and I was sure I looked like it too. The thick coating of sweat and grime covering my skin seemed as if it was the only thing holding me together. As the sun fell below the horizon and the moon claimed its position above us, I began to lose hope.

"Shouldn't Liam have sent help by now?" I asked, hugging my arms around myself.

Dad nodded, then lowered his head.

Darla's colorless lips puckered. "I thought the park rangers would have arrived before dark."

I peered toward the trail. "What if something happened to Liam? What if no one knows we're out here?"

"Let's not panic." Pete took a few deep breaths in and out as he massaged his forehead. "If help doesn't arrive by daybreak, I'll hike out. All this sitting around is pointless."

My teeth clenched. "But you don't know the way."

"I brought the map with me. It's in my pack." Pete motioned at the supplies.

His statement offered some relief. But I'd seen the map Liam had provided. It was a crude black-and-white drawing, only outlining the major trails while leaving out the lesser-traveled ones like the one we'd taken to get here.

Kenny stretched his elbows behind him, groaning. "I'm starving."

"I have one more bar we can share." Dad stood and hobbled to his pack, unzipping a pocket.

"Does anyone else have anything to eat?" Darla asked, her gaze pausing on each of us.

I shook my head, noticing the others doing the same. My trail mix had run out yesterday.

I heard Pete's grunt of disapproval. "I'm hungry too, but if we only have one bar left, we should save it until tomorrow. Just in case they don't show up right away."

Dad stopped fumbling and returned to his seat on the fallen log. He looked as horrible as I felt. Pete and his parents weren't faring much better, shoulders hunched and eyelids drooping.

I stifled a yawn with the back of my hand. "We should rest. It's getting dark. The rescuers will wake us up if we're sleeping when they get here."

Everyone agreed.

Pete looped his arm around me as I eyed my tent beyond our circle. I couldn't bear the thought of leaving Pete's side, of abandoning Dad. "Darla, I'm going to sleep with Pete and my dad tonight. You and Kenny can have our tent."

"Of course," Darla said as she and Kenny gave each other a nod.

"I'll get my things," Kenny said. He ducked into the men's tent and exited with his sleeping bag.

We abandoned the lantern, leaving it glowing in the clearing so that other hikers or the authorities could locate us. Pete retrieved my belongings from my former tent before Darla and Kenny crawled inside. I imagined them taking up the empty space where Mom should have been sleeping, and the vision sent a fresh wave of grief surging through me. I turned away from them, squeezing my eyes closed as tears leaked out. I was too exhausted for niceties, too entrenched in my tragedy to wish them a good night. Pete escorted me over to Dad, who waited by the lantern. I followed them into the other tent, positioning myself next to Pete and zipping us inside. As my legs slid into my sleeping bag, I was thankful for the warmth of Pete's body next to me, the steady rise and fall of his chest. I closed my eyes and gave in to the fatigue, letting sleep swallow me whole.

* * *

I awoke with a start, the hoot of an owl yanking me back to consciousness. Beside me, Pete's heavy breathing maintained an even rhythm, and Dad's every other breath was coupled with a nasally wheeze. My head ached as I lifted it, eyes blinking through the darkness and my jumbled thoughts reordering themselves. The memory of where I was and what had happened slammed through my mind. Mom was dead. No help had arrived yet. What the hell was taking Liam so long?

My stomach groaned, aching with hunger. I envisioned the single granola bar remaining for the five of us, just one or two bites per person. Unless help came soon, it wouldn't be enough. Suddenly, I had more empathy for that skeletal hiker, although I wished Mom hadn't given him those bars because we certainly needed them now. The memory sparked an idea that made me sit up. Mom's pack sat just outside with the rest of our packs. There wasn't much room inside the tents, so we'd been leaving our extra gear out there. I hadn't checked her pack for food because I'd assumed help would have arrived by now. There was a chance it held an additional granola bar or two.

I held my breath as I slipped out of my sleeping bag and quietly unzipped the doorway before crawling outside. The inky night sky offered little light, but the lantern splashed a faint glow across the clearing, illuminating the shadowy outlines of our tents, the trees in the distance, and our bags of supplies. A moth fluttered into my face, but I batted it away as I crept toward the line of backpacks, trying to stay quiet even as I hobbled in my uneven gait. My fingers grazed over the top of each pack before landing on Mom's. Kneeling down, I unzipped the main pocket first, rooting through her clothes, smelling her T-shirt, running the fabric over my cheek. *I'm sorry, Mom.* Tears built behind my eyes, but I pushed them back, forcing myself to set down the shirt and continue the search. Beneath more clothes, there was an extra pair of shoes, but no food. I discovered additional items in the side pockets —bug spray, sunscreen, hand sanitizer. Nothing edible. My fingers dug into one final pocket, hitting something hard and flat. I pulled it out, finding a miniature notebook, spiral-bound with a dark cover. Mom had always been big on journaling, a practice she often recommended to her patients to get in touch with their feelings and tap into their creativity. She'd encouraged me to journal too, although I hadn't kept up with it in recent years. So many times she'd said, *It doesn't matter what you write. Just write something!* My hands trembled as I flipped open the tiny notebook and angled it toward the glow of the lantern, expecting to get a private glimpse into the mind of the mother I'd lost. I hoped it wouldn't be too much to bear.

On the first page, she'd written about our visit to Mackinac

Island, detailing every activity and meal matter-of-factly, as if for a travel log.

> Biked 8.2 miles around the island. Ate lunch at the hotel (a Caesar salad). Abigail barely ate anything. She seemed nervous about this weekend. Played mini golf in the afternoon overlooking the water. We took a walk by the old cottages after dinner. John held my hand.

The next page read:

> Feeling apprehensive. Camping isn't my thing. I hope things go better than at Applebee's. Oh, the things we do for our kids ☺

The next page was merely a list of types of trees she'd seen on our hike the first day of the camping trip:

> White Pine, Maple, Hemlock, Spruce, Birch.

My fingers flipped the page again, tilting the notebook to the side to catch more light. Next came a five-line poem about pink flowers, which I realized must have been referring to the lady slippers. My mouth filled with grief. If only Mom had known where those flowers would lure her. I took a second to compose myself before turning the page.

> So many red flags. Should I tell Abigail about my concerns? I have to. I'm her mother.

I lowered the journal, realizing Mom must have written that before she pulled me into the tent and begged me not to marry Pete. I turned the page, finding the remaining pages empty. But when I flipped through the journal again, I realized two of the written pages had stuck together. I'd accidentally skipped over the second-to-last entry. I pressed the page flat and read Mom's words, one line written in all caps:

DARLA IS A FRAUD!

A sleepy sigh from nearby made me jump. My pulse raced as someone turned over inside Darla and Kenny's tent, covers rustling. I froze. A minute passed as I stood still, desperate to pore over Mom's things alone. Another minute passed, my heart pounding in my ears. At last, a man's light snoring replaced the silence. I tucked the notebook into my waistband and sifted through Mom's backpack once more, disappointed to find I hadn't missed anything.

I stepped back, preparing to return to my tent. A moth flitted past my face again, circling the air before landing on a pack with a smear of mud in the corner. I recognized it as Kenny's pack. He'd already stolen Dad's medication. Now I couldn't help wondering what else he had in there. I tucked my hair behind my ear and crouched down, hoping to get in and out as quickly as possible.

Ever so slowly, I pulled at the zipper, opening one notch at a time. Each metallic click seemed to echo through the trees, making my molars clench. At last, I'd opened the main compartment, and angled the bag toward the lantern. The pots and dishes had already been removed, and Kenny's clothes filled the bottom. I pulled out a dirty pair of shorts and three T-shirts, which were wadded into balls, and damp to the touch. That's when I saw a glint of something shiny at the bottom. The corner of a foil wrapper. I leaned closer, reaching down and dislodging the bounty. I held the goods up to my face, fingers gripping granola bars in silver and green wrappers, oats-and-honey flavor. There were four bars, unopened. I tipped my head back, gasping as my last bit of faith in Kenny drained out of me.

Kenny had claimed he didn't have any food remaining. He'd lied again.

Frantically, I began unzipping all the other pockets of Kenny's pack, digging through the contents. For all I knew, he was stashing a block of cheese and a jar of peanut butter in here too. I was about to give up when I remembered the hidden pocket on the interior of my pack. It was where I'd stashed a few pads and tampons just in case. I located the same pocket inside Kenny's pack and unzipped it, pulling it open and peering inside. I nearly fell backward at the contents.

Liam's red-and-black canister of bear spray stared back at me, looking more like an undetonated bomb. Liam believed it had fallen off his broken carabiner as we hiked, but that wasn't what had happened at all. While I wasn't all that familiar with bear spray, I knew the stuff was toxic, similar to pepper spray but likely even stronger. It could blind a person. My trust in Kenny had dwindled to nothing, and I couldn't help wondering if he'd used the spray to stun Mom before shoving her to her death.

With a trembling hand, I reached in to recover the stolen object.

"What are you doing?"

A twig cracked behind me. I choked on my breath, dropping the pack as I spun around. Kenny stood facing me, glaring.

"I was hungry. I was looking for food." My eyes traveled downward to the open backpack. "I thought this one was Mom's and then I saw a bunch of granola bars inside."

Kenny's lip snarled beneath his unkempt mustache. "You shouldn't go through other people's things." He stepped toward me, hands twitching like they wanted to wring my neck.

"You lied." My voice shrieked, splintering through the night. I suddenly felt threatened, and I hoped the commotion was enough to wake the others. "You said you didn't have any food."

Movement rustled from inside one tent. Pete popped out, rubbing his face. He looked from Kenny to the granola bars in my hand. "Dad. What did you do?"

Now Dad and Darla emerged from opposite tents, hollows under their eyes.

I motioned at Kenny. "He was hiding granola bars from all of us. He was going to eat them while we starved!" The image of the bear spray lurked in my mind, but I wasn't sure if I should mention it. The backpack sat at Kenny's feet. I didn't want to provoke him, potentially causing him to do something stupid. Something violent. With my ankle the way it was I wouldn't be able to run.

"Everyone lay off." Darla shook her head. "It's a behavior he learned in prison."

Dad released a weary breath. "What is?"

"Food hoarding." Darla stumbled toward Kenny and looped their arms together, giving her husband a squeeze. "It's okay. I know you didn't mean anything by it."

Pete touched his forehead, eyes squinting as if he was in physical pain. "Are you serious? Don't we have enough problems here? This is not okay!" Pete leaned over to me and snatched the four bars out of my hand, then handed one back to me, tossed one to Dad, and gave one to Darla. He leered at his dad in a way that almost made me uncomfortable. "How about everyone gets a bar, except for you? How's that? I think that's more than fair."

Kenny muttered something under his breath, arms pulling away from his wife and dropping to his sides.

"There's one more bar in my pack," Dad said. "So, I guess we all get one. Even Kenny. We should save them for the morning."

"Yeah. Whatever." Pete pressed his palms into his eye sockets. "I just need to get out of this place." He looked as if he was about to lose it.

I rubbed his back, feeling the heat of his body. "Help is probably on the way right now," I said, hoping my words were true.

Darla glanced at the moon. "Well, I guess this was all a big misunderstanding." She thumbed toward the tent. "Maybe we should all go back to sleep."

Darla and Kenny's tent jostled in the wind, appearing more like a secret hideout than a simple shelter. I eyed Kenny's pack, envisioning the compact canister of bear spray inside, wondering again why he'd stolen it from Liam. In the depths of my pocket, my fingers found the smooth coating of Mom's acrylic nail along with its jagged edge. The final entry in Mom's notebook scrawled through my mind. *DARLA IS A FRAUD!* My gaze lifted toward Pete's parents. What were they up to? Although I had no solid proof, I couldn't shake the notion they'd been involved in whatever horrible things were happening out here, including Mom's death.

I motioned for Dad and Pete to join me off to the side as Darla and Kenny eyed us. "I think we should all go back to bed." I kept my voice to a whisper as my eyes flicked toward Pete, who gave a nod.

Darla tugged on the raggedy ends of her hair, staring at me, her eyes growing smaller by the second. In the dim light with long ropes of hair hanging around her face and the scowl on her mouth, she resembled a witch from one of the fairy tales Mom used to read me, the type of woman who lured children inside with candy, only to lock them in an oven. A chill slid down my spine and I had to look away.

Kenny grunted and grabbed his backpack, taking it into the tent with Darla trailing behind him.

I only let myself breathe once I was inside the other tent with Pete and Dad. Pete pulled me closer to him. "I'm sorry about that. Let's try to get some sleep. I'll hike out at first light if no one's shown up by then."

"Let's hope it doesn't come to that." Dad's voice wavered, and I felt horrible about this trip, about all the tragedy I'd caused.

"Okay." My body was rigid, my eyes wide open as the troubling thoughts continued to pour through me.

Pete lifted himself halfway up. "Abigail, is there something else?"

I hesitated but decided I couldn't keep this to myself. "Liam's bear spray. The bottle that went missing. It's in your dad's backpack."

Pete gasped, head dropping forward. "What the hell?"

Now Dad propped himself up too, frowning. "Kenny took the spray? This is unbelievable."

Pete placed his hand on mine. "He has a problem with stealing, not that that's an excuse. I'll go get it from him."

Dad pressed his lips together, motioning for Pete to stay put. "Maybe it's best not to start something when we're all on edge."

My temples throbbed, dizzy from the swirl of grief, fear, and guilt inside me. The last thing we needed tonight was another charged run-in with Kenny. "Let's deal with it in the morning. Maybe he was worried about bears."

Dad chuckled in disbelief. "Right. I'm sure Kenny's motives were nothing but pure."

TWENTY-FIVE

ABIGAIL

Daybreak came, at last, the morning sun trickling through a gap in our tent and awakening me from a splintered sleep. Dad and Pete lay on either side with eyes open. My mouth was dry and my ankle throbbed. A bird chirped outside. I could tell by the deadened look on their faces that no help had arrived.

Pete sat up with a purpose, locating his water bottle and taking a swig. "I'll pack a few things and get on the trail as soon as I can."

"Are you sure?" I asked.

"Yeah. Something must have happened to Liam. We'll be out of food soon, and you can't move. I have to go."

I knew he was right, but the thought of me and Dad stranded here alone with Darla and Kenny made me uneasy.

Pete exited the tent. Zippers opening and closing and rustling fabric sounded from nearby. He returned and grabbed the three bars we'd saved for ourselves in the corner of the tent, motioning us outside. Dad followed, and I scooched out on my butt behind him. In the distance, Darla and Kenny wandered along the edge of the pond, glancing over at us with no expression. I wondered how long they'd been out there.

The foil wrappers crinkled in Pete's hand. He handed us each a bar. "We should eat half now. Save half for later."

The lining of my stomach burned as if it had started digesting itself. I tore the wrapper open and took a giant bite, then slowed to a nibble as I reached the bar's halfway point way too soon.

Darla and Kenny approached, unsmiling. Kenny picked at his cuticles, averting his gaze as we ate, perhaps ashamed by his dishonesty the day before. I caught Darla staring at me and I forced a tight smile in her direction.

"Did you sleep well, Abigail?" Darla's voice held an edge.

"Not really."

Darla jutted out her chin and rotated her shoulders away. It seemed she felt offended by something, but I was no longer concerned about her feelings. I only cared that I'd lost my mom. I wanted to get out of this place, back to our safe suburban lives. Everything was taking too long. The rescuers needed to remove Mom's body from the gulch before the vultures found her.

Kenny stroked his wiry beard. "Darla and I are going to leave and get help."

Pete lifted his backpack. "No, Dad. I'm heading out now. I can get there faster."

"You don't always know better than us, son."

"This time, I do." Pete removed some of the bulkier items from his pack and flung it onto his back, securing the front clasp on his chest. "I'm going. You're staying here." He and Kenny locked eyes, nostrils flaring, neither one backing down. "And, while you and Mom were over there looking for pine cones, I took your bear spray." Pete paused and smiled, letting the statement land for full effect. "Oh wait, not *your* bear spray. It was Liam's bear spray that you stole. So, you might want to stay with the group."

Kenny's shoulders slumped. He muttered something to Darla, waving Pete away. He'd been found out. Again. Unlike the incident with Dad's medication, this time he didn't even try to deny it.

We stood there, not looking at each other. The tension in the air seemed to carry an electric charge as if the first person to make a wrong move would be zapped by a bolt of lightning.

Finally, Pete turned to Dad, extending a hand, which Dad shook. "John, I'll send help soon."

Dad dipped his head. "Good luck."

Then Pete stepped toward me, hugging me close and whispering in my ear. "I love you and I'll get us out of here soon."

Just as I squeezed him tighter, something rustled from beyond the tree line. My body went rigid at the noise. Pete pulled away from me, widening his stance as if ready to fight. I prepared for the creepy hiker to lunge at us or a mother bear to release a protective roar. Instead, a uniformed man emerged through the trees, pulling a stretcher with a wheel on the bottom. Another man, wearing identical clothes, pushed the stretcher from behind. "Hi, folks. I'm Rich. This is Hank. We're part of the park's rescue team. We have food and water for you." His eyes scanned across us. "I understand someone has an ankle injury."

I blinked to make sure I wasn't dreaming, a rush of relief heating my face and stinging my eyes. It had taken longer than expected, but Liam must have made it back and alerted the Park Service to our location. I raised my hand as Dad helped me over to the stretcher, where the two men lifted me onto it and buckled me in.

"Oh, thank goodness," Darla said, fluttering her eyelashes. "My crystals worked."

Up above, another noise reached my ears; the choppy sound of a helicopter cut through the quiet of the wilderness. I couldn't see it, but the whirring of helicopter blades was unmistakable, and it was coming from the direction of the gulch.

I felt Pete's hand on my arm. "I think they're getting your mom."

"Please!" I said to Rich and Hank. "Push me over there. It's not far." I had a sliver of hope that maybe she was still alive, still clinging to life, and that she could somehow be revived.

The two men looked at each other, unsure.

"C'mon." Pete picked up a fast walk, pulling my wheeled stretcher and yelling at the rescuers to follow. Dad scrambled behind us, along with Darla and Kenny. We arrived at the edge of the gulch a minute or two later, where a surreal scene unfolded: a rope ladder lowering from the side of the hovering helicopter, a man and a woman climbing down, then a stretcher lowering from the end of a cable. Mom's body was unmoving as they strapped her into the stretcher, extinguishing any hope that she was still alive. The rope lifted her body into the cab of the helicopter. The rescuers saw us standing up above and yelled something we couldn't make out. They climbed back up into the open door, raised the ladder, and shut themselves inside. Then the helicopter disappeared over the horizon.

Dad and I clung to each other, tears flowing freely as one of our final glimpses of the woman we both loved vanished. My arm flung across my face, covering my eyes as ugly sobs heaved from my chest. A piece of my hair stuck to the corner of my mouth and Pete brushed it away.

Hank rolled my stretcher backward a few feet. "They don't have anywhere to land, so it's too risky for the rest of us to climb up. But don't worry. We'll get you back as quickly as we can. We've got ATVs waiting for us a few miles from here."

As they rolled me back toward camp, Rich said, "I'm so sorry for your loss."

"Thank you."

The tears wouldn't stop as the others followed the rescuers who pushed me along the trail.

Hank told us how Liam had arrived at the visitors' center

hours earlier heavily under the influence of drugs. He'd taken a wrong turn along the way, had gotten lost, but had eventually found his way back to safety. Despite his impaired state, Liam was able to tell them where we were and what had happened.

"Where's Liam now?" I asked.

"He told our co-worker to call his dad, who he said would come and get him. I'm not sure where they were headed next."

Dad, Pete, Darla, Kenny, and the two men from the rescue team hiked for another two hours, guiding me along rough terrain and lifting me over streams and rocks. At last, the trail widened. Up ahead, two more rangers and four all-terrain vehicles waited for us.

"We'll be back at the visitors' center within the hour. There's going to be an investigator there from the local police department to take statements about your mom's fall into the gulch. It's standard protocol. There's no reason to think it wasn't an accident."

I reached into my pocket, touching Mom's broken nail and remembering the message at the first campsite: *WATCH YOUR BACK!* I wasn't so sure.

TWENTY-SIX

DARLA

Darla huddled underneath a blanket in a side room at the Hiawana National Park Visitors' Center, clutching an onyx crystal in one hand and gripping a mug in the other. The nice man had brought the hot tea she'd requested. But even after drinking half of it and changing into dry clothes, the chill wouldn't leave her bones. The head park ranger and a local police detective called Detective Leeman had introduced themselves, explaining how they would question everyone individually about Kristen's death. The others sat in another area outside, resting their heads against the wall or sipping cups of water after returning from their interviews. The ranger had explained a few minutes earlier that no one was under investigation for any wrongdoing. This was only a fact-gathering session. It was important to follow protocol in situations like this.

Now a kind-eyed Detective Leeman sat across from Darla, who was the last to be questioned. They'd already gone over the basics of the trip, including Pete's engagement to Abigail and their family bonding experience out in the wilderness.

The detective leaned back, crossing his arms. "Abigail said

that you seemed to know something bad was going to happen to Kristen. You even told her as much." He shook his head. "How did you know?"

"I was only referring to the lines on her palm. They indicated an abrupt change in her health."

A smile pulled at Detective Leeman's lips. "Okay. So, you didn't really know."

"Not specifically. But the signs were there." Darla bit her lip. "It's a shame she didn't pay attention to them."

"Did you and Kristen get along?"

"We didn't really know each other. We only met once before this trip. We had a couple of minor disagreements over the wedding planning, but other than that, things were fine."

"Do you have any idea who left those messages at your campsites? According to the others, the first one said, 'Watch your back' and the second one said, 'Someone is lying.'"

Darla's mind traveled back over the events of the last few days. She should have turned around and hiked straight back to the car at the sight of those messages. She wished she'd forced the others to do the same.

"I have no idea. We came across a desperate-looking guy in the woods on the first day. He seemed like he wasn't in his right mind. Maybe he was following us. That's the only thing I can think of."

The detective nodded, and Darla assumed her statement matched those of the others. In truth, a terrible suspicion grew inside her. But she wouldn't tell the detective because she so wanted to be wrong, so hoped the messages were only a coincidence. After spotting that first warning, she'd even hiked alone into the woods trying to find solid evidence, but there hadn't been anything there. She'd returned with an armful of pine cones, pretending that's what she'd been doing instead. Although she yearned to disprove her hunch, those messages written in stones and scrawled in the dirt hadn't allowed her to look the other way. The more she thought about them, the more she knew they couldn't have been written by a stranger. Those warnings were the work of someone closer to home. A person who had known about the wedding, who was familiar with their route, and who had been one step ahead of them the whole way. Darla knew who it was, but at first, she hadn't understood why he'd killed Kristen, instead of Abigail.

As the detective scribbled something on his notepad, Darla pictured Trent, her firstborn child, the one with a troubled soul. She'd convinced herself Trent had been doing better the last few years. He'd gotten a steady job, moved into his own place, and joined a bowling league. He still came over to their house every Sunday, when he tinkered around the house and the garage and usually stayed for dinner. During those visits, he was often alone for stretches of time. She remembered the email Liam had sent three weeks earlier with the guidelines, forms, releases of liability, and a map of the National Forest with their highlighted route. Darla had printed everything and placed the papers inside a red folder on her desk, the one she'd clearly labeled "Camping Trip."

Detective Leeman cleared his throat, raising his eyes to meet hers. "Do you know what Kristen would have been doing so close to the edge of the gulch? Why she might have been over there?"

Darla nodded. "The pink flowers. She was drawn to them, and they grew over there. It was one of the items on the scavenger hunt Liam put together for us."

"Was anyone with her?"

"I don't think so. I was off by myself trying to locate the items on the list. As far as I know, that's what everyone else was doing too."

More nods and scribbling from the detective. She could tell that she was once again confirming what the others had told him.

"Can you think of any reason why someone would want to harm Kristen? Push her to her death?" He cocked his head, face solemn. "I'm only covering all the bases here."

"No." Darla blinked rapidly, covering her lie. Kristen had been wearing Abigail's fleece coat when it happened. Abigail and her mom were the same height and their hair was about the same length and color. Darla realized that if he'd approached from behind, Trent could have mistaken Kristen for her daughter.

Darla recalled the venom in Trent's voice when he'd told her and Kenny that Pete and Abigail had asked him to serve as an usher in the wedding, that he'd have the "important" job of handing programs to the guests and leading them to their seats in the rows of pews.

"As if people can't figure out where to sit on their own." Trent had bitten his lip until it bled.

She and Kenny knew the usher role was a cop-out, a work-around to prevent Trent from standing next to Pete as he and his bride recited their vows in front of a crowd of onlookers.

Rejection had been the one thing that had triggered Trent in the past, and Darla sensed that this recent brush-off by Pete and Abigail had been more dangerous than either of them might have realized. It had occurred to her when she saw that first message written in stones that Trent might have spotted the red folder lying on her desk and gone through the papers. He could have snapped a photo of the route. He could have lied about his bowling tournament. Her gut told her he'd followed them out into the wilderness to get revenge. But she was protective of her son. Trent had been good to her, even if he didn't always act that way toward others. She couldn't tell the detective any of this now.

Detective Leeman tapped his pen on the table, reading a message on his phone. "Excuse me, Darla. I need to go check on another issue. I'll be back in a minute."

Darla nodded as the detective exited the room, leaving her alone, her thoughts tumbling back to Trent's childhood. She didn't like to admit that she'd seen troubling signs in Trent from very early on, even before his best friend, Freddie, died in the canoeing accident. Like when Mr. Flynn's dog went missing.

Her boys loved that dog named Molly. She was a scruffy retriever mix who knew how to roll over on command and lived to play fetch. Trent sometimes saved bits of his lunch or dinner in his pocket, so the dog was especially drawn to him, jumping all over him and wagging her tail. One day, Mr. Flynn knocked on their front door, his face drawn, asking if any of them had seen Molly. The boys said they hadn't seen her that day, but they helped him search for two solid days, walking the neighborhood streets, traversing fields and patches of woods, and screaming Molly's name until their throats were raw.

But the sweet dog was nowhere to be found.

After the second fruitless day of searching, they'd all but lost hope. That night, a pale-faced Pete found Darla alone in her bedroom and, looking over his shoulder, whispered he had to tell her something. Pete's complexion appeared almost green and Darla thought he was sick, that he needed to tell her that he was going to throw up. But instead, he told her he'd seen Trent through his bedroom window, leading Molly out of the yard the same afternoon the dog went missing. He hadn't said anything before because he didn't want to believe his brother could do something so horrible. Darla took a second to gather her breath, then told him he was brave to tell her what he'd seen, but that it was likely a simple misunderstanding or an unfortunate coincidence, and she'd speak to Trent about it.

When she confronted Trent later, he admitted to having taken Molly out for a walk but said he returned her to the yard less than an hour later. Darla wanted to believe him, but Trent had a nervous way of speaking, a whole demeanor, that created doubt. He refused to look her in the eye when he talked, he thought too long about his words before he said them. She couldn't help wondering why Trent hadn't shared the information about the walk with Mr. Flynn when he'd questioned the boys a few days before. Still, she chose to believe her son because the alternative was too troubling. Too gruesome.

Four months later, while digging in an overgrown flower bed she'd abandoned years earlier, Darla was surprised when her shovel hit something solid about a foot below the soil. She scraped away the earth, spotting the dirt-encrusted red collar first, then the flash of ivory. Clearing more dirt away revealed a narrow skull, not from a human. Her hand flew to her mouth as the realization stole the air from her lungs. It was Molly. She took a minute to step away and find her footing, blinking back the tears. In a burst of panic, she covered the poor dog back up, promising herself she would tell no one. Maybe one of their neighbors or another outsider had sneaked into their yard during the night and done this. Still, the sinking feeling in her stomach never went away.

So, it had been even more disturbing when she and Pete had walked through the front door one sunny morning to find Trent's eyes gleaming, his foot hovering over a tiny field mouse, about to stomp down on its quivering body. But when he'd spotted them and heard Darla gasp, he'd slowly lowered his foot and taken a step back, focusing his attention on something else. Pete had shoved his hands in his pockets, hurried toward his bike, and pedaled away, an action he'd repeat often in the years that followed.

The door opened, drawing Darla's eyes toward the detective, who popped his head inside. "I apologize. Just one more minute and I'll be back to wrap this up."

"That's fine." The door closed, and Darla breathed in the stuffy air of the room, letting her thoughts circle back again, to a couple of years after she'd discovered that dog in the garden.

It was a week after school let out, and Trent and his best

friend, Freddie, wanted to take the neighbor's canoe out on the lake at night. The lake sat within walking distance, and Pete had tagged along despite the older boys' protests. Trent and Freddie had been going through a rough patch because Freddie hadn't invited Trent to a recent last-day-of-school bonfire at his house.

Darla had hoped they'd repair their friendship that night, but it wasn't in the cards. Trent and Pete came back from the lake just before 11 p.m., soaking wet and crying. Freddie wasn't with them. There'd been an accident. Trent had been rocking the boat as a joke. He said he'd wanted to scare Freddie. But the boat tipped. Her boys swam to shore, but Freddie hit his head on the way in and drowned.

Trent was distraught at the loss of his friend. She and Kenny told him that it was a tragic accident, it hadn't been anyone's fault, but nothing could console him. Trent blamed himself for his recklessness. He retreated inward at home and started acting out in school. The few friends who used to invite him to go fishing or to the movies stopped calling.

A month or so after the canoe accident, Pete found Darla alone in the kitchen and, once again whispered that he had to tell her something. She recognized the traumatized look on his face from the last time he'd cornered her. In a hushed voice, he told her that Trent had tipped the canoe on purpose, that he'd smiled at Pete right before he flipped it. Darla didn't want to believe it, but she remembered the dog she'd found buried in the garden. She instructed Pete never to repeat what he'd just told her to anyone, that his brother could go to jail.

Maybe she shouldn't have said that.

Because there was a third death. Once again, Darla didn't have any solid proof that Trent had been responsible, and she was grateful for that. But the timing had been suspiciously coincidental. Five years ago, when Pete was a senior in college and living in an apartment, he invited Trent for a weekend visit. It had been a welcome relief for Darla and Kenny to get Trent out of the house for a couple of days, for him to have plans that didn't include his parents. The boys had attempted to arrange a visit the previous fall, but Pete's girlfriend at the time, Megan, hadn't felt comfortable sharing her space with Trent, which made Darla wonder how much about the past Pete had shared with her. Trent had overheard Megan saying she would leave if Trent came to visit, and he'd later repeated Megan's hurtful words to Darla. But Pete had since broken up with Megan and she'd moved out. So, Darla had lent Trent her car for the weekend. He'd returned it two days later with a large dent on the front bumper.

"What happened?" she asked, running her finger over the bent metal.

Trent stared at the murky garage window. "I don't know. Pete must have hit a pole when he went out to get groceries. He probably won't admit it if you ask him though."

"Were you with him?"

"No."

"Doesn't Pete have his own car?"

"Yeah." Trent paused, frowning. "I guess he does."

"Why was he driving my car? Was there something wrong with his car?"

"Maybe. I don't think so." Trent grimaced, a sign Darla attributed to catching him in a lie. "Maybe I bumped into something and didn't realize it."

Darla had been annoyed with Trent for lying, but let the conversation drop after speaking to Pete, who swore he hadn't driven Darla's car anywhere. She'd enlisted a friend of Kenny's to do the repair for a reduced fee. About two months later, Pete called her one afternoon, saying he'd just found out his ex-girlfriend, Megan, had been killed in a hit-and-run as she rode her bike along a side street. He couldn't believe he hadn't heard about her death when it happened. He felt guilty for breaking up with her, and terrible for missing the funeral.

Darla googled Megan's name and found information about the memorial service, which had already happened weeks earlier. It was the date of her death that caused a shiver to flutter across her skin and her stomach to fold in on itself. Megan had been killed the same October weekend Trent had been visiting. Megan had prevented Trent from visiting the previous year—had rejected him—and now she was dead.

Darla's motherly intuition knew something was seriously off with her eldest son. She thought she'd kept him close enough, maintained a watchful eye. After Freddie's death, she'd doubled down on her studies of Tarot and palm reading as a way to forewarn her of troubling things to come, events that might be avoided. And she'd chosen to focus on Trent's softer side, which could be so gentle and sweet. She even kept a card Trent had made for her when he was eight in the drawer of her nightstand to remind herself that Trent was a good person at his core. The card contained a poem entitled "Mothers are Precious" that Trent had written all by himself. But he was a grown man and Darla couldn't be with him all the time. She'd foolishly believed they were in the clear now that he had a job and had moved into his own place. But she should have nipped his troubling tendencies in the bud and gotten him the help he needed the moment she'd discovered that dog. She'd let his problematic behavior go on way too long—years too long—and now the situation was out of her control.

Over the years, Darla had observed Trent's quiet jealousy toward his younger brother. She'd noticed the way Trent's lip quivered when Pete brought home his annual report cards lined with As, or whenever Pete's friends picked him up to go to a party or a movie while Trent stayed home to play video games by himself. She recalled how Trent had hung his head and marched out of the room when Pete received a full-ride scholarship to college, and how Trent's face had frozen when Pete called home, ecstatic about his new position at the commercial real estate company. It was clear Trent had always been comparing himself, always falling a thousand steps short. And now Pete had found an intelligent and beautiful bride, something that Darla had to admit was unlikely to happen for Trent. Pete and Abigail had poured acid into an open wound when they cut Trent out of the wedding. Darla wondered if that decision was the final strike of the match, igniting a raging fire inside Trent, one that had been smoldering since childhood.

But the animosity between her boys cut both ways. She was sure that Pete sensed that something was off with his older brother too. It seemed he was even a little scared of Trent. That was likely why he'd worked so hard to get away, to escape to a new life, and separate himself from this family. But, as it turned out, he hadn't done it fast enough. Because now Abigail's mother was dead. And it was only a matter of time before Trent realized he'd killed the wrong woman. Then Abigail would be next.

TWENTY-SEVEN

ABIGAIL

I remained comatose on the living room couch. My mind idled in a thick fog, aware of nothing but my tightly wrapped ankle and Pete bumbling around the kitchen, banging pots and pans. It had been less than two days since we'd escaped the woods and returned to our townhome. Pete had insisted on taking me to urgent care right away, where they did an X-ray and diagnosed my injury as a sprain, not a fracture. "Such good news," the doctor had said, completely unaware of the larger tragedy surrounding me.

Now a text buzzed on my phone. My heart pounded when I saw it was from Liam. I propped myself up from the sea of cushions and hobbled up to the bedroom, not wanting Pete to read whatever had been written.

Relieved to hear everyone else made it out okay. I'm so sorry—more than words can say—about what happened to your mom. Just wanted you to know I didn't tell anyone about our history or your real reason for the camping trip. The secret is safe.

I released a breath, even as my fingers squeezed the life out of my phone. Liam's discretion offered a sliver of relief as far as my dark secret was concerned. But I was too angry about Mom's death to respond to his message. Nothing about it was okay. Liam might not have pushed her over the edge, but he'd been reckless to bring us to that spot, to put us in that situation. He'd made all of us sign dozens of waivers and releases of liability before the trip, almost as if he'd expected something tragic to happen. Another message came through.

Sorry again.

I deleted the messages. Then I blocked Liam's number from my phone.

The doorbell rang from the front of the house, and I limped out of the bedroom and down the stairs.

"I got it," Pete yelled. He hurried toward the door, pulling it open as I reached the bottom step. "Mom?" he asked.

Darla stood in the doorway, a suitcase resting near her feet and a casserole clutched in one arm. The unexpected sight of Darla at my house ushered in a fresh wave of grief and anxiety. I'd only just gotten away from her. What was she doing here?

"I'm here to help." Darla smiled at me as if she'd read my mind. "The funeral planning is going to take a lot out of you, honey." She reached forward and squeezed my hand. "I'll help you get through the day-to-day stuff so you can focus on healing."

I was too stunned to speak. Dad had already talked to the funeral home and scheduled a tentative date for the burial on Saturday, conditioned on approval from the coroner's office. That was still six days away because the medical examiner needed time to perform the autopsy.

Pete stepped to the side, eyes darting between me and Darla. "Mom, you should have asked us before driving all the way here."

I stared at Darla, but instead of her features, all I could see were the words in Mom's journal. *DARLA IS A FRAUD!* The note had left a permanent mark on my mind. I didn't fully trust this woman, wasn't convinced she hadn't been involved in Mom's death, and I didn't want her in my house. She must have seen the true feelings stretching across my face.

Darla held up a defensive hand. "Now I don't want to be a burden. In fact, I'll sleep in my car if that's easier. You won't even know I'm here."

Pete threw an unsure look my way, apparently leaving the decision to me.

As much as I didn't want Darla around, she was Pete's mom. She had driven nearly four hours to get here. She was offering to help. I was barely functioning as it was, and Pete had been bending over backward to accommodate my every need. Maybe having her around for a few days wasn't the worst idea, if only to allow me to observe her behavior. But I wasn't going to make her sleep in her car, which would only exacerbate my guilt. "That's okay, Darla. We have an air mattress. Pete can set it up in the den for you."

"I just wish you'd asked us first," Pete said again as Darla stepped past him, setting the casserole dish on the kitchen counter.

She returned to the front door, turning the deadbolt and peering out the narrow side window as if searching for something. "You would have told me not to come," Darla stated matter-of-factly. "Kenny has to work this week, but he'll be here on Saturday morning before the funeral."

I nodded, but the room seemed to spin around me.

Darla pointed toward the kitchen. "I brought a veggie casserole for dinner. And I can go to the grocery store and pick up anything else you need. Just put together a list for me."

"Thank you," I managed to say, but even the thought of constructing a simple grocery list felt too overwhelming. Pete massaged my shoulders and kissed me on the cheek. "Hey, why don't you go upstairs and lie down? I'll get Mom organized. Maybe then I'll drive over and check in on your dad, too. See if he needs anything."

"Okay, thanks." I looked at Darla, who nodded at me as I forced myself up the stairs. Mango prowled in the hallway, and I scooped her into my arms. Then I closed myself and the cat inside the bedroom, locking the door behind me. Lying in bed for the rest of the day was about all I could handle.

* * *

I stayed in bed for most of the day and evening, leaving the cocoon of my darkened bedroom only to join Pete and Darla for dinner. I picked at Darla's casserole, which contained spinach, pasta, and a cream sauce with several spices I couldn't quite identify. She shifted in her chair and peered toward the blackened windows every minute or two as if expecting someone. Pete filled the silence, telling me how he'd spent an hour with Dad, and had helped him make a few decisions about Mom's funeral.

"Your dad chose one of the higher-end coffins," Pete said as I pushed the casserole around on my plate. "And he'd like your input on some of your mom's favorite poems to be read at the funeral. And some Bible verses too. He'll email them to you tomorrow."

"Okay," I said, but I could barely comprehend his words. It all felt like a horrible dream.

A car engine sputtered outside and Darla sat up straight in her chair, craning her neck toward the noise.

Pete gestured toward the window. "That's our neighbor's truck. It's super loud."

Darla released a breath as she looked down at her plate. "Have you ever thought about installing a home security system? They have all sorts of fancy ones with cameras that you can control from your phone. I saw they were on sale at the store. I'm happy to pick one up for you tomorrow."

I looked at Pete, who made a face. "There's no need, Mom. This is a very safe neighborhood."

I pushed my knife forward. "Actually, Darla, I wouldn't mind having something like that."

Pete turned to me, his face morphing from surprise to embarrassment. "I'm sorry, hon. I wasn't thinking." He placed his hand on mine. "Of course, we can get one if it makes you feel safer."

"I'll pick one up the next time I'm out," Darla said, bobbing her head up and down. "Consider it an early wedding present."

* * *

The next afternoon, I had locked myself in the bedroom again, hoping to sleep the remainder of the day away while Pete drove to his office to grab a file. Darla had already run out to purchase the security camera and now lingered downstairs doing who knew what. I woke with a start as my phone buzzed. I'd saved Detective Leeman's number to my phone, and now his name flashed on the screen.

I rubbed the sleep from my eyes. "Hello."

"Hi, Abigail. It's Detective Leeman."

"Yes." I swallowed, preparing myself for whatever news he was about to deliver.

"I just got off the phone with your dad but wanted to call you too. We received the results of your mom's autopsy."

I crumpled the edge of the sheets in my fingers. "What did they find?"

"There was no evidence of foul play. No unusual marks other than what would have been expected from a forward-facing tumble off the cliff."

"What about her eyes?" I gripped the phone, glancing at the door. "Did they check for bear spray?"

"Yes, they checked. No chemical residue of any kind was detected anywhere on her body."

My fingers loosened. At least one of the scenarios I'd imagined—of someone stunning her with bear spray before shoving her to her death—wasn't true. "What about her broken nail?" I asked.

"That's still with the lab. They are checking it for DNA along with all of her other acrylic nails, but it will take a few more days to get the results."

"Okay."

The detective cleared his throat. "Abigail, obviously, we'll wait for the DNA results on the nails before deciding whether to officially close the case. But there are dozens of innocent reasons your mom's nail could have broken off."

I closed my eyes, remembering how Mom's other nail had ripped off when she'd stumbled during the river crossing and realizing the detective wasn't one to jump to conclusions.

"As for now, it appears that your mom stepped too close to the edge of the gulch and lost her footing. Unfortunately, accidents like this aren't all that uncommon, especially in a rugged and unfamiliar setting. It might help to know that she was likely knocked unconscious on the way down. I can say with near certainty that she didn't suffer."

My throat went dry as the horrible image spiraled through my mind. During our initial interview, the detective had appeared to take me seriously when I shared my suspicions about Darla and Kenny. Now I wondered how he'd discounted them so easily. I clutched the phone to my ear, lowering my voice. "So, you don't think Darla and Kenny were involved in this?"

"Not after talking to them. Their statements were consistent with the evidence we found, and their version of events matched what everyone else had reported. No one seemed to be near your mom when she fell. Darla and Kenny are strange birds, for sure, but that's not nearly enough reason for us to make an arrest, much less get a conviction. As it stands, I have no way of even placing them at the scene."

"But Mom's nail might provide the evidence."

The detective sighed, then hesitated. "It might. Or it might not."

Hot tears formed in the corners of my eyes, and I wiped them away. I wasn't sure why I was crying, but I supposed it was a relief to get some answers, to find some reassurance that maybe my future in-laws hadn't murdered my mom.

"What about that hungry guy we ran into in the woods?"

"There's been an extensive search of the park. We couldn't find anyone matching his description, and not surprisingly, he never registered his route."

I slouched forward.

"The park rangers are keeping an eye out though. And I'll be sure to call you as soon as I hear anything on the fingernail test."

"Okay. Thank you." I ended the call, feeling disappointed by the lack of clear answers. Now I questioned everything I thought I knew. I'd dreamed up so many evil scenarios surrounding Mom's death. Maybe I'd merely needed someone to blame, had imagined things that simply weren't true. After talking to the detective, it seemed more than possible that Mom's death had been nothing more than a tragic accident. Still, I wouldn't be convinced of that until I saw the DNA results.

TWENTY-EIGHT

ABIGAIL

The next morning, I awoke with my head slightly less foggy than the day before.

Pete sat on the edge of the bed, checking his phone and raking his fingers through his hair. "Do you mind if I head into the office for a few hours today? I just have so many phone calls to return." He leaned toward me and squeezed my arm. "You can call me if you need anything. And I'll come home early."

"Yeah. That's okay." I propped myself up, noticing the sunlight filtering in through the curtains. I wasn't sure if I could stand another day spent locked in my bedroom, but I also hoped to avoid spending the day with Darla. "I'll go over to Dad's and help him finalize the details for the funeral."

Pete nodded, surprised. "That's a good idea. You okay to drive?"

"My right foot still works." I lifted it in the air.

Pete smiled, looking relieved by my slightly elevated spirit. "That's a good point. I'll go make some coffee and give Mom instructions to stay out of your hair."

* * *

I spent the entire morning at Dad's house, where we sat in the sunny kitchen reading through poems and spiritual verses, discarding the ones that didn't quite fit and saving the few that reminded us of Mom. Dad's face looked worn, purplish bags swollen beneath his eyes. The thin scratches on his face had healed quickly and were barely visible.

It felt strange to be in the house without Mom. The kitchen was clean and organized like always. Mom's jackets and sun hats still hung on the hooks near the door, a row of her shoes underneath. Mom smiled at me from a photo on the wall, an image of her and Dad standing on a beach from the trip to Miami they'd taken two years earlier.

"What will you do with her things?" I asked, staring at her shoes.

"I don't know." Dad touched his throat. "Nothing for now. I just can't bear to get rid of anything."

"I can help you when you're ready," I said, and he nodded, eyes filling with tears.

For lunch, Dad and I ate the white bean soup that Darla had cooked the night before and packed up for us, insisting it contained healing ingredients. I had to give Darla some credit because it was the first food I'd eaten since the camping trip that hadn't made me feel like throwing up. Even Dad commented on how good it tasted.

Four hours later, I made the short drive back to our townhome, feeling proud of myself for getting out of the house, not to mention helping to ease Dad's suffering a tiny bit. Mom had always said that helping others was the key to surviving any tragedy, and I wished I could tell her she was right. I parked out front, pulling behind Darla's dented station wagon, then hobbling my way to the front door, where I let myself inside. I'd expected to find Darla on the couch watching TV or cooking something in the kitchen, but she wasn't in either room. I popped my head into the den where the air mattress took up most of the room. She wasn't there.

My hand tried to stifle my third yawn in so many minutes. I decided I'd go upstairs and read or take a nap until Pete returned. When I reached the top step, I heard a drawer open and close. The noise was coming from our bathroom, the one attached to our bedroom. I crept into our bedroom. Through the partially open bathroom door, I spotted Darla's wide back, the braid hanging down the middle. Now she opened the medicine cabinet, the one above my sink. She reached for something.

"Darla?"

She jumped, slamming the mirror closed and spinning toward me. "Oh! Abigail. I'm sorry. I just... I was looking for a Band-Aid."

"A Band-Aid?"

"Yes. My toe." She glanced at her foot, but her breathing was heavy. "My shoes don't fit me the right way."

"They're on the top shelf of the linen closet." I pointed behind me. "In the hallway."

"Of course. I should have checked that closet first." She ducked past me. "I didn't mean to intrude."

"It's okay."

The door to the linen closet opened and Darla rustled around. "Here they are. Thank you."

"Sure. I'm going to take a nap."

"I won't bother you." I heard Darla's heavy footsteps plod down the stairs.

I stood still for a second, an uneasy sensation draining through me, tipping me off balance. I got the feeling I'd walked in on her, that I'd caught her doing something she shouldn't have been doing. I stepped forward and locked the bedroom door. Then I hurried into the bathroom and opened the medicine cabinet above my sink. Darla had been about to reach for something, and I had a horrible feeling I knew what it was. My packet of birth control pills sat front and center on the bottom shelf, over two weeks of pills to go. I remembered Darla's strange insistence that I have a baby right away. My legs felt as if they might give way.

What had she planned to do?

* * *

I remained locked in my bedroom until Pete returned from work. Pete hadn't had a chance to install our new security camera yet, and even if he had, it didn't protect me from Darla. As soon as Pete returned from work, I told him in hushed and frantic tones what I'd seen and that I suspected his mom was somehow trying to tamper with my pills or swap them out. Pete tipped his head back, closing his eyes. Then he stormed downstairs and spoke to his mom in a forceful voice. I inched forward, listening through a crack in the door as Darla claimed she'd only been looking for a Band-Aid. She showed Pete the blister on her foot, and forced him to look at it. Darla was sorry if she'd accidentally stumbled into a private area, but she hadn't been doing anything sinister. Pete returned a few minutes later. "Sorry, hon. I think it was all a misunderstanding. She really did need a Band-Aid."

"Oh." I placed my fingers on my throbbing temple. "Maybe I got it wrong." I'd been getting so many things wrong lately.

"I made it clear that she's not to go into our bathroom again. She has the one downstairs, anyway."

"Okay." I clutched my elbows. "Is she mad at me?"

"What?" He shot me an incredulous look. "No. It was a misunderstanding. That's it. End of story."

I tucked in my chin and closed my eyes, refusing to let

myself cry again. I would make a point to be extra nice to Darla tomorrow.

* * *

The morning before the funeral, my phone buzzed with Detective Leeman's name.

"Hello."

"Hi, Abigail. We have the DNA report from your mom's nails."

I squeezed the phone, afraid to breathe. "What did it say?"

"There were trace amounts of your DNA on the surface of the broken nail, which we expected to find because you carried it back to us. Besides that, there was no DNA other than her own detected on the broken nail or any of her other nails."

I swallowed. "So—"

"So, she didn't scratch another person prior to her death. That's not how her nail broke." He breathed in and out a few times, letting me process the news. "We're going to officially rule her death as an accident."

I bit my lip, thinking again about how I'd gotten so many things wrong. "Thank you for letting me know."

TWENTY-NINE
ABIGAIL

Six months later

I lifted the high-speed blender from the box, showing it off to Pete, who oohed and aahed at the shiny appliance from his spot next to me on our living room couch. A few feet away on the floor, Mango twisted around and licked her orange fur, seemingly annoyed by our antics. I'd returned from my bridal shower thirty minutes earlier, which had been hosted by my maid of honor, Betsy. Betsy had gone all-out for the party, telling me privately that I deserved the best after everything I'd been through. She adored Pete and hadn't known about my brief fling with Liam. Thankfully, no one except me knew about that extreme lapse in judgment. Liam hadn't even bothered to show up to Mom's funeral. And when I checked the Team Wilderness website a few weeks after I'd blocked his number, I noticed his profile had been removed and I assumed he'd been fired.

Pete let out a low whistle. "That's quite a blender. It'll be perfect for my smoothies."

"That's what I was thinking."

After so much pain and sadness from losing my mom, it was a relief to focus on something happy. I tried not to spend too much time envisioning exactly how Mom had fallen off that cliff. Dad had met with an attorney to discuss potential negligence lawsuits against Team Wilderness and the Hiawana National Forest, but after hearing the whole story and looking over all the waivers we'd signed, the attorney had advised him of the pitfalls and expenses of pursuing such actions. We really had signed our lives away with those waivers. And, apparently, the National Park Service was protected from most negligence claims by a special governmental statute. So, Dad decided it wasn't worth the time, money, and emotional stress to move forward. It had grown tiresome and frustrating to constantly blame everyone, including the wild animals who lived in the forest. Because of her death, at least that stretch of trail near the gulch had immediately been closed down by the park until a guard rail could be added.

Now six months had passed since Mom's funeral, which I'd experienced in a blur of despair. Darla and Kenny had been there, sitting in the front row next to me and Pete. Once the suspicion around them had officially been lifted, they'd taken on the role of helpful and supportive in-laws. They visited often, never requiring anything in return, although I secretly locked up my valuables when Kenny was around. But sometimes Darla acted strangely. She always seemed to be looking over her shoulder, jumping at any movement outside the window, and asking us how the new security camera worked. It was as if she didn't feel safe in our house.

Still, Darla had been the one who contacted everyone on the wedding guest list to let them know that due to the family tragedy, we'd postponed the wedding ceremony and reception for an additional three months. Kenny had insisted on taking on a few extra shifts at the warehouse so he could contribute to the cost of the rehearsal dinner. Dad had buried himself in work and encouraged me to continue with my plans and marry Pete. "Mom would have wanted you to live your life, not wallow in sadness." It seemed Mom had never had a chance to share her desire for me to call off the wedding with Dad. Sometimes I still heard the frantic whisper of her voice in my ear, telling me to run in the other direction or, at least, pump the brakes. But that was only because I'd set things up that way. Mom hadn't known the whole story.

Any lingering and unwanted suspicions about those scratches on Dad's face were erased first by the DNA results, then again when I'd visited him a month after losing Mom. He encouraged me to go up to their bedroom and collect a few pieces of Mom's jewelry that had been special to me. Just like the coats and shoes downstairs, Mom's belongings remained exactly as she'd left them, even the indentation of her head on her pillow. Dad hadn't even moved the clothes she'd left on the drying rack. As I walked down the hall, I noticed Dad's alarm clock, book, and reading glasses resting on the nightstand in the guest room. He stood at the top of the stairs, touching his lower back when he noticed me looking. "The firmer mattress in here is better for my back." He glanced toward the main bedroom, eyes watering. "Now I don't have the heart to replace the one your mom and I shared."

Finally, I'd fully accepted the conclusion that everyone else had already come to—that Mom's death was nothing more than a tragic accident, the kind that sometimes happened to people when they least expected it. The universe had taught me a painful lesson about deceiving those I loved.

Now my hands picked through layers of tissue paper as I made a conscious effort to enjoy the small moments. "Look what your mom gave us." I made a face at Pete as I removed a yellow-and-green striped onesie from a gift bag and held it up. It looked impossibly tiny, even for a baby.

Pete tipped back his head and sighed. "Are you kidding

me?" He snatched it from me. "I'm so sorry. We'll just ignore her until we're ready to start a family. Until *you're* ready."

I waved him off. "I've decided to let the baby stuff roll off my back. Your mom has been great in so many other ways." I winked. "And I've hidden my birth control pills."

Pete patted my leg, then sighed. "Trent sent us something too."

A tinge of nausea seared through my gut at the mention of Pete's brother, but I reminded myself to be nice. "What is it?"

"I don't know. I haven't opened it yet." Pete went to the console table and returned with a square package wrapped in silver paper. He held it away from him with his fingertips as if it were filled with toxic chemicals.

I nodded toward the box. "Go ahead and open it."

Pete tore at the seams as he tossed aside the paper and lifted the lid. A frown overtook his face as he peered inside.

"What is it?" I asked again. When Pete didn't respond, I reached inside and pulled out a shiny vinyl collar, candy-apple red with a heart-shaped silver tag inscribed with the name *Mango* dangling from the middle. "A new collar for our cat?"

Pete rubbed his temples. "He's such a creep."

"It's kind of thoughtful though, isn't it?" I asked, glancing at Mango, who was now asleep on the armchair.

"Not really. Not when you consider his past."

I took another look at the collar, my stomach folding as I remembered the story Pete had told me about the neighbor's missing dog—the one with the shiny red collar.

"We can throw it away." Pete pushed the box aside.

I didn't argue with him.

He draped his arm around my shoulders and pulled me close. "Can you believe we're getting married in one week?"

I looked into his eyes, seeing my reflection in them. "Not really. But it's happening whether we're ready or not."

Pete chuckled and kissed the top of my head. "There's no turning back."

THIRTY

DARLA

Darla flopped into bed, exhausted after driving over three hours home from Abigail's wedding shower, thinking about the single path that might ensure a happy future for Abigail and Pete, despite what the Tarot cards had shown her, despite the unusual break in Abigail's Line of Life, the exact same break that had shown itself on her deceased mother's palm. There were always alternate paths to choose, paths that could result in a more agreeable outcome.

Darla had come to wholeheartedly believe Kenny's repeated claims that he'd had nothing to do with Kristen's death and that he'd never mentioned any details of their camping trip to Trent. Nonetheless, Darla hadn't been able to shake the suspicion that Trent had followed them out into the wilderness on his own, that he might have been responsible for Kristen's deadly tumble into the gulch, having mistaken the woman for her daughter. But when they'd arrived home from the forest, Darla had found the file with their route locked inside her cabinet, the key sitting in the exact same place she'd left it, facing straight up and down and touching the right edge of the drawer. Of course, that didn't mean Trent couldn't have discovered the papers and the map in the weeks before they'd left or put the key back in the same place.

The day after they'd returned home, Trent had stopped by to pick up the sunglasses he'd left in the living room a couple of weeks earlier.

"How did the bowling tournament go?" she'd asked.

"Good. It took up the whole weekend."

"How'd you do?"

"I came in second place." Trent turned away from her.

"That's great." Darla tried to study Trent's face but couldn't get a good view. "Did you get a trophy? I'd love to see it."

"No." He shuffled toward the window. "They must have run out of them or something."

"Oh."

Trent made a fist and smacked it into his opposite palm. "I've got things to do, Mom. I'm gonna get going."

Darla said goodbye but couldn't stop turning over the exchange with Trent in her mind, weighing its truthfulness. Did bowling alleys often run out of trophies when hosting a tournament? She didn't know. When she'd pressed Kenny for information about the tournament the day before, he only said that he didn't know the details.

To keep her imagination in check, Darla had called the bowling alley that Trent frequented—the only one in town.

"Oakwood Lanes. How can I help you?" a chipper voice had asked.

"Hi. Did you host a tournament this past weekend?"

"Hm. No. I worked Saturday afternoon and there was no tournament. As far as I know there wasn't anything on Sunday either."

"Okay," Darla had said as her insides dropped. She'd located the next two closest bowling alleys online, each one about thirty minutes away, and called them too. Neither of them had hosted a tournament the previous weekend either.

There weren't any others in the area. She feared Trent had lied and there'd never been any tournament at all.

Now Darla reached across her chest and pulled open the nightstand drawer, studying the heartfelt card Trent had made for her so many years earlier. *Mothers are Precious.* There'd been dozens more similar cards that followed on birthdays and Mother's Days. Trent had a soft spot, not just for Darla, but for mothers in general. He'd always been so sensitive that way. She remembered the way he'd been about to stomp on the mouse in the backyard, but then stopped when he saw her. After Pete had raced off on his bike, Darla noticed the real reason Trent had stepped back. A tiny nest of baby mice sat in a hollowed-out spot beneath the shrubbery. He'd left the mother mouse alone, entranced by the little ones she'd brought into the world. "She's magical," he'd said, eyes wide with wonder. "Just like you."

Darla had seen the sideways glances earlier today when Abigail opened her gift at the bridal shower, her face reddening as her friends widened their eyes and giggled at the onesie. And it was true that a few months earlier she'd attempted to swap out Abigail's pills for the fake ones she'd purchased online. It had been a stupid move. Too risky. But Darla had only done those things because she was trying to protect her future daughter-in-law. Trent would never harm a woman with a baby. She was sure of it. The sooner Abigail got pregnant, the sooner she'd be safe.

THIRTY-ONE

ABIGAIL

I paced around the waiting room bordering the church's entryway, "Ode to Joy" playing from the chapel. The flower girls meandered up the aisle, sprinkling pink and white petals around themselves as they walked. Now Betsy waited in the doorway for the best man, Oliver, who was Pete's friend from college.

I fiddled with the pearl bracelet encircling my wrist. Something borrowed from Mom. She'd worn it on her wedding day, and I wished she was here. A haze slowed my thoughts. I hadn't slept last night. I'd thrown up twice this morning. But I'd told myself to stop being ridiculous. How many times could I remind myself I was doing the right thing?

Betsy wavered in the doorway, giving me a wink. On the other side of the room, something caught my eye. The white corner of an envelope peeked from my purse. I'd found the letter wedged into the driver's side door of my car this morning, but when I saw 'For Abigail, From Liam' written on the outside of the envelope, I'd stuffed it into my purse without opening it. Liam was the last person I wanted to think about today. If it hadn't been for him, Mom would be here with me.

Betsy turned to smile at me, then followed the directions of the wedding coordinator just outside the door, stepping forward as the music continued in the background. I rushed over to the envelope and picked it up. I shoved it down into the nearby bag with my extra clothes so I didn't have to look at it. Then I went to the doorway, where Dad waited for me, all smiles.

He stepped toward me, eyes glistening. "You look beautiful, sweetie."

"Thank you." I felt the hot tears burning down my cheeks and I wiped them away.

"Why are you crying?"

"I don't know." I sniffled and forced a smile.

"Mom's here with us."

"I know." I looped my arm through Dad's.

"Are you ready to get married?" He gave my hand a squeeze. "'Til death do us part and all that?"

I nodded and we stepped forward, the petal-filled aisle stretching before us. Up ahead, Pete, handsome in his black tuxedo, grinned at me from beside the minister. Betsy and Oliver stood on either side of him, smiling. I kept my eyes straight ahead as we paced slowly down the aisle, our footsteps matching the pull and lull of the music. I felt as if I'd left my body and was floating above myself as we passed rows and rows of people, all of whom watched me, joyful and expectant. Trent perched on the pew in the front row, craning his neck to leer at me as I neared. The way he stared gave me the creeps. Darla and Kenny sat next to him, their faces a rosy pink. I tried to only look at Pete and not his brother.

When we finally reached the front of the church, Dad kissed me on the cheek, removed his arm from mine, and took his seat. Pete grasped my shaking hands. We said our vows and then we kissed and embraced. People cheered. We were married.

I rolled back my shoulders and let my eyes travel across the smiling crowd, at all the happy people. And I wondered if all brides felt this terrified on their wedding day.

THIRTY-TWO

DARLA

Darla yawned, exhausted from yesterday's festivities. The wedding had been splendid, the dancing, drinking, and well wishes lasting late into the night. There'd been a decadent brunch this morning at the hotel, and Abigail and Pete had made an appearance, wearing matching "Just Married" T-shirts. She'd kept Trent in her sights the whole time, even as she and Kenny had hugged the newlyweds goodbye and wished them well on their honeymoon.

Now Darla was back at her little house after she and Kenny and Trent had driven back together the day before. Their house wasn't much, especially compared to the house Abigail had grown up in, but it had a comforting aura, and she was glad to be there. Kenny was outside shoveling snow. Trent had returned from his apartment an hour earlier, enticed by Darla's offer of a home-cooked meal, and he rested on the couch next to her.

She noticed that Trent was quieter than usual, which only worried her more. "I'm sorry they didn't include you in the wedding party, honey." Darla patted her son on the knee, at least thankful he was staying for dinner. "Maybe you, me, and Dad can plan a fun trip somewhere."

He shrugged. "It's fine. I didn't really expect Pete to include me. He only cares about impressing people." Darla studied Trent's face as he stared at the wall, searching for any indication of guilt but finding none. After a minute, he straightened up, face brightening.

"Hey. I got something in the mail while we were gone. It's an award." Trent stood tall, puffing out his chest. "Do you want to see it?"

"Award for what?" Darla asked.

"Bowling. I was in a tournament a few months ago. Remember? They finally sent me the certificate."

Darla sat up straighter, remembering her troubling phone call to the nearby bowling alleys many weeks earlier. "Sure. I'd love to see it."

Trent jogged outside to his truck and returned a minute later with a rectangular piece of paper. He placed it on the table in front of his mom. "I was the runner-up."

Darla's eyes scanned over the writing. She smiled at the sight of Trent's name in the fancy black ink. But when she got to the date at the bottom, she nearly lost her breath. The award was dated six months ago, the same Friday night that Abigail's mom died.

"Where was the tournament?"

"Over in Cadillac. I had to drive almost an hour to get there."

Relief washed over her at the realization, rinsing away her poisonous thoughts. Trent hadn't been lying. She had called the wrong bowling alleys. She hadn't thought to search for a bowling alley this far away. Trent couldn't have followed them into the woods. It would have been impossible for him to earn this honor at the bowling alley on the same night the rest of them had been hours away. Her body shuddered with a new kind of fear displacing the relief she'd experienced a moment earlier. If Trent hadn't done that terrible thing, did that mean someone else had been responsible?

Trent grunted. "What do you think?"

Darla pinched the paper between her fingers. "It's wonderful." She pulled her eyes from the award and looked at her son. "I'm very proud of you."

Trent raised his chin. "Pete can't take this away from me."

"Of course he can't. Why would you say that?"

"Pete's always saying things are different than they are. He thinks he's smarter than everyone else. But I know he's just a liar."

Darla shook her head, lips pinched. She'd never heard Trent talk this way about Pete so openly before. "What do you mean?"

Trent tapped his heel against the floor. "Like when I visited Pete at college a few years ago, he said I dented the car. He tried to convince me that I'd done it. But he took the car to the grocery store. I wasn't even with him. I think that's when it happened."

"Yes. You mentioned that before."

Trent raised his chin. "But you didn't believe me. You always believe him. He told me I was stupid so many times that I finally said that I dented the car just to get him to stop." Trent shook his head. "Pete was being a jerk all weekend because his girlfriend dumped him. Even months later, he just couldn't get over the fact that she wouldn't take him back."

Darla's stomach lurched. "Megan? She dumped Pete? I thought he broke up with her."

Trent swung his head from side to side. "She was smart not to trust him."

Darla's molars clamped down on the inside of her cheek. Maybe Pete had lied to her. He'd always been a smooth talker. He'd known how to charm people and play to people's doubts and weaknesses. She thought back to the palm readings she'd attempted on Pete in the past, the way he always pulled his hand away as if he was afraid of what Darla would see.

Sitting there now, she wondered if she'd been wrong to trust Pete's version of events over Trent's. "What about the canoe accident?" she asked, finding her voice.

"Huh?"

"The canoe accident when Freddie died."

Trent slumped forward. "You said we weren't allowed to talk about that."

"Well, I'm telling you something different now." Darla lowered her face, forcing Trent to look at her. "It's okay to talk about it. Tell me everything that happened again."

Trent slid his palms down his legs and leaned forward. "It was dark. Freddie was making fun of Pete, asking why he had to tag along and ruin our fun. I started rocking the boat to make him shut up, but I rocked it too far and it tipped over. I'm so sorry I did that." Trent's lip quivered and tears streamed from his eyes.

"It's okay. It was an accident." Darla rubbed his arm. "What happened next?"

"We all fell in. I swam to shore. I thought they were right behind me."

"Where was Pete?"

"Under the water. I thought he'd drowned at first because there was so much splashing. Finally, Pete's head popped up and he made it to shore too. But I couldn't see Freddie anymore. There wasn't much light. It was hard to see like I said."

Again, a dark knowing twisted in Darla's stomach. Had she gotten things wrong all these years? Pete had told her a different version of events—that Trent had gotten angry about something and tipped the boat on purpose, that Freddie had hit his head and never resurfaced as Trent and Pete swam to shore. She'd believed Pete—the straight-A student, the popular kid, the articulate one—over Trent, the one who couldn't focus in school, the one who'd been so distraught he hadn't been able to speak. The accident had set him back so much that he'd had to repeat eleventh grade, which he barely passed the second time. But now Darla examined the accident through a different lens. Pete had always been a strong swimmer. She would have expected him to be the first to get to shore, not Trent whose swimming had been mostly self-taught because he'd thrown a tantrum every time she'd tried to take him to a swim lesson at the local YMCA. And while Trent had been distraught over Freddie's death, she couldn't remember seeing Pete ever shed a real tear. She'd let her beliefs about who had buried the dog in the garden taint her view. But now she wondered if she'd even gotten that right.

"Trent, I have to ask you something that I've never mentioned before, and I need you to promise to tell me the truth. I swear on my life that I won't be mad at you no matter how you answer."

Trent tilted his head and blinked.

"Do you remember Mr. Flynn's dog? The scruffy one who liked to play fetch?"

Trent nodded. "Molly?"

"Did you have anything to do with Molly's..." Darla hesitated, the horrible image of the buried collar, the narrow skull, reeling through her mind. It was the first time she'd talked about her discovery out loud. "With Molly's disappearance?"

"No!" His face stretched with horror. "Why would I hurt a dog? I would never do that."

"Maybe you hurt her by accident and didn't know what to do."

"No. I didn't. I loved Molly. She always looked so fancy in that shiny, red collar. I went across the street to give her a cookie one day and she wasn't there. I never saw her again. We looked everywhere, remember? Pete was always jealous of Molly because he thought I loved her more than him."

Darla nodded, but her ribcage felt as if it was collapsing in on itself. She sensed that Trent was telling the truth—that, once again, Pete had lied to her when he said he'd seen Trent leading the dog out of the yard. He'd used his cunningness against his own family. The realization stunned her. She felt as if she'd been thrown off the edge of that gulch right alongside Kristen. She'd spent her whole life trying to protect others from Trent. But now she had to face a new, more troubling understanding. All these years, she might have been shielding the world from the wrong son.

THIRTY-THREE

ABIGAIL

"Are you ready for Hawaii?" Pete hauled our suitcases from the bedroom to the front door of our townhome.

"I can't wait!" I searched my purse, realizing I'd left my sunglasses in the car. "Hold on. I need to get something." I slipped through the door and tiptoed down the icy walkway out to the street where I always parked. Grabbing the sunglasses from inside the armrest, I was relieved to find no further attempts by Liam to contact me. A couple of hours earlier, I'd come across the envelope he'd left wedged in my car door on the morning of my wedding. It remained unopened in the bottom of my carry-on bag, the same bag I'd used to hold my extra clothes and makeup on my wedding day. Although I'd promised myself I wouldn't read Liam's note, wouldn't give him any more power over me, my curiosity had pulled at me. So, I'd left the envelope buried in the bottom of the bag, instead of throwing it away.

Back inside, I placed the glasses in my carry-on, which now bulged with books and snacks. Leaning down, I kissed our cat on the head, double-checking to make sure her food and water dishes were full. "Don't worry, Mango. The cat sitter will be here later. And I'll be back in ten days."

Pete shifted his weight. "Let's go."

"Aren't you going to say goodbye to Mango?"

Annoyance flashed across Pete's face, but he bent down to pet the cat. She skittered away and darted under the couch to avoid his touch. Pete threw up his hands and huffed. "Stupid cat."

"Pete! She's not stupid. She's our baby."

He lowered his eyes. "I forgot to tell you that I booked a half-day sailboat cruise for Monday. Just the two of us."

"I thought you didn't like boats?"

"No. That was you."

"I know *I* don't like boats. But when I told you that, you said you didn't like them either."

"I did?"

"Yes."

Pete placed a hand on his hip. "Well, I like boats in Hawaii. And hopefully, you will too. It's cooler on the ocean."

I picked at the stitching on my purse, wondering why Pete had booked a boat cruise when he'd known I didn't like boats. I was terrified of them, actually. Especially sailboats. I didn't want to go out on the boat but now didn't seem like a good time to start an argument either. At least he'd gone to the trouble of planning something for us.

"It'll be fun." His arms ensnared me in a hug. "We should leave now."

A warning darted through me, and my feet wouldn't move. It was the same surge of cold doubt I'd been feeling regularly in the last few weeks. Little things weren't adding up and even as my mind convinced myself it wasn't a big deal, my gut refused to let it slide. Sometimes when I looked at Pete, he seemed more like a stranger, and I found myself wondering if I really knew him at all.

Our packed suitcases and my eager husband waited near the door. There was no choice now but to make the best of things. What was wrong with me, anyway? What kind of person was nervous about going to Hawaii? I swallowed back my doubts. Maybe the boating experience wouldn't be as bad as I feared.

My phone buzzed and I dug it out of my purse. Darla's name showed on the screen. "It's your mom."

"Don't answer it. We'll talk to her when we get back." He waved me forward as I ignored the call. "Let's go."

I blew one last kiss to Mango and followed my husband out the door.

* * *

Four hours later, the back of my head pressed into the seat as I stared through the airplane's cutout window. We were one hour into an eight-hour flight, and clouds hovered below us. I'd been skimming through a book, but couldn't stay focused, so now I was attempting to take a nap. It wasn't working. Even though I'd reclined the seat, it remained at a nearly upright angle.

Pete rustled next to me. "I'm going to use the restroom."

I craned my neck toward the aisle behind us, seeing two people waiting. "There's a line."

"That's okay." He unbuckled and stretched, then slipped away.

There was a little more elbow room with Pete gone. My carry-on was wedged underneath the seat in front of me and I pulled it forward to look for a snack. The unevenly weighted bag tipped sideways, the contents spilling at my feet. "Shit," I said under my breath, scooping the magazines and packets of chips back into their place. The edge of a white envelope slid forward, catching my eye, and sending a prickle through me. I glanced toward the rear of the plane, where Pete still waited for the restroom several rows back. A breath of courage gathered in my lungs as I bent forward and plucked Liam's letter off the floor and onto my lap. I shoved the other items back into the bag and held it upright with my feet, scanning over the other nearby passengers to make sure no one was watching. Then, I ripped open the envelope. Obviously, I'd changed my mind about not reading whatever Liam had placed inside. It was better to know what it said, so I could throw it away and move on. I worried Liam might have mentioned something about our extra-curricular activities, so I had to open it while Pete wasn't around, read it quickly, and crunch it into a ball, which I'd throw away at my first opportunity.

I removed a single, white piece of paper, which unfurled before me, Liam's black, chicken-scratch writing lining the page.

Dear Abigail,

I'm sure I'm the last person you want to hear from today.

Uh, yeah. No kidding. I breathed in the recycled airplane air, forcing myself to read more.

But I have something urgent to tell you. I tried texting and calling you earlier today, but you blocked my number. You probably didn't get my first letter because I just realized I accidentally sent it to your old address. This is my last-ditch effort to reach you. I left rehab two days ago (182 days sober) and just found out that you're getting married tomorrow. I hope I'm not too late. Please (PLEASE!) read this entire letter before you say "I do."

I gritted my teeth, wondering if this was some kind of desperate ploy by Liam to try to sleep with me again. Well, he was out of luck. Too late. It wasn't happening. I didn't know anything about another letter, and I was glad I hadn't opened this one sooner. But I kept reading.

The first thing I want to tell you is that I'm sorry. I've lied to you from the start. Our first meeting at Team Wilderness was not accidental.

My mom was a former patient of your mom's. She suffered from chronic depression. She died by walking in front of a bus after your mom took her off her medication.

My breath hitched in my throat as I reread the previous sentences, trying to understand the words. Liam's mom had been my mom's patient? Liam hadn't met me by chance. He'd set me up. I didn't want to believe I'd been so stupid, so trusting.

My mom's death was ruled an accident, but I know it was suicide. I have never gotten over losing my mom or the fact that your mom never faced any consequences for her recklessness. That's why I tried to get close to you and wanted to mess up your life (and hers too).

My palm pressed into the armrest as my heartbeat throbbed through my temples. What a bastard! I peered back at the bathrooms, spotting Pete entering the one on the right. Liam had been playing me this whole time. He'd been using me to target Mom. What if he'd gotten his revenge by killing her? By pushing her over the edge of that cliff, just like he'd described in that ghost story? A flight attendant rattled a cart of drinks toward me, stopping two rows ahead. The words on the page blurred in front of me. I steadied my hand and refocused on Liam's confession.

My head is clear now, and I realize that befriending you was childish and wrong. I can see that you are a good person who was doing her best to get out of a difficult situation without hurting anyone. I shouldn't have taken advantage of you or helped you create conflict between your parents and Pete's parents. I shouldn't have slept with you or taken your family on a wilderness outing, and I'm sorry for my part in it.

Ha! I swallowed against my dry throat, unwilling to accept the apology.

But I need you to hear this more than anything: your instincts were right! Do NOT marry Pete! HE IS A MURDERER!

"Would you like a drink?"

The sound of a bubbly voice made me jump. A blue-eyed woman with a name tag and too much eyeshadow stared at me.

"No." I flipped over the letter and looked away, hoping she hadn't seen the mix of horror and confusion on my face. I stared straight ahead, waiting for her to move forward. A chilled sweat formed across my skin and black spots floated before my eyes, the same way they had when I'd discovered Mom laying at the bottom of the cliff. But I didn't have much time before Pete returned. I had to pull myself together and get through this letter, determine its truthfulness. My hand slowly turned the paper back over.

Pete shoved your mom over the edge of Norton's Gulch and straight to her death. The attack was totally unprovoked. I saw the whole thing with my own eyes.

Was this for real? My heart pounded inside my chest as I glanced at the restrooms again. Pete was still inside. He'd return in a minute or two. I reread the last few lines to confirm I hadn't imagined the sickening words. Was Liam telling the truth? I wasn't sure as my eyes flew over the rest.

I didn't say anything about what I'd seen out there. I was high and in shock when it all went down. I convinced myself that

Pete had done me a favor by ridding the world of the woman who caused my mom's death. I know I'm no angel either. But at the end of the day, I'm not a murderer.

I've had a lot of time to think these last six months and I realized that you are not responsible for your mom's actions. You should not marry Pete just because it's the path of least resistance, especially knowing what I know. What we both know now.

My eyes squeezed closed. But I had married him. Pete was my husband. He slept in my bed. He was the perfect son that Dad had never had. The restroom door clicked open, and Pete's body emerged. I crouched low, needing to finish the letter.

I have no idea what Pete's motive was. Maybe he sensed you were pulling away from him. Maybe he overheard us talking or your mom telling you to call off the wedding. I don't know.

My whole body went numb. I closed my eyes, remembering the shadow outside the tent as Mom pleaded with me to call off the wedding. I'd convinced myself it had been Darla lurking out there. But had it been Pete? I'd always sensed something about him wasn't quite authentic, but he covered himself so well. I'd buried my doubts. Time and time again, I'd listened to other people's opinions over my own instincts. Still, Liam was a liar. That was a fact.

Pete was heading toward me, just a few steps away.

"You'll have to wait a second, sir." It was the flight attendant, blocking the aisle with the cart. Quickly, my eyes skimmed the rest.

Please believe me. As far as everyone else is concerned, your mom's death was an accident and I have no reason to lie about what I saw. You need to run in the other direction NOW and contact the police. But it is your life and I'll leave that decision to you.

I hope this gets to you in time.

Take care of yourself,

Liam

P.S. The creepy guy in the woods had nothing to do with any of this. He was a colleague from Team Wilderness who I paid to set everyone on edge. It turns out he was the one who left the messages at the campsites.

I gulped for air. The plane could have dropped out of the sky and I wouldn't have noticed. The cart rattled away from me. I shoved the letter back into the envelope and stuffed it deep into my carry-on bag, unsure what to think.

"Hey." Pete retook his seat, securing the safety belt loosely around his waist. "That was an ordeal. Did I miss anything?"

"No. Nothing." I blinked and tried to smile, but I felt like I was going to vomit.

"You feeling okay? You look a little... green."

"Just a little motion sickness, I guess."

He reached into the seat pocket. "Here. You can have my water."

I took it, hiding the tremor in my hand, which was now reverberating through my whole body. I didn't know what to think. What to do. Who to believe. I stared at Pete and tried to discern some dark, murderous secret hiding behind his thick eyelashes and day-old stubble. But his face gave nothing away.

"Man, I can't wait to hit the beach."

I gripped the water bottle. "When's that boat ride again?"

"Tomorrow morning. It'll be perfect. Just the two of us out on the open water."

I nodded. My head was dizzy from Liam's accusation, plus the altitude. I wasn't sure if I believed the horrible thing Liam had written in that letter. He'd lied to me from the first day I'd met him. On the other hand, his story matched with what my gut had been screaming at me for months: that something wasn't right. I tucked the water bottle into the seat pocket in front of me and decided to act normal until we landed and got to our hotel. Then I'd sort out the truth, figure out what to do. But just to be safe, maybe it wasn't a good idea to get on that boat.

THIRTY-FOUR

ABIGAIL

At ten thirty the next morning, the boat's hull cut through the choppy, blue waters, the wind filling the sail. Every time the vessel tipped too far sideways, my muscles tensed, and I clung more tightly to the solid ledge. The wind rippled my hair and droplets of saltwater sprayed across my skin. Under different circumstances, the ride might have been thrilling. But we'd drifted too far out, beyond the volcanic rock formations and well into the prohibited area. There was no one else as far as I could see. Pete insisted we didn't need to wear the lifejackets. "We'll be too hot in these. Besides, we know how to swim," he'd said, tossing them into one of the storage compartments. I waited for an alarm to sound or a patrol boat to speed up next to us, but nothing like that happened. It was only me and Pete out on the open water, just like he'd promised.

It had been Pete's idea to sail in this direction, almost as if he'd mapped it out. Planned it. And when I'd asked him why we were heading this way, instead of the route recommended by the guy who'd rented us the boat, he'd hesitated, placing his sunglasses atop his head. Maybe it was the glare of the tropical sunlight or the accusation from Liam's letter imprinted in my mind, but I glimpsed something different in my husband's eyes today, something cold and two-dimensional. They lacked humanity.

Pete's empty stare only confirmed what I'd realized after reading through Liam's letter a second time in the middle of the night and, again, when I'd gone through Pete's things while he was in the bathroom this morning. I'd spotted a bulge in the interior pocket of his swim bag, the one he'd packed to bring with us on the boat. My fingers had pinched the tiny zipper, sliding it to the side to open the pouch. My twisting intestines knew what the hidden object was before I moved it into the light. I didn't have to ask myself twice why my fiancé had packed Liam's canister of bear spray for our romantic boat outing. I'd been stunned by the discovery, unable to do anything but eye my phone which rested nearby. I remembered Darla's phone call as we'd left for the airport. It was odd she'd called me instead of Pete. She always called Pete. Suddenly, I had a feeling her voicemail contained more than just well wishes. But the voicemail wasn't in my inbox anymore. Someone had deleted it. Pete was the only one who had access to my phone, who knew my passcode. That's when I'd changed my mind about getting on the boat.

"Just a little further." Pete stared at the horizon, then back toward the shore. He'd lowered his mirrored sunglasses over his eyes, but I knew exactly what he was searching for—witnesses or lack thereof. He let out the sail as the boat drifted beyond the line of rocks. A three-foot-long metal pole rested inside the open bag of supplies secured to the deck. Pete had pulled the object out of a storage compartment and put it there before we'd left when he'd thought I wasn't looking.

I'd been sailing with Mom plenty of times when I was a teenager. I'd hated the activity ever since we'd capsized in rough waters, but I'd learned a few things along the way. I'd never seen a piece of equipment like the pole resting near Pete's feet before. This time, I didn't ignore the sensation of a thousand spiders skittering across my skin. All night long, the same realizations battered me, crashing my body against a rocky shoreline. Each time I came up for a breath, they slammed into me again. Pete had murdered Mom. Liam must have written the truth about what he'd seen at the edge of Norton's Gulch. He had no reason to lie, especially after he'd confessed his damning connection to my mom, and his true reason for befriending me. All night long, the shadow outside my tent as Mom begged me to call off the wedding had wavered through my mind. Pete must have overheard her. He must have also heard me express my doubts. Or maybe he'd discovered my illicit relationship with Liam, the stunt we'd pulled. There was more than one reason Pete could have planned this surprise outing today. The only thing I knew for sure was that he wanted to make my death look like an accident too. I could see the picture clearly now, without everyone else's approval and adoration clouding my vision. Pete was a narcissist, a psychopath whose constant shows of charm and empathy had been nothing more than well-rehearsed acts. I must have always known on some level, but I'd talked myself out of my feelings again and again. I hadn't wanted to hurt anyone, to make anyone mad. Instead, much worse things had happened.

The ocean stretched wide on all sides. We were completely isolated, and I knew I didn't have much time left. I waited until Pete's back was turned, perhaps as he calculated his next move. I sensed my time was running out and I took a wide stance, stabilizing myself and struggling to keep my panic from consuming me.

Pete's voice cut through my thoughts, projecting over the waves. "I received an interesting letter about a week ago. It was addressed to you at your old place, but the guy who took over your lease brought it over. Said it looked personal. He wasn't sure why it hadn't been forwarded." Pete turned to me with his mouth pinched. Then he rotated away again as if he couldn't stand to look at me. "I should have known about you and Liam."

My body tensed as I thought of everything Liam had outlined in his second letter—what we'd done, what he had witnessed. Surely, the first letter had been just as revealing. "It was a—"

"Shut up!" Pete slammed his fist against the side of the boat, and I jumped. "I will not be rejected by a wife who doesn't love me, who cheated on me with a drug-addicted loser, whose mother thought she was too good for me. It's humiliating."

I heard my breath in my ears as I inched toward the metal pole, keeping watch on the back of Pete's head, his hair sticking up in the breeze.

The muscles in Pete's arms flexed as he gripped the ledge and leaned over the water, spitting into the waves. "The good news is that no one will ever find out about any of it." His tone was eerily calm, and his back still turned. But now I glimpsed the canister of bear spray he'd positioned in a cubby nearby.

My time was definitely running out. Pete was going to kill me, and probably Liam too. But he had underestimated me. I was done second-guessing myself. I found my footing along the floorboards, the waves rocking underneath. The hem of Pete's Hawaiian print bathing suit fluttered in the wind as he watched a flock of seagulls fly past. My legs were unsteady. The metal rod was heavy, but I lifted it and wound it up like a baseball bat just like Dad had taught me. I envisioned the way Mom's face had lit up when she'd first spotted the pink lady slippers, how she hadn't had an opportunity to defend herself. Then I clenched my teeth and whacked my psychopathic, piece-of-shit husband over the head as hard as I could. *Watch your back.* Pete's body seemed to move in slow motion as he toppled over the side of the sailboat and splashed in the water. I braced myself against the low ledge, stunned by what I'd done. But it was him or me.

Always trust your instincts. It was Darla who'd told me that. But I'd done exactly the opposite for many months. Until now. A stubborn knot in my gut had been warning me, letting me know I was going to die on this boat ride. I'd felt a flash of fear the moment Pete mentioned he'd booked the private sailboat. It was so strange that he hadn't discussed it with me first. And why had he booked an activity he'd known I'd hated? And then there'd been Liam's letter and the bear spray hidden inside Pete's bag. And Darla's mysteriously deleted message. How many more red flags could the universe wave in front of me?

I peered over the edge into the water where Pete's designer sunglasses bobbed along with the waves. His dark hair had sunk below the surface. I'd always sensed something was off with him. Mango sensed it too, hadn't wanted Pete to touch her before we'd left. Over the last two years—but in the last week especially—there'd been moments Pete had let his mask slip, the look on his face sending a chill down my spine. But then he'd flip a switch, talk himself out of whatever had just happened. Pete had always been able to talk himself out of everything. He must have been shocked by the contents of Liam's misdelivered letter, but he'd hidden it well even as he'd complimented me, held my hand, nuzzled my neck, had sex with me, recited his vows, and married me. If it weren't for Liam's second letter wedged into my car door, Pete might have fooled me completely.

I dipped my hand into the seawater, watching it oscillate and reflect around my wrist. My body shook, but I felt nothing inside. Straightening up, I tightened the sail and guided the boat away from the scene toward deeper water, then tossed the metal pole and canister of bear spray, watching them disappear. *Leave no trace.* I shifted the boom around again and sailed back to the approximate location where Pete had gone overboard. Then I pulled my phone from my pocket and dialed three numbers.

"911. What's your emergency?"

"I need help right away." I injected panic into my voice, remembering the story I'd concocted about the gust of wind that whipped the sail around and slammed my unsuspecting husband in the head, knocking him off the boat. Maybe it was the same story Pete had planned to tell about me. "There's been a terrible accident."

EPILOGUE

JOHN

John peered around the open refrigerator door, to the spot where Kristen used to lean her hip against the counter and gaze out the window toward the red maple tree, commenting on the cardinals or the blue jays at the bird feeder. Sometimes, he could feel his wife's ghost still haunting this kitchen. Or maybe he was just paranoid. A pan clanged against the burner, yanking him from his thoughts.

"How about I make us some eggs?" She smiled at him, her hair still mussed from their romp up in the bedroom.

"Sure. That sounds great."

"You look sad. Are you thinking about Pete again?"

John had been living in a fog these past few months, ever since he'd heard the news that his son-in-law had died in a boating accident in Hawaii. The tragedy had left him stunned and bereft. How could someone so ambitious and full of life die on the first full day of his honeymoon? It didn't make any sense.

John sighed. "Yeah. It feels like I lost my son."

A different woman occupied his house now. John had been secretly seeing Janie Metz for nearly two years. He looked forward to the day when she wouldn't be a secret. He'd only recently started letting her over to the house. But Kristen hadn't been gone long enough and he had to keep the whole thing under wraps a little longer to avoid the whispers.

He leaned his weight against the wall, wishing Pete was here. Pete was the only one who'd known about John's affair, who'd seen first-hand how his friendship with Janie had bloomed into something more, a truly authentic kind of love he wasn't sure he'd ever really felt with Kristen. And Pete had understood John's predicament. Asking for a divorce hadn't been an option. John would be seen as a cheater and would be shunned by his family, friends, and colleagues. Losing his daughter's adoration wasn't worth the risk.

So, a few days after Abigail had booked the camping trip, John found himself at the office late one night, feeling trapped by the life he'd constructed for himself. Everyone else had gone home, except for Pete who often put in a few extra hours at the end of the day. They chatted about their planned outing with Team Wilderness and the weather in the upper peninsula. John paused, mentioning an idea under his breath, one that could be interpreted as a joke. "There's a good chance Kristen won't make it back from the camping trip alive."

Instead of laughing or looking perplexed, Pete simply shrugged. "Accidents happen all the time."

John looked up, detecting a sinister note in Pete's voice. They stared at each other for a beat too long.

"Would you like an accident to happen?" Pete's tone was calm and composed as if he regularly caused accidents to happen.

"Yes," John found himself answering. For the first time, John saw a flicker of light at the end of the tunnel. Pete was on his team. Pete was someone who put his ideas into action.

In hushed voices, they discussed a variety of ways a death in the wilderness could appear accidental—from sneaking unfiltered water into Kristen's water bottle to an unstable tree falling on her tent at an inopportune time. Because there'd be other people around, they decided they didn't need to force anything. They would play it by ear and see if an opportunity presented itself. But when they heard Liam's ghost story about Norton's Gulch, they knew they'd found the perfect plan, one that was so easy to execute. Any of John's second thoughts were extinguished the second Pete told him he'd overheard Kristen telling Abigail to call off the wedding. John had been waiting his whole life for a son like Pete, and he wasn't about to let Kristen's impossible standards ruin it for him.

The scavenger hunt began a few minutes later, and the time had finally come for John to make his move. He found Kristen standing alone near the pink flowers and strode toward her with what must have been a wild look in his eyes, forcing her closer to the ledge. She'd stumbled at first, catching her fall with her hands, breaking a nail. But she quickly righted herself, her animal instinct to defend herself kicking in. As John approached again, she kneed him in the groin. The stun of the pain snapped him back to reality. He was frightened of himself and what he'd just attempted. So he'd darted into the woods, feeling like he was going to throw up. He hadn't seen the brambles there waiting for him, catching the skin on his face.

John had huddled behind a line of trees, panic overtaking him. He was terrified that the plan had failed and that Kristen would tell everyone what he'd tried to do. He clutched his head, concocting a lie to tell Kristen about why he'd approached her like that. Maybe something about Darla and Kenny, who made easy scapegoats. But it turned out John didn't need a story because, a few moments later, he spied through the branches as a younger and stronger Pete arrived at the gulch, intercepting a sobbing Kristen and pretending to help her. Pete calmed her by looping one of his arms around Kristen's shoulders, guiding her back to the scene so she could describe what had happened. With his free arm, Pete gave one final shove, sending Kristen

over the edge to her death. Then he marched back to the campsite. And no one suspected a thing. At least, that's what John
had believed.

John handed Janie the carton of eggs, the organic, free-range
kind that Kristen had always preferred. Janie turned back
toward the stove and John was ever grateful his lover had never
directly questioned him about Kristen's death. She'd taken his
story of an accidental fall at face value, which was reasonable
given that Kristen's cause of death had been corroborated by the
park service and police investigations. And his grief in the after-
math of the camping trip had been real, although his emotions
had been influenced more by Abigail than Kristen. He felt so
terrible about the loss his daughter had suffered.

As Janie cracked eggs into a bowl and beat the life out of
them, a vision of Pete surfaced in John's mind. John had grown
increasingly suspicious of his daughter. She'd seemed happier
than ever in the days since Pete's funeral. Abigail had moved
out of the townhome she and Pete had shared into a one-
bedroom apartment at the first opportunity, doling out many of
Pete's belongings to Darla and Kenny.

John suspected that Pete hadn't died in a tragic accident.
Abigail was smart. Always had been. Everyone else gobbled up
her harrowing story about the gust of wind and the sail whipping around, and the boom nailing Pete in the back of the head.
Even Pete's parents took the tale at face value, asking far fewer
questions about their son's death than John would have
expected. Darla and Kenny hadn't given Abigail the cold
shoulder or demanded any further investigation. But John
didn't buy it. Why hadn't Abigail and Pete been wearing lifejackets? Abigail had taken a full summer of sailing lessons when
she was a teenager. His daughter knew how to react to an emergency. So why hadn't she jumped in after her new husband?

A dark knowing lived inside John, like a tumor spreading its
poison through his body. Abigail must have figured out that Pete

killed Kristen. She must have gotten revenge for her mother out there on the open water of the Pacific. But how had Abigail known? That was one of many questions that kept John awake at night. John wondered if Abigail had seen more than she should have the night of the scavenger hunt, or if Pete had said too much, inadvertently showing his hand. John prayed that Abigail never found out about his role in Kristen's death. Especially, not after what he suspected she'd done to Pete.

He suddenly felt light-headed. "I'm going to run to the bathroom for a second."

Janie nodded as she hummed to herself, pouring the eggs into a pan.

Inside the powder room, John ran the faucet and splashed cold water on his face. On the other side of the door, a doorbell rang, causing John to jump. He patted his face dry with a hand towel as Janie's light footsteps flitted past. Unlike John, she was done with the months of secrecy and wanted everyone to know their status as a couple.

"I've got it," she said at the same time John yelled, "Wait!"

He barged out of the bathroom and down the hall to find Janie opening the front door. Abigail stood on the front step, holding a box of muffins from his favorite bakery. She looked from Janie to John, smile fading.

"Hi, hon." John stepped forward, trying to act casual, somehow managing to keep his face still. "I didn't know you were coming by."

"I picked up some muffins." She gave her dad a sideways glance. "Who's your friend?"

Janie stuck out her hand. "I'm Janie Metz. Nice to meet you."

Abigail nodded, but she looked up and to the side like she was trying to remember something. "The accountant?"

"Yes." Janie placed her hand on her heart. "Have you heard of me?"

"Um." Abigail raised her eyebrows, and her face had lost its color. "Just once, I guess."

John found the courage to glance at his daughter just as her eyes sharpened on him. Her stare seemed to pin him to the wall, tighten around his throat. He couldn't speak. Abigail's glare unleashed an overwhelming fear that crowded out everything else. It was clear that she knew he'd lied. Maybe she hadn't uncovered everything yet, but his affair was now exposed. Abigail was like a Rottweiler with a scent. She would follow this treacherous trail wherever it led. Just like she'd clearly done with Pete.

"Why don't you come inside and eat some breakfast with us?" Janie asked, oblivious to the ticking time bomb she'd set in motion.

Abigail stretched her neck to the side, a bone cracking. She flashed a steely smile toward Janie as her voice lowered a pitch. "Yes. Let's get to know each other."

John sucked in a breath, unable to think of any gathering he wanted to host less. He'd hoped to postpone this meeting between his daughter and his girlfriend for another six months, at least. It took the power of every cell in his body not to sprint out the back door and hide behind the shrubbery. Instead, he exhaled, planting his feet on the floor.

Abigail stepped into the foyer. She extended the box, locking eyes with her dad again. Despite her calm demeanor, John glimpsed a storm raging behind her irises. He wondered what she saw in his.

"Take it," Abigail said, demanding he accept the muffins. "They're your favorites."

As John grasped the flimsy box, he hoped it was a sort of peace offering, even if a deranged one. Abigail was his only child, after all, and he couldn't bear losing her affection.

She slipped past him, her slender arms hanging by her side. To Janie, she probably appeared, innocent and breakable. John thought about Abigail's loyalty to her mother and about what she'd done to Pete. He would never physically harm his daughter. He wasn't capable of it. But he wasn't sure if the reverse was true. He had to set things right with her, and the sooner the better. Because once Abigail decided to get revenge, there was one thing John knew for sure.

He wouldn't see it coming.

A LETTER FROM LAURA

Dear reader,

I want to say a huge thank you for choosing to read *The In-Laws*. If you enjoyed it and want to keep up to date with all my latest releases, just sign up at the following link. Your email address will never be shared and you can unsubscribe at any time.

www.bookouture.com/laura-wolfe

I strive to write stories fraught with tension, and I could think of very few scenarios more disquieting than a fast-approaching wedding, a nervous bride, and future in-laws who do not get along. This was a fun novel to write because nothing was as it seemed and nearly everyone had a secret agenda. I plucked the flawed characters in my story from their usual domestic lives and placed them in the wilderness to level the playing field. Then I threw in a wilderness guide with his own ulterior motives and a few outside threats. Darla's character developed from my casual interest in the mystic arts—Tarot and palm reading, crystal healing, and astrology. I often thought how creepy and unsettling it would be to have someone who claims to see your future glimpse something horrible... and then not want to tell you. So of course, I had to make that part of the story! Darla's unfettered belief in the mystic arts made her the perfect foil to Kristen's logical and science-based background.

I hope you loved *The In-Laws,* and if you did, I would be very grateful if you could write a review. Reviews make such a difference in helping new readers discover one of my books for the first time.

I love hearing from my readers – you can get in touch on my Instagram, Facebook page, or my website. To receive my monthly book recommendations in the mystery/suspense/thriller genre, please follow me on Bookbub.

Thanks,

Laura Wolfe

www.LauraWolfeBooks.com

facebook.com/LauraWolfeBooks
instagram.com/lwolfe.writes
bookbub.com/profile/laura-wolfe

ACKNOWLEDGMENTS

While writing a novel is mainly a solitary endeavor, there have been many people who supported and assisted me in various ways along the journey of writing and publishing this book. First, I'd like to thank the entire team at Bookouture, especially my editor, Isobel Akenhead. She helped to smooth out my novel's rough edges and continually reminded me to raise the stakes. Her insights into my story's structure, pacing, and characters made the final version so much better. Additional gratitude goes to copyeditor, Dushi Horti, and proofreader, Shirley Khan, for their keen eyes, and to Bookouture's top-notch publicity team led by Noelle Holten and Kim Nash. Thank you to the friends who continuously support my writing and provide inspiration and encouragement. Thank you to the many book bloggers who have helped spread the word about my books. I'm so thankful for the authors in the Bookouture Authors' Lounge Facebook group, who are always there to prop me up, offer laughs, and answer questions. It's a joy to be a part of such a supportive group of talented writers from around the world. Thank you to my parents, cousin, mother-in-law, and other family members who have supported my books. I appreciate everyone who has taken the time to tell me that they enjoyed reading my stories, has asked me "How's your writing going?" or has left a positive review. I also owe gratitude to my canine "writing partner," Milo. He sat by my side (and only occasionally barked) as I wrote every word. Most of all, I'd like to thank my kids, Brian and Kate, for always cheering for me and for finding creative ways to occupy themselves, especially over the past summer so that I could have time to write, and for my husband, JP, for supporting my writing. As always, I wouldn't have made it to the end without his encouragement.

Printed in Great Britain
by Amazon